ROUGH WATERS

THE LIFE OF A NAVAL INTELLIGENCE OFFICER

Part One

DOCTOR JAC

abbott press

Abbott Press books may be ordered through booksellers or by contacting:

Abbott Press
1663 Liberty Drive
Bloomington, IN 47403
www.abbottpress.com
Phone: 1-866-697-5310

ISBN: 978-1-4582-1637-3 (sc)
ISBN: 978-1-4582-1638-0 (hc)
ISBN: 978-1-4582-1639-7 (e)

Library of Congress Control Number: 2014909682

Printed in the United States of America.

Abbott Press rev. date: 11/3/2014

DEDICATION

Branching out into a new specialty can be a daunting
endeavor. Success depends not only on one's ability, but also
the support and direction that others have to offer. In my
case, my magnificent wife Laura stepped in during a difficult
period and took on a myriad of responsibilities that freed me
to concentrate on this project. Without her encouragement
and collaboration this book could not have been written.

ACKNOWLEDGEMENTS

Throughout this project my wife Laura offered story ideas and critical overview. She is my story editor. Insights and data on military matters were provided by my brother Col. David Fitz-Enz USA ret. Early manuscript review and technical assistance data on Vietnam came from my best friend Bob Coon. My ninety-one year young mother-in-law Laura Sanchez Dubois was my Spanish guide. Derek Ling played the same invaluable role with Hong Kong remembrances, Chinese customs and language passages. Dr. John Rashkis provided detailed guidance on medical issues. After having written a dozen business books I had to start anew and learn how to write fiction. For that I am very much indebted to my editor Lynn Weber who taught me and guided me through this project.

CONTENTS

1

HOT LAUNCH

An early June Morning in 1942 - - the last week of school. The blacktop in front of our house at the corner of Downer Street and Huron Boulevard is already steaming. The smell of tar is everywhere. Even the cement sidewalk is hot. I start walking the two blocks on Huron to Sacred Heart School at 8 am. I'm wearing a short-sleeve shirt and short brown pants, but feel like I'm in a bearskin coat. Along the right side of the sidewalk is a block-long vacant lot. There's only one house, and it's a little white thing on the opposite corner. In the middle of the lot is a pond made from rain water with an inviting layer of cool mud. Tempting, but I'm late already. The day is turning into a scorcher. Little do I know how hot it's going to make me.

I've done well in the first two grades and am looking forward to the summer. Final tests have been taken and the inmates are anxious to escape their confinement. I imagine that the nuns in their long black robes and starched white head gear are even happier to see the term ending. As I climb the stairs to the second floor classrooms over the church I'm excited too.

When I enter my classroom Sister Mary Clare tells me that Sister Mary Frances, the principal of our little citadel of education, wants to see me. This can only be bad news. On the short walk to her office I nervously play back what I've been doing the past week. I can't think of any rules I've violated. I'm innocent. I knock on sister's open door and she beckons me into her stiflingly hot office. The window is open, but it's still hot and will be sizzling very soon inside and outside that little closet. There are the usual decorations on the wall of the Blessed Virgin Mary, Jesus Christ of the Sacred Heart and a crucifix with a dried out palm leaf wrapped around it. There is a faint odor of incense. It could be Sister Mary Francis. She daubs the sweat off her face as she fusses with the mountain of paper in front of her. In the corner a small electric fan pushes the heat around the room.

Sister is a round little thing seated behind the standard worn yellow oak desk. She's generally serious and has a smile that can go from angelic to satanic in a split second. While I sit stewing, she mines the mountain. At last, she finds what she's searching for, digs it out and looks up. She starts with a semi-angelic smile beginning to tell me why she wanted to see me.

"You've done very well, Michael" - - - that's my name, Michael Still. I'm momentarily relieved. "I've been looking at your grades, and you have an A in every class. You scored 100 on every one of your final exams." My stomach starts to relax, and the beginnings of an actual smile edges at the corners of my mouth. It's not to last. "That is perfect. I've never seen it in over thirty years of teaching. But this is a problem. You know don't you that perfection is not possible in this world, Michael? Only God in heaven is perfect." With that her expression cools and she lays it on me. "I'm going to have to lower your arithmetic grade to 95". From that moment on I've hated math and I don't care much for Sister MF thereafter either.

I skulk back to Sister Mary Clare's class. The other kids look at me for a clue as to how bad it's been. Sister MF never brought good news. They can see I'm crushed. Fortunately, no one is grading my attitude that morning or I'd have had an F minus. How can they do this to me? What is the point of being a good boy, doing everything you're told and working hard when in the end you get conned?

After stewing in the classroom pressure cooker for another four hours we're freed, finally. As I trudge back down Huron Street toward home I struggle to hold back the tears. Remember, mother told me boys don't cry. Okay, so I turn the frustration into anger. Passing the vacant lot, I look at that pond again. This is the perfect place to blow off some of my steam and take a measure of revenge. I walk right over and start jumping up and down in the dirty water. I don't know the right curse words then, but in retrospect they would have been something like *son-of-a-bitch*.

When I get home I leave my dirty shoes on the back step. I find Mom in the kitchen sweating over a pot of boiling spaghetti sauce. I tell her, "Mom, sister Mary Francis said I had perfect grades but that only god is perfect. So, she cut my math grade from 100 to 95. It's not fair to be cut for being too perfect". But Mom, who is quite religious at the time, agrees with Sister MF and on top of that is mad at me for my mud-caked shoes. She gives me a stiff brush and commands, "Go outside and brush those shoes off. Make sure that you get every last spot of mud off them. Then, you ask Dad for his polishing kit and polish them so they look brand new." I'm going from bad to worse.

When Dad comes home from work I look for sympathy from him as well. He doesn't share my mother's religious viewpoint, but his cynicism is just as useless. He just lights another of his endless chain of cigarettes and chuckles, "Son, life isn't fair. This won't be the last time someone screws you. The world is full of idiots. Just do your best, and leave the garbage behind."

Still looking for an ally, my last hope is my new baby brother Bob, who is about a year old. Lying in his crib, he looks up at me with big innocent eyes as I explain to him what has happened to me and how unfair it is. All my hard work, all my beautiful perfect scores have been stolen from me by the black habit thieves at Sacred Heart, backed by my spineless parents. Bob just smiles up at me, gurgles and drools.

* * *

My parents have reason for their desperation. They were married in the heart of the Depression, 1933. My mother, Irma, delivered me on a blisteringly hot July 30th in 1935. The hospital was not air conditioned. The stuffy delivery room must have been a hundred degrees adding to the pain of child birth. She never tires of telling me how difficult her labor had been and how insensitive the nurses were. She talks as though the nurses and I had somehow conspired to make it difficult for her. I tire of hearing it, but she never lets it go.

Now, in 1942 the worst of the Depression is over, but the effects still linger. We're among the lucky ones because my father has a job at a local factory that makes farm machinery. He's in the accounting department. It's not an exciting job unless you're an accountant, which he isn't. He's good with numbers so they start him out as a bookkeeper and he's thankful for the job. When he gets home at night he tells us stories about the people and the job.

We're happy to have Dad's paycheck every two weeks. Once a month he and Mom sit down at the dining room table after dinner and get all the bills out to see if they have enough money to pay them. I like to watch them do it and hear what they have to say to each other. I always like to listen to the big people when they sit at our house and talk. My parents make sure that with his salary of $200 they can always keep up with the $30 monthly rent for our brown shingled bungalow. All other bills come after that. I remember one night when we've had some unexpected medical expenses there isn't enough money to cover all the bills. They talk about it a long time. Mom say, "We could cut down on meat for dinner for a week. That will save two dollars. Dad says, "Why don't you cut my hair? That will save fifty cents." Back and forth they go looking for a few pennies here and there so that they won't be late or be in debt. Finally, Dad says, "There's no way out of it. We have to dip into our savings for fifteen dollars." Mom starts to cry, "That money is for us to go to the lake for a week next summer." Dad agrees, "Yes, but maybe we can stay for five days instead of seven. Maybe I can find an odd job to make it up." Mom jumps up and says, "I forgot about that. Mrs.

Solis is looking for a housemaid for a week to help her with spring cleaning. She's getting old and can't do it all by herself. Mr. Solis is almost bed ridden now and he can't help her. She told me that she would pay someone ten dollars to help her for four days. I can do that and still have time to take care of our house." Dad smiled and said, "I think old Mr. Burns at work was hinting that he could use some help picking cherries in his yard. He had two or three trees and they are too much for him to keep up with. I can probably get at least five dollars doing that for him." They sit back and smile. Then they hug, which they don't do very often. "We're gonna make it hon," he shouts with a big smile. The pressure was off, at least for another month.

Mom and Dad are very proud that they always pay their own way. If someone invites them on a trip, even if it is only one day, they always insist in paying their share. One time Dad is invited to go on a short golf trip with some of the executives of the company. He declines because he won't let anyone else pay his expenses. He tells me, "You've got to be responsible for yourself. Self-reliance is important. If you can't afford to do something don't expect someone else to pay for you. Be a man and take care of yourself."

While we're lucky to have a roof over our heads, even if it is small, old, frequently drafty or leaking, it requires endless labor to maintain it. The landlord said," You live in it you take care of it." The little brown shingled house had a small porch in front, two bedrooms and one bath, no shower. In the basement there was a coal-burning furnace, a coal bin, laundry sink, work bench and space for a reclaimed pool table.

On warm nights I like to sit on the porch with Dad after dinner and watch the sun go down. He smokes his cigarettes and blows smoke rings for me. I try to put my fingers into the hole but the ring always breaks up. As the sun sets the shadows creep slowly up our street from the west. Then, the street lights go on and the bugs start buzzing around them. Sometimes we talk about life and how to live it. Even though I'm no more than eleven years old I have lots of questions about the world, people and myself. Dad answers my questions if they aren't too obtuse. His basic advice is always, "Pay attention to what is happening around you. Watch people carefully to know if they are honest with you. Then do what you think is right."

If we have rain sometimes we go out onto the lawn with flashlights and look for night crawlers, big worms. If there's a lot of rain the worm holes are flooded and they come out onto the grass. When someone is going fishing we give the worms to them for bait. Dad, Pa and I go fishing a couple times on the river that divides our town. We hook the worms with our fish hooks and drop them into the murky river water. I remember the only things we catch are a couple of small bass, too small to cook, so we throw them back. Once we caught a bullhead. It is a bottom feeder that is thick, dirty gray, with whiskers like a catfish and pretty ugly. It was only about eight inches long so it went back into the river too. Even if we had kept it no one would have wanted to eat it except a cat.

In the basement of our little place I often help Dad shovel coal, scooping out the dusty pellets and dropping them into the hopper that feeds the furnace. It makes me proud to help with this because this is what my grandfather does for a living. He shovels coal for the railroad. The hopper feeds the coal pellets into a large donut shape in the furnace. Every day or two Dad reaches into the furnace with a long hook and pulls the burned coal out. The hot donut is about twenty inches in diameter and is called a clinker. Dad breaks it into a couple smaller pieces and drops them it into an ashcan. Once as I turned from the coal hopper to get another shovel full from the bin, Dad turned with his shovel and hit me in the forehead. I was showered in coal dust and pellets. The impact made me see stars. Dad dropped his shovel and went to his knees, checking my head. When he was sure he hadn't nearly decapitated me, he helped me take off my dirty clothes, gave me a big hug and said he was sorry. Then, he sent me upstairs for a bath. My head pounding, my legs shaking from the impact, I open the basement door to the kitchen where Mom is toiling over her second hour of ironing. Turning toward me with fatigue covering her body she snaps, "What happened to you?

You're a mess. Get into the bathroom and take a bath this minute. And make sure you don't leave coal dust all over everything for me to clean up." She never asks about the red bump on my forehead. I grit my teeth and do as I'm told.

While my dad's week is regulated by factory work and house maintenance, my mom's week has its own seemingly endless cycle of chores. There is an unending pile of washing, daily cooking meals for a husband and son . . . later two boys, beating back the dust and grime her husband and sons bring into the house, day after day. Every Saturday it is laundry day. We have a blue enamel, round washing machine on wheels with a hand wringer on top. Soap comes from shaving off a large bar of pure white soap about four inches long. Clothes go into the tub with the soap shavings and hot water from the laundry tub. A small electric motor turns the rotor in the tub. This draws the hot soapy water back and forth through the clothes to release the dirt. After washing a load, rinsing it in the two tubs and running it through the hand wringer Mom gives the clothes to Dad and me to hang while she continues to run more heavy loads through the machine. We must do at least a dozen loads counting clothes, linens and towels. In the summer we hang the clothes outside on a couple of lines that run from the house to poles next to our detached garage. In the winter we have to hang the clothes in the basement. It takes several days for them to dry that way. The basement, with its cement block walls and concrete floor smells moldy all winter. About the time the clothes are dry it was time to start laundry day again. The cycle of heavy labor was enough to break the spirit of some people. But for most of us it was the only choice.

Like most households my mother has a small Victory Garden during the war. She continues it until brother Bob goes to school. Then, she goes to work at an office and doesn't have time to tend a garden. Although it wasn't very big it took a good bit of labor to dig, fertilize with real cow manure, plant, weed and harvest. That is just the beginning. Then, she still has to prepare and serve meals using the produce. Behind the garage, where the garden is located,

Mom grows lettuce, peas, corn and other vegetables I don't care for. Our daily meals are basically northern European style, namely meat, potatoes, bread and butter, milk or coffee and, in the winter, canned vegetables. In the summer, along with vegetables, Mom's garden produces my favorite, strawberries. On Thursdays, the entrée is usually liver and onions, which look, smell and taste like the sole of a shoe. Since we're Catholic, Friday is fish day. Living in the Midwest the seafood selection is limited. The local rivers produce only a few fish that you really don't want to eat. Mostly we eat frozen halibut that has the consistency of thick cardboard.

We have a small yard on the front and west side of the house. It's big enough for Dad and me to play catch after work. He bounces the ball at me or throws it as high as he can. I run under it and try to catch it. It's fun and helps develop my baseball fielding skills. In the back is the fence and a double garage. The owner rents the other half to someone who often leaves disgusting things in the bed of his dump truck. I recall vividly the smell the night he left a dead horse in it.

On the east side of the house was Huron Street, a very busy road that leads north to my father's factory and south to Sacred Heart church and school. During the War Dad's factory switches from farm machinery to cannons. Because he has two kids, is in his thirties and works in a defense factory he's exempt from the draft. I remember well trucks going past the house towing army drab green 105 millimeter howitzers off to war. Morning and night people speed to and from work along Huron. I get many lectures about not going into the street after a ball. In good weather Dad walks the five blocks over the hill to work. Across Huron Street is Mr. and Mrs. Burken's little cream colored grocery store. They look like Ma and Pa Kettle. He's small and quiet. He dresses in a clean work shirt and wears suspenders that he likes to hook his thumbs into when he's just standing looking out at the traffic. His principal job seems to be stocking shelves and sweeping out. Mrs. Burken, who never stops moving, distributes two hundred pounds in lumps over her six foot frame. When he thinks she isn't looking Mr. Burken will sneak me a small piece of candy. If she catches us she yells at him, "What are you doing? Do you think money grows on trees?" Few people like Mrs. Burken, but they patronize her store since it is convenient. Beyond the store there are only a few clustered houses half submerged in a sea of corn fields that seem to stretch to infinity. On a hot, humid summer day you can smell the sweet scent of corn. You could almost hear it say, "It won't be long now until you can pick and eat me."

During those difficult Depression and prewar days there was an attitude of helpfulness. Paychecks are small, if you even have one. With a couple million people still out of work people help each other. If Dad needs someone to help him repair the house there is usually a neighbor or relative who has the requisite skills and makes time to lend a hand. It's expected that everyone should help out. Even right after the war I remember the family and friends erecting a prefab house for my uncle, free of charge. I lend a hand picking up scraps and throwing them into someone's truck to take to the dump. By the fifties the country is prosperous for the first time in thirty years. Most people have jobs and through the GI Bill many are able to buy a house for the first time. As the basic economics of the country change so to, gradually, attitudes change. It's the dawning of a new, more prosperous, but more self-centered America. The pioneer spirit that marked America as unique in the world is dead forever.

* * *

My dad's mother, Ma, dies in 1945 when I'm in fifth grade. We have to move across town to live with Pa. Ma's house is a gray and white Victorian across the street from McGowan Park. It has a large bay window that looks out on the park. Ma's first husband, Mr. Weisman had run a small brush and broom factory and was well off, although not rich. Ma is a whirlwind of a housekeeper. Mom said she would work up a sweat cleaning every crevice in the place. I don't remember anything ever out of place. Ma had been sent by her family from Luxembourg to America alone when she was only nine years old. She had been settled with a distant relative on a nearby farm. Throughout her life she is very angry for having been sent away alone to a foreign place and unknown people.

The move means a new school for me. Its name is Saint Nicholas. Although I'm unsure about moving and meeting new kids, I find life in Ma's house much easier in some ways. The rooms are large. There are easy chairs and a sofa, and best of all a large radio and windup record player. Ma used to make remarks occasionally about how good Mr. Weisman had been to her. I think they are aimed at Pa who is a common laborer and who often frustrates her with his cigar ashes on the carpet. She's about the same height as him. I used to have a picture of the two of them standing in our yard. Side by side they resembled a couple of fireplugs. I like Ma because I am her first born grandchild and she pampers me. Her baking specialty is cinnamon and oatmeal cookies. They're both about three inches in diameter, thick and chewy. The cinnamons are lightly covered with brown sugar. The oatmeal has raisins and sometimes little pecan chips buried inside. What is it that gives grandmothers these great culinary skills?

Pa's name is Johann Baptiste Schullatsch. It was shortened to Still when he came through immigration. Pa is 5'5" tightly packed with 200 pounds of muscle. For over twenty years he shovels coal to keep the boilers going and provide steam power at the rail yards across the river. Family lore has it that when someone teases him about being short, he picks the man up and throws him into the coal bin. Pa loves to drink. Ma keeps a close watch on him. She knows exactly when he gets off work because they blow a loud, shrill whistle at the end of each shift. In an effort to thwart her when he leaves work he runs as fast as his stubby little legs can carry him and stops in at the bar on our side of the bridge. He chugs a couple beers and then runs the rest of the way home. When he arrives he is sweating like a horse and doesn't smell any better. I idolize Pa because he is direct, tough, strong and irreverent. He doesn't take sass from anyone except Ma. Unlike Dad who just laughs it off, Pa will fight back. He belongs to a croquet club in McGowan Park. The club has two perfectly level, hard packed clay courts, lightly sanded and surrounded by a cement curb. It serves the dual purpose of keeping balls in play and gives the players a border on which to bank their shots. The club has a neat little shack that houses a couple card tables and racks of the member's customer made mallets. In the early hours Pa sneaks me into the club to play a game before the other members show up. To me, it's like playing in Yankee Stadium. There is nothing Pa couldn't or wouldn't do except drive a car. He for sure wouldn't let a bunch of nuns cheat him out of a perfect score. My mother and Pa don't get along well because he laughs at her piety.

Mom's family lives across the river on the east side. While Dad is an only child, Mom has three brothers and two sisters. The family has fantastic longevity genes because almost all of them live into their nineties. Grandma makes it to a few days short of 100. Mom's father, Jeremiah, owns a sheet metal business and does quite well. To avoid paying craftsmen, whenever he needs something done he uses his sons, sons-in-law, and grandsons as an ad hoc workforce. Grandmother Emma is a very small woman with several crooked front teeth housed within an easy smile. While Mom seems overwhelmed by the demands of her small family and her house, Grandma is imperturbable. She has been born and lived her whole life in this house. Her memory of the neighborhood is legendary. One time she tells me about the flu epidemic of 1918 that killed millions of people around the world. It wreaked havoc on her street as well. She started her narrative by telling us that on a Monday one of the girls at the Weiland's house took sick and died in four days. On Saturday the family took her to St. Mary's three blocks east for burial. When they got home Donny took sick and he was gone before the next weekend. Grandma went through the whole neighborhood reciting the epidemic's tracks. It was truly a plague.

The floors creak throughout her house. She has a real ice box and a stove with a wood-burning chamber in her large old-style kitchen. When she needs a block of ice she puts a cardboard sign on the pillar of her porch. Depending what number shows on the card the iceman chips a chunk off a big block in the back of his horse drawn wagon. Then he carries it on his leather shoulder pad up the steps and into the house, depositing it in her ice box. If you want ice for anything there is an ice pick on top of the box. You just open the ice door and chip off what you need. Invariably chips fly onto the floor. Grandma just laughs and kicks them aside where they'll eventually melt and dry up. This attitude undoubtedly contributes to her longevity. In the backyard is a large, black trunk, cherry tree that produces beautifully scented white blossoms in spring and large, dark red, sweet cherries in summer. Grandpa finds someone to pick them of course. Grandma turns them into the richest, sweetest cherry pies in the Western Hemisphere. She bakes fresh bread every day because Grandpa won't eat store bought. She also makes "fry cakes", her name for doughnuts. They're light, fragrant and crispy on the outside, steaming on the inside. Eating a doughnut immediately after it comes out of the hot oil with a glass of cold milk is indescribably delicious. The aromas of her baking fill the old house.

On holidays the whole clan of aunts, uncles and cousins descend on Grandma's house on Fall Street. Hordes of grandchildren run through the house, banging on tables, the piano or each other. One Easter my youngest uncle, Ed who is a chemical engineer, shows us a new type of army canteen. It isn't the typical gray metal we're used to. Instead, it's sort of dull green, smooth and much lighter than the typical canteen. The surface has a texture that we never felt before. He extolls the advantages of this vessel, telling us how it is almost indestructible. My know-it-all uncles are skeptical, so he says, "Stand back". He jumps up on the porch and throws the thing down as hard as he can onto the brick path leading to Grandma's porch. It bounces up to eye level where he catches it. Then, he holds it out and lets us examine it. Instead of cracking or denting it's unmarked. Amazing! He explains to the incredulous group, "This is plastic."

2

SMOOTH SAILING

My middle school years at Saint Nick's are some of the happiest of my life. The nuns here are a looser, more pleasant group than the black-clad sisters of Sacred Heart. The Dominicans wear light cream robes with a less severe head gear. They smile and even play a bit with us. If a ball comes their way on the playground they pick it up and throw it back. At noon, rain or shine, they're on the playground with us, especially Sister Midget, as we call her, who plays kickball and runs the bases gleefully with her stubby legs. Cheering on their classes in softball, they seem to be on our side, Sister Teresa is ever hopeful as she yells, "Run, Michael, run!" at my tortoise-like pace around the bases.

Early in the school year I'm appointed captain of the school patrol. This is no small honor. It consists principally of standing in the middle of the highway at lunch and the end of the school day stopping traffic so the kids can cross safely. I have a white web belt running around my waist and across my chest with a brass badge on it. I also have a paddle that says STOP in big red letters. I ask one of the sisters what should I do if a car or truck doesn't look like it's going to stop. She tells me to stand my ground and hold up my sign. That night I tell Dad what she commanded. He rolls his eyes and says, "If a truck looks like it isn't going to stop, you get the hell out of the way."

A high point of the school year is our one and only field trip. In those days kids went to school. That was it. But we're lucky. Some kind hearted person donates money to the school to take the eighth graders on a one day trip to the museums in Chicago. This is a very big deal. Chicago was about one hundred miles from Nowhere where we live. Most of us have never been there. In 1949 the interstate highway system was nonexistent. Most roads from small towns like ours were two-lane concrete with tar filling the sections and cracks. It would be a slow trip but all the better for us. A school bus is rented and the twenty some kids plus the assistant pastor and two of the nuns climb in. There's great anticipation. We're all higher than kites. Sister gets us to sing our school song, which I don't remember. All I recall was that it's loud and repeated many times. The bus driver has a hard time with the din in his ears for the two and a half hours it takes to get to the big city. When we got back on the bus to come home he smelled like he had stopped at a brewery. I can't blame him.

The first stop is the Museum of Science and Industry along the shore of Lake Michigan. Obviously, we've never seen the Lake either. It's awesome. The museum is the largest building we've ever seen. It's a huge, granite, castle-like fortress that stretches a couple blocks. Inside, the exhibits blow our small town minds. In 1949, television is a black and white five inch box that isn't on more than about six hours a day. We've not been exposed to the outside world yet. We race around this marvelous place testing the patience and legs of the priest and nuns. There were model ships, planes, trains and the latest farm machinery. We climb on everything that we can. We also ride the rails into a coal mine. In one room I whisper something into the wall and kids standing on the other side can hear me. This is truly a magic castle.

Most of the time my friend, Patsy Black is with me. When we left Ma's Victorian across from the park we moved into a house next door to the Black family. They had two girls, Mary and Patricia. Everyone called Patricia, Patsy. It turns out that she is in the same class as me at Saint Nick's. Patsy has long, raven black hair to match her name, ebony black eyes, a pretty face, and a twinkle in her eye that attracts and intrigues me. She's a really nice girl, clearly the prettiest in our class, and bright in ways not included in the subjects we study. Patsy's older sister has clearly taught her some things I don't know. You might say that she is very mature for a girl her age. In her white *Peter Pan* collar, pullover cashmere sweater, and pencil skirt, she's a delight to see, be with and talk to. At school during recess, while the other girls are playing hopscotch, sometimes Patsy will be at the softball lot watching me play. At school functions, we often find a way to sit together. We're best friends. We talk about little personal things like what high school will be like or what we'll do after we graduate. We get teased by our classmates over how much time we spend together. But I don't care. If I had a sister I would want her to be just like my friend Patsy.

When we stop for lunch at the Museum cafeteria Patsy doesn't go with the other girls. We sit together and share our lunches. I order a hamburger with everything and she has a toasted cheese sandwich. We have a taste of each other's lunch and giggle at nothing, but ourselves. The sisters notice our friendship and are a little apprehensive about how far it might go. They needn't worry.

After lunch we get back on the bus and go to the Field Museum. When we get off the bus and go through the front door I almost fall over. There, behind the small information desk, is a large dinosaur skeleton with its mouth open staring right at me. Next to it on a raised rock platform are two huge elephants. They must be twenty feet tall at the shoulder. One of them with huge curved tusks raises his trunk to the sky and I can hear him roar all the way from Africa. Patsy grabs my arm. "Are you sure they're not alive?" She's a little scared that the elephants aren't really just models. I'm not so certain myself.

The museum is filled with exhibits of animals from Asia and Africa. There are zebras, lots of different kinds of antelope, giraffes, tigers and lions and little wart hogs with their tails sticking straight up in the air as they run. We have a guide in this part of the museum. Once she stops in front of a display and asks us, "Do you know what animal that is?" There are several guesses but none of them are right. She tells us, "That is a cheetah. It is the fastest animal alive." Mr. Know-it-all Billy Hunter pipes up and challenges her, "I think a horse is faster. It can run twenty miles an hour or faster." Then the guide says, "That's pretty fast alright, but a cheetah can run up to seventy miles an hour for a short distance." Billy shuts up.

The last thing we see before we have to leave is the display of native people who lived in America thousands of years ago. Patsy says, pointing at one of the sullen statues in a display, "He looks like Father Connor, doesn't he?" Father Connor is our head priest at Saint Nick's. The assistant hears her and says that isn't very nice, but she's right.

By now it's going on four o'clock. When we come outside our well-lubricated driver was waiting for us. "Let's go slow pokes. We've got to get going before the traffic gets bad." He knows there will be a lot of traffic all the way across Chicago as we head west out of town. The return trip is nothing like the outward bound revelry that morning. It takes about a half hour for the adrenalin to work its way out of our systems. Then, it's nap time. Although some of the kids hang on, most of us fall asleep. I'm sitting by the window toward the back of the bus. Patsy is next to me and one of the nuns is right behind us. Soon Patsy starts to nod off on my shoulder. I shift around a little and see that Sister is also falling asleep. Her head falls forward. In a few minutes she catches herself and sits up. This lasts about sixty seconds and off she goes again. In about thirty minutes we clear Chicago. Then, the drum of the tires on the road gets to me and I'm a goner. We're home in time for a late supper.

A couple weeks after we get back Dad has a recurrence of his chronic stomach problems. He tries different home remedies, but it gets worse so he finally visits the doctor. Immediately, he's sent to the hospital where they test him and confirm an ulcer. It turns out that Dad's not as cool as he acts. He just keeps his anxieties bottled up in his stomach. The diagnosis is that his ulcer is bleeding badly and they need to operate on him. This is scary for me. When I see him get really sick and have to go into the hospital it's the first time he isn't there for me to lean on. I see him before the operation. He says, "Mike, don't worry. The docs here are very good. I'll be fine in a couple of days." Mom is no help. She vacillates among anger, fear and tears. Fortunately, the operation is a success, but it's not to be the last one Dad will undergo.

A month after the field trip it's time for graduation. I do very well at St. Nick's. I'm very involved in school activities from softball, to the Christmas pageant, school patrol captain, serving mass and am in the school choir. I win the American Legion medal awarded to the top all-around student. Given Dad's disdain for the nuns, he's relieved that I'll soon leave St. Nick's for my new high school, The Academy. At graduation Mom is almost satisfied. Her comment is, "Well it's good that you got the medal, but if you'd worked a little harder you would have had the best grades too." Dad's too weak to do or say much of anything except, "Nice going son."

After graduation I don't see Patsy for a couple of years. Her dad is transferred and they move away. When I was a junior in high school they move back to Nowhere. It's great to see her again. She has grown up in more ways than one. She tells me something that gives me more impetus to leave Nowhere behind.

She said, "We moved to California. Our house was in Santa Clara a small farm town in a valley about 50 miles south of San Francisco. Once you get out of the main section a lot of the roads are just gravel. Daddy worked with the farmers to help them fight insects and grow more fruit. The valley is covered with orchards. If you go up on the hills in the spring you can look down and see miles of blossoming fruit trees. It looks like clouds. They call it the Valley of Heart's Delight. It never snows except in the mountains. All winter long it is about 40 to 60 degrees. They grow apricots, cherries, almonds and lots of flowers. In the summer everyone who is old enough works in what they call cutting cots; that's apricots.

17

After they pick the apricots they cut them in half and put them on long tables to dry in the sun. Then they package and ship them to stores. It is really hot in the summer there and you can smell the cots almost everywhere. I loved living there. I wish we could be back." This is like a fairy tale. It's Shangri La. I'll have to learn more about it. It might be a good place to go to college, if we can afford it.

* * *

We have a park in town, creatively named City Park, which sprawls over rolling hills south of town and is surrounded by the ubiquitous corn fields. In the heat of the Midwestern summers the pasture that the city calls its golf course features unwatered fairways as hard as a concrete highway. There were no carts. We walk the course carrying our clubs. Walking four or five miles with steel spikes on rock hard surfaces often we're rewarded with a fine set of shin splints. When it gets really hot we soak towels in water and droop them over our heads, taking them off only to hit a shot. The good news is that the ball rolls forever on those concrete fairways. Even a skinny kid of 15 could hit drives 250 yards in August.

There's a swimming pool in the park. It's about 20 feet by 40 feet and at the deep end plunged to a depth of 4 feet. Hardly anyone ever uses it because it isn't too clean. If you take a chance jumping in you never know what you might meet. One summer day while at a picnic Bob and I go exploring. We're walking along the pool's edge when I turn to say something to him and see this 4 year old face down in the pool thrashing feebly. Like superman, I leap into the abyss at the three foot mark and pull Bob out. He looks at me with wondrous eyes. I've saved his life! If he had swallowed a mouthful of the pool water I don't think my heroics would have mattered. Thirty years later he still thinks I'm a hero.

The third main feature of the park is the baseball diamond. The infield is brick hard dirt. Batted balls bounce in every direction at varying heights. Fielding is more a matter of survival than athletic ability or grace. We just try to get a glove on the ball to knock it down before picking it up and throwing it somewhere. The pitcher's mound and the batter's box have great holes dug by generations of players' cleats. From a distance the pitchers and batters look like they had tiny legs. No one ever thinks about filling the holes.

I'm a great sports junkie. Baseball is my favorite. I'm too small for football, too slow for basketball or track. But I can't hit a balloon with an ironing board so baseball is out. Golf is a minor sport at the Academy. In fact, when I was a freshman and sophomore we didn't even have a golf team. I go into golf by chance. Dad has a mismatched, cheap set of clubs. One day he says that we should go to the golf course and he will show me how to play this game. We hack our way around nine holes before we wear ourselves out. Nevertheless, I really like it. One of the best parts is that golf is a game that you can play alone. Being a bit on the shy side means I don't have to find someone to play with or be embarrassed about how poorly I play. To this day I enjoy being on the course by myself. In good weather it's like a walk in the park.

There was no practice area at our city's golf course. The pro, Mr. Carburry, doesn't have time to teach, because he has to handle the whole operation. So, I just go out on the course and dug it out of the dirt, through constant, unrelenting practice. The first round I play by myself I struggle through with a 136. The second round I shoot 110. Then, I get the hang of it and my scores drop into the mid 90s. Considering that the average player shoots close to 100 I was doing well. Being a natural student I look for instruction books, but there isn't much at that time. Nevertheless, I seem to have a knack for this game and am physically more suited for it than any of the team sports. I play every chance I could. Over the years I play competitively in school, in the Navy and afterward. But in the early days I'm always aware of what my playing partners or the onlookers are thinking about me—the exact opposite of what I should be focusing on.

My best friend in high school, Buddy Forest, is an excellent golfer. When he learns I like the game he recruits me to play with him. In time, learning from him, I bring my scores down into the low 80s. Buddy keeps urging me to play competitively saying that I'm better than most people and will improve from the experience. By the end of high school, I feel confident enough to enter our city championship. It's match play. That is, you play elimination matches against individuals rather than comparing your aggregate score for the whole field. I win the B flight, which frankly surprises me. Emboldened by that I sign up to play in the Western Junior Open, a major amateur event. The tournament is at the esteemed Medina Country Club outside of Chicago.

I start well. In the practice round I shoot an 82. For the first time on a championship course this was quite an accomplishment. I'm feeling very confident; overconfident as it turns out. The qualifying round is the following week. Waiting to tee off each player is introduced to the gallery with their name and club affiliation. Country Club this and Country Club that, these boys, surrounded by their smart aleck friends, were all beautifully dressed, have large tournament size golf bags filled with matched sets of the latest equipment. They're out for a fun day at a prestigious country club that is like home to them. I, on the other end of the fashion stick, wear plain cotton slacks, a regular short sleeve shirt and plain brown golf shoes that have seen many rounds. I have a simple, small canvas bag that is fine for home, but out of place in this company. After the litany of country club affiliations I'm introduced as being from City Park Golf Course. To say the least I'm embarrassed and feel very out of place. My rearing, instead of helping me cope with my lower status, reinforces that I don't belong in this crowd. I'm extremely nervous as I walk onto the first tee. They call my name and I tee up my ball. Setting the driver down behind the ball my nerves twitch and I knock the ball off the tee. I bend over and retee the ball. Talk about nervous now. Without wasting any more time on a practice swing and anxious to get away from the crowd I promptly duck hook my drive into the woods. Needless to say, I don't qualify. Later while navigating my way through the Navy's golf world I learn that concentration turns out to be a very effective tool.

* * *

The local military academy is run by the Benedictine monks, which, while not ideal for Dad, it does seem to him a slight step up. The Academy requires uniforms and I'm looking forward to my spiffy appearance as I pass the girls on the way by the general high school. But, my excitement for the uniform is short-lived. My parents make me wear a hand-me-down from a cousin who is a year older. He is slightly shorter and thinner than even me. I look like a scarecrow in it. By my second year the jacket sleeves are halfway up to my elbows. While I'm fifteen years old and trying to impress girls I look more like Little Lord Fauntleroy than Jack Armstrong, the All American Boy. When I mention my appearance Mom and Dad say they spend a lot of money to send me to the academy and I should show some appreciation rather than complain.

This, although it may be true, doesn't help my fragile self-esteem. Then I grow seven inches and add 30 pounds in the next two years and get new uniforms. The academics are not too difficult and my record is well above average. Frustration comes in extracurricular activities. I aim at making captain and commanding the precision drill team. This is a group of a dozen cadets who show off their ability with intricate marching maneuvers, twirling their rifles and carrying out march commands smartly. I don't work hard enough and settle for lieutenant, which isn't bad, but it isn't the goal either. Later, brother Bob fulfills the dream by becoming the drill team commander.

* * *

My social life begins to pick up in the Academy. I'm a slow starter in this game. At age 16 I have my first real date with a girl named Nancy Phillips whom I've known at St. Nick's. She is a year behind me there. Nancy has no great talent and no noticeable flaws, in the beginning. I can't remember why I choose her or how I get my courage up to ask her out. On the other hand, I don't know why she says yes. She's nice enough looking, but I was to learn soon enough her flaw. Generally speaking, whenever I'm around girls my age I stammer, blush, stumble and otherwise am very cool.

Our date is on a typical Midwestern summer night, meaning hot and humid. I start my 1930 Model A Ford coupe and am so nervous driving over to her house that my foot keeps jumping on the gas pedal, making the black buggy buck and hop. Fortunately, I get it under control before I arrive. Nancy and I go to a drive-in movie in a big field outside of town, to see a Fred Astaire and Ginger Rogers film. In those days you get a newsreel, a cartoon and a feature film, sometimes two, without having to sit through twenty minutes of previews. We arrive just before sundown. When I try to hook the speaker on her side of the car window I slip and punch her breast. Neither of us knows what to do, so we ignore the misstep. Very quickly I head to the refreshment counter and buy some cokes and a large popcorn for us to share. We chat a bit nervously while we eat the popcorn and wait for the movie to start. There are periods of silence broken only by the sound of popcorn crunching. We're not exactly Clark Gable and Claudette Colbert in It Happened One Night. There was nothing happening this night. Although I sense that the protocol is to put my arm around her, I have no idea what to do after that. If I tried I probably would have knocked the popcorn over. So, I decide to be cool. After the speaker incident I don't want her to think I am some kind of sex fiend.

Following the movie I go around to her side and disconnect the speaker without another blunder. When I try to start the car old reliable Model A won't kick over. After many tries finally, I have to get out, go around to the front and crank the motor. I instruct Nancy to pull the spark lever down about an inch and once the car starts shove the lever back up and step lightly on the gas. She gets it all correct except the lightly part. Nancy must have been a bit nervous also. When she hit the gas hard the car bucked and roared, nearly knocking me over, scaring her and me and drawing stares and laughter of people driving out. Finally, everything calms down and we head for the only drive-in restaurant in town, the kind with carhops on roller skates, where all the cool guys and gals hang out and flirt. The cool kids are making fun of my Model A. "Hey, is that thing made of cast iron? Nice color, what is it, black? How do you start it, push it down a hill?" When the carhop skates back to the car with our order she asks if we want ketchup and mustard. Nancy replies yes to the mustard, but no to the ketchup, explaining that she has an acid condition. Good-bye, Nancy. I wasn't going to date a girl with an acid condition, whatever that means! After I drop Nancy at her house, permanently, it starts to rain and I can't get the driver side window up. Soon I'm all wet in both senses. Great romantic evening.

Even with its poor showing with Nancy, the Model A is my boon companion through my high school years. Yes, it's painted black, like every other Model A. It has a rumble seat and cost $75. Dad bought the car for me when I turned sixteen since we live several miles from the Academy. Mom thinks it is an extravagance. Taking the bus should be good enough for me. As one of the few kids with a car in high school, I drive my friends everywhere. If there are more than one, the others sit in the rumble seat with no seat belts, going slightly airborne every time I hit a bump. In an effort to dress it up a little I spend hours with the roughest sand paper available to scrape the paint off the black wire spokes and repaint them red. It is 20 years old when Dad buys it, but through two winters Mr. Ford never fails to start. You just have to know how to do it. A crank sticks out in front just below the radiator. I turn the engine over a couple times. This loosens the almost solid oil and the transmission from their overnight sleep. It makes it easier for the cold engine to turn the drive shaft. The next step is to move a lever on the steering column to retard the spark. If I do one and two and hit the starter, this ancient mechanical marvel coughs and starts. You would cough too if you had sit outside in a Midwestern winter night.

* * *

The Model A gives me freedom. Also, it allows me to make money on my own. Dad builds a wooden platform that hooks onto the rear bumpers. I lash our red gas-driven Toro lawn mower from Sears and Roebuck to it and spend the last two summers of high school driving around town mowing lawns. Gas is less than 20 centers a gallon, and I charge anywhere from $1.00 to $1.75 per lawn. That leaves enough money to go to a movie and have popcorn and a box of Jujubes. I'm also able to put aside a little money to take to college.

My lawn-mowing gig takes me into heretofore unknown corners of Nowhere life. One of the more memorable examples is on a hot August day when I'm mowing the lawn for a middle-aged widow; she seems advanced in years at the time but is probably only about 35. When I stop to cool off and she hears the motor stop, she comes out and asks me if I would like some cold lemonade. How nice of her! She comes out a few minutes later with the drink and sits down next to me. She's wearing a thin cotton dress that was rather low cut and bulging out loosely. It didn't seem like she's wearing a bra, although I don't dare look. She tells me what a good job I'm doing. What a hard worker I am and, oh yes, how cute I am. She says her name is Lilly and she leans on me until I almost fall into her cleavage. She puts her hand on my knee and suggests I take a break and come into the house where it's cool. If I hadn't known what to do with Nancy, I sure don't know what to do with Lilly! I jump up, give her the glass with a quick "thank you," and mow the rest of the lawn in record time. When I tell Dad about it he just laughs. Mom notes that if I had gone inside it wouldn't have done the poor widow any good. When I tell my buddy Johnny Burton, who delivers bakery goods for a local company, he grins and tells me this is what delivery guys call a "couch stop."

* * *

The most interesting experience of my high school years is Mary Bridget Harrington. Irish as the Blarney stone, she's fair-skinned, reddish blonde and blue-eyed—an early version of Doris Day except she can't carry a tune in a bucket. Of course, she is Catholic, which delights my family. I meet Bridget casually at a mixer for Academy boys and St. Mary's girls. We talk a little bit and I like her. She is easy to be around and uncomplicated, not like some of the girls who are always scheming. Bridget doesn't ask for much and laughs a lot. I see her a couple more times, but am too chicken to ask her out. No one would mistake me for Casanova.

One night I'm at the local East-West Club, a supervised meeting place for teenagers. We can dance and meet up in a supposedly wholesome environment. The old building had originally housed the city hall, courtroom, and jail and is a red brick monstrosity with white granite lintels and eaves. The first floor courtroom has been converted into a dance hall with subdued lighting and a small movie theatre, whose promising atmosphere gave it the nickname; the Passion Pit. The dance floor has a ratio of about ten girls to every boy. Mostly the girls dance with each other. The boys gravitate to the basement, a concrete dungeon that had been the jail. The cells have been removed and ping pong tables installed.

After rehearsing my speech a hundred times I decide to make my move. I ask Patsy Black to dance and lead her to the floor for my version of a two-step. After stepping on her toes a few times and losing the beat of the music, I blurt out, "I want to ask you something." Her dark, knowing eyes light up, and she tilts her face up to me. I look deeply into her pretty face and ask, "Do you think Bridget Harrington would go out with me?"

I can't adequately describe the look on Patsy's face at that moment, but it's somewhere between a hurt kitten and an angry elephant. I never saw a woman's eyes flash like that before or since. Although I'm not too smart when it comes to members of the other gender one look at the oncoming stampede and I get out of the way. Two-step Michael, exit right.

Despite this narrow escape, eventually I manage to get a date with Bridget. She's only my second date, and, unlike Nancy, already has my heart in her hand. I ask her to a Saturday party being held by Academy boys for St. Mary's girls. With butterflies in my stomach, I hop into the Model A and drive to her house. Her small, lop-sided, gray farm house of none-too-distinct style obviously needs a new paint job. It's set among a cluster of elm trees that help shade it from the hot summer sun. Mr. Harrington, Paddy to his friends, is a husky, hardworking farmer tending this small place of about 125 acres. Padraig is unquestionably Irish in every aspect. He is red haired and very outgoing. Always talking, singing Irish ballads and making Irish jokes, he is the center of attention. He loves to tell stories of his childhood in Ireland.

On that unforgettable first date when Bridget introduced me to her mom and dad he grabs me tightly but gently around the neck and mutter, "Well, me bucko, so you're tinkin you're takin me Bridget to a party tonight are ya?"

I reply breathlessly and a bit apprehensively, "Yes sir it's at the Academy," figuring this will make it sound very wholesome.

"Well, I presume there'll be priests there to keep you young hot bloods out of trouble, will there?

"Daddy!" Bridget exclaimed.

Her mother chimes in supporting her alarm. "Padraig you know of Michael. He's a fine catholic boy."

"Aye, that he is. I'm just wantin him to know that I'll be watchin."

With that we leave, me sweating still from the picture of Mr. Harrington breaking me in two. Bridget explains as we get into the car, "You know daddy was only teasing you. He does that with any boy that comes to see me. He really wouldn't hurt you." The memory of that date is all about Mr. Harrington, not about his daughter. All I can think of is his huge hands around my neck.

Later in my relationship with his bonny daughter whenever I arrive at the Harrington place I will be greeted by him with song.

"Oh Danny boy the pipes the pipes are calling." He'll start.
"From glen to glen and down the mountain side," I reply in my teenage croak.
"The summer's gone, and all the roses falling." He'll howl sorrowfully.
"Tis you, 'tis you must go, and I must bide." I finish with a warble.

Then, he'll give me that bone crushing handshake and a paralyzing slap on the back again.

The big man is so sentimental that he tears up at any tender scene from the birth of a calf to a basket of kittens. One time his sentiment gets the better of him in a big way. Padraig won a shot putter's spot on the United States 1936 Olympic team headed for Berlin. He figured this is a good, and perhaps only, time he can stop in Ireland to visit family. So, along the way he drops in on Mum and Da and all the cousins, aunts and uncles. Mrs. Harrington told me, "The dear boy was so taken by his return to his roots in the old sod that he niver didn't make it to Berlin, the poor divil."

Bridget's mom is a small, pretty, black-haired and freckled colleen who works side by side with her husband. She tends their garden, milks their two cows and shushes their small herd of Angus cattle around. They grow corn and raise a flock of chickens, They scrape by year after year, praying that beef and eggs prices won't drop. I become very attached to her. Whenever I visit she will always give me a hug and take me into her fragrant kitchen for some pie or cake. In the winter, sitting in front of a warm oven eating Mrs. Harrington's creations, is a delicious pleasure.

In tried-and-true Michael style, my shyness is one catch in my plans for a Grand Romance with Bridget. In the beginning we mostly hang out with our friends, going to movies, picnics, house parties. Drinking is minimal except when the guys get together without the girls. Eventually, I ask her to go steady, mostly to be like the rest of my friends, I think. After several months, our connection matures. But it becomes more familiar and less romantic. I like girls a lot, but I'm just not up to being Don Juan. The other factor is that as I get to know her better it becomes apparent that she is what might be described unsympathetically as an airhead. A truly nice girl, always pleasant and smiling, but only slightly connected to the real world. The relationship is restricted to a hug and peck on the cheek, almost like a sister whom I love. Nice girl, but no future there, again.

* * *

Finally, high school comes to an end. I finish second in my class, to my parents' disappointment and my own frustration. However, generally I have a good time. I learn a lot about myself, which is the best education one can obtain. I learn from my little lawn mowing business that I like to be my own boss. This leads to focusing on golf, an independent activity that covers my inherent shyness. I love learning but am unfocused. I have no idea of what I want to be when I grow up. Underneath it all I'm a little scared about my future and I'm a bit lonely. But no one knows this.

3

SURF CITY

After hearing Patsy's description of life in California I do some investigating. Everything I read sounds great. I watch televised football games from Los Angeles. In November while we are putting on coats and boots for impending Midwestern snow storms they are going to games wearing white shirts and chino pants in 70 degree weather. Cold weather has never appealed to me. I don't like to ice skate or ski. I like to play golf, which is difficult through snow drifts.

Throughout my senior year I make strong and continuous arguments with Mom and Dad for going to UCLA in Los Angeles. "UCLA is a great school. It is highly ranked nationally, particularly in political science and economics."

Dad counters with, "There are lots of great schools here. How about Notre Dame? It has a long tradition and a beautiful campus. Plus, it's only four hours away."

Mom chimes in with, "Al, I think he just wants to get away from us."

"Mom, this has nothing to do with you. It is about the school I would like to attend."

The question is moot for the time being. I need to work for a year or so to make enough money for college. Dad's career has stagnated as a result of his chronic ulcer. It causes him to lose some time at work and not perform as well as he used to. I find a job at a paper box factory. It's housed in an old brown brick building on the south side of town. We get printed and embossed paper from the mills and cut it into shapes that fit around small boxes. Then we cut the cardboard and match the paper to the box. The end product goes mainly to retail stores to wrap purchases. The work has a bit of danger for the cutters. These men stack up piles of paper and cardboard and cut them to shape in large cutting machines. The machines are set up with two buttons that must be pushed simultaneously before the big knife can drop down and slice through the stack. In order to cut more paper faster and earn a bonus, some of the cutters rig one button on permanently so they can shove the paper through with one hand while pushing the other button with their second hand. Occasionally, their timing is off and so are their fingers.

The workers are for the most part lightly educated. Many of them went to work right out of high school; some even before that. As a result they're not too refined, but they are a great group to work with. The ladies on the shop floor are especially funny. They gossip constantly about who's coming in early to screw who behind the cardboard bales in the warehouse. They even bet on it. When I walk by they have fun teasing me with words, gestures, and exposed cleavage, "Hey Mikey, take a look at this! Hey Mike, what's that in your pants?" I start as a gopher and eventually graduate to the shipping dock. Both are good jobs. Gophers have the run of the place, and shippers make comparatively good money.

The argument at home over college goes on for weeks. After my persistent, resolute harangue, Mom and Dad give in with some reluctance accompanied by a good bit of guilt tripping. When the time finally comes to leave, Mother's parting words are, "Well I guess you don't need us any more, except of course for money." To a small degree she is right. But I would have liked more guidance, a little love and less criticism.

The last week in August 1955 Dad drives me to Chicago to catch the California Zephyr bound for the Golden State. The train is a string of a dozen silver-sided cars each with a name such as Silver

Mustang, Silver Saddle, or Silver Lariat. A few cars in the front of the train have what are called Vista Domes. These have seats and sky lights on top of the passenger cars. We go up a few steps and are transported to the top of the world. As the train pulls out of Union Station, I feel the power of the great locomotive as it makes the cars shudder. Slowly, the train gains speed and starts west out of the big city and across the flat prairie of northern Illinois. In half an hour we are passing through the beginning of a sea of cornfields that extend across the state, jump the Mississippi River, and continue unstopped through the state of Iowa. It's a two-hundred-mile carpet of corn. After a couple hours in the Vista Dome I need to move. I go down to the platform between the cars. From here I'm sometimes as close as twenty feet from the cornfield. I can smell the corn. The six-foot stalks with foot-long drooping green leaves are the base of the yellow tassels sticking out of the top. I know that within a month the people in Nowhere will be harvesting the corn. They will pull the ears off the stalks, shuck the leaves from the ears, and pick off the silk that grows along the kernels. Then, they will throw them into boiling water for a few minutes while they warm some butter and have salt handy. The memory of that feast is almost enough to turn me back. After Iowa we transition into the wheat fields of Nebraska. Just as in Illinois and Iowa the waving fields of now golden wheat stalks go on to the horizon. Farms here are not a hundred or two hundred acres; they're a thousand.

The next morning we arrive in Denver and I sit in a Vista Dome as the train glides through a washing system to get rid of the road dust. After watching the shower I go to the dining car for some breakfast. The car is nearly full so they seat me at a table with a man that looks to be an old cowboy. He's dressed in well broken in jeans and the typical western shirt complete with string tie. "Mornin son." He says as I take a seat. "Where ya headed?"

"I'm going to California, how about you?"

"Me, ah'm jist heddin home to Cheyene. Been in Chicago at a rodeo. Rode one bronc for eight seconds, but the second one like to throw me inta the cheap seats. Got a medal and a check in the calf ropin though. All in all had a good time."

"That sounds pretty exciting. Have you been rodeoing a long time?"

"Ever since I could git on board one of those ornery critters."

I figured this might be a chance to learn something from a man who has spent his life roaming the country. He must have seen a lot. "Tell me sir, what have you learned from your travels. It must be an interesting life."

"Interstin? You could say that. I'd say more like educational. I seen and worked with all type people; some good, some not so good and some downright ornery. Layin in the dust with a thousand pound bull tryin to kick ya to kingdom come does cause ya to wonder why you're doin this. You know what I figger?"

"No, what?"

"I figger ya gotta do what ya like to do even if it means getting kicked once in the while. Why stay home warm and safe when there is so much to see and do in god's great world. It ain't all fun, but it beats settin on the porch watchin other people go by. Young fella, as you come to deciding which trail you're gonna pick for your life remember this; getting kicked once in a while is still better than rottin on the porch."

The Denver and Rio Grande Western takes over here and adds a couple locomotives to power the train through the Rockies. Turning north, paralleling the front range of the Rocky Mountains, we are like immigrants looking for a way through this impregnable mass. After passing through over twenty tunnels we reach Cheyenne, Wyoming. Then, it is west again toward Salt Lake City. We cross northern Nevada and enter California from the north down the Feather River Canyon. It was named Feather River by settlers because of the thousands of birds in the area whose feathers floated on the river. This is the northern tip of the great central valley of California. It is a true cornucopia garden nearly one thousand miles long south to the Mexican border. This fertile valley is contained on the east by the Sierra Nevada range and on the west by the Coast range. In between there are seemingly endless farms producing every type of fruit and vegetable including orchards of plums, peaches, apricots, cherries, almonds, and of course oranges. In the southern end there are great cotton fields that cover one thousand acres or more along with date palm farms in the desert.

At Marysville, which is at least a hundred miles north of San Francisco and four hundred miles north of Los Angeles, I get my first glimpse of the fabled land of California. However, Marysville is not typical twentieth-century California. It had been Gold Rush territory, not Surf City. Nevertheless, at the tiny Marysville train station I see my first red-tile-roof adobe building and my first palm tree. The palm is no more than five feet tall, but it's a real live palm tree. At last we reach Oakland and are transported across the bay by ferry to San Francisco. On the final leg of the journey from SF to LA, I ride the Southern Pacific Daylight train along the coast and inland. We go back and forth from beaches and ocean views to miles of vineyards stretching up and down the hills of the coastal valleys. In Los Angeles the sun-tanned, blonde beach babies are sporting bikinis, which I've never seen except in movies. I'm distracted, so to speak. No competition here. I'm a couple light years behind the hip southern California boys.

In the 1950s orange groves radiate for miles out of Los Angeles to the mountains on the east and south to the Mexican border. Outside of LA there are only small towns. The rush to the Golden State is just beginning. Within twenty years it will be the most populated state in the nation. One of my uncles settles in Laguna Beach in the early 50s. I borrow a car one weekend and drive down Pacific Coast Highway to see him. He meets me at the street: "Hi Mike, did you have any problem finding us?

"No Unc, it was just the way you describe it." We enter his house. I can see through from the entry right out the back. I'm awestruck. His house is three stories built into the cliff. This is the same uncle who introduced us to plastic on Grandma's front steps. His neighbors are the famous Nelson family: Ozzie, Harriett, David, and Ricky. Uncle

33

Ed's view is a 180 degree panorama of the Pacific Ocean including some huge rocks to the south where the surf crashes continuously. When we step out of the bottom level of his place we're actually on the beach about fifty yards from the water's edge. This is truly the paradise I'm seeking.

"This is fantastic. What a view and to live right on the sand. It's unbelievable."

"That's why I bought it," he says, smiling like a cat that just caught the mouse.

The weather is superb in the fall, naturally. There is no stifling heat and best of all no humidity. Every day the sky is cloudless and the sun is brightly transiting the sky. Great beach cities circle the Los Angeles basin from Malibu on the north to Long Beach on the south. My first experience with ocean swimming doesn't come until the so-called winter. Winter to me is leaden gray skies, cold wind, black leafless trees, and snow on the ground. In LA winter is a lot like summer only a bit cooler, with some rain and less smog. The sky is blue and the sun is out. During a school break a group of us drive thirty-five miles from west LA to Long Beach. A broad sandy beach runs the length of the city that is fast becoming a retirement town because of its great weather.

On the beach the temperature is very close to 80. I ask the guys, "How's the water?"

"Nice," they tell me. So I decide to go for a swim. I run down the beach to the water's edge and dive in. Ice! What a shock! The ocean is not like Wisconsin's summer lakes. The water temperature is about 60 degrees. I can hardly catch my breath. I can't come running back out in front of my friends so I take a couple strokes and then stand in the water up to my waist for a minute. Then I notice I am the only fool in this arctic sea. As slowly as I can while retaining my dignity I come out onto the beach. Someone says to me, "Pretty cold, huh?" To which I reply, "Yeah, but not too bad."

UCLA is located in Westwood, an aptly named western section of Los Angeles. It's in the middle of a mix of commercial buildings and upscale residences. The Pacific Ocean is about five miles straight west and the campus sits at the foot of the San Gabriel Mountains. It's not the typical tree-covered Ivy League campus and the students are not trust fund babies of rich Eastern families. The student body is different from what I expected or anything I've experienced till now. Instead of the typical group of eighteen- to twenty-year-olds we've got people of all ages and backgrounds. There are WWII veterans in grad school and Korean Vets who have just been discharged, people who have seen it all and are not easily impressed. They are mature well beyond their years. I feel like a child among them.

When I check in at the Registrar's office there is a very long line. It takes almost two hours to reach the front and pick up my materials. They give me a map of the campus and a note telling me where my dorm is. After a quarter mile slog across campus lugging my suitcase and getting lost once I find the building and go up to the second floor to my room. The room is about twelve by twelve feet. On the far side are bunk beds. The lower bunk has someone's duffel bag on it. There are two desks by the window overlooking the east section of the campus. The desks face each other. Along one wall are two well-worn dressers and a closet big enough for a couple person's clothes, provided one person doesn't have any to hang there. There's a small room with a toilet and sink. The showers are down the hall. I throw my luggage on the top bunk and sit down by the window to catch my breath and cool off. Suddenly, a big, blonde, muscular fellow bursts into the room. He says, "Hi roomie, I'm Roger. What's your name?"

"Hi, I'm Mike."

"Where you from Mike?"

"I'm from a small town in Illinois. Where're you from?"

"Hard to tell. I just got out of the army. I was a paratrooper serving in Korea. My parents live in Fresno, but I don't know where I'll settle when I graduate. I've only got two years to finish my degree. Uncle Sam plucked me out of school when Korea was hot. Now I'm back on the G.I. Bill."

We're both political science students although I have to get the basic courses out of the way before they let me tackle the interesting stuff. Roger is a force of nature. He's a natural leader attracting people all the time. We have a constant stream of young men, and once in a while a woman in the room, discussing the state of the world. It's a great opportunity for me to hear viewpoints different from those I grew up with in Middle America. The discussions center around the best form of political philosophy. Being young idealists we don't all believe the party line that democracy is the best for everyone. In addition, we have students from all over the world. Some come from countries where tribalism is the dominant form of government. In fact, when you really examine it, outside of Europe, tribalism is very common. Before the arrival of Europeans in North America tribes were the norm here as well. After we eliminated or subjugated them we built a democratic system. Still, there is an undercurrent of tribalism in America between the north and the south. Could it be that this is the natural state of governance for human beings? Democracy has worked pretty well for us, but must it be the best for everyone? Roger makes the point that the Korean War was not about territory, it was about imposing a political philosophy on South Korea. Meeting people like the cowboy, Roger and foreign students opens my eyes to the possibilities the world offers. I'm lucky that I get a chance to experience it before buying into the get a job, get married and get kids syndrome.

I don't find classes at UCLA very difficult. Additionally, I have no idea of what I want to do with my life except play second base for the Chicago White Sox. During the summers at home I play on a number of teams in various leagues. I settle on second base because I don't have a strong enough arm for shortstop or third base. I'm proud that throughout these summer leagues I never make a single error. On the other hand, I can't hit a baseball out of the infield. My disappointment is overshadowed by my Dad's who had been a good athlete in high school and in the AAU basketball league.

I decide to major in political science and economics since the White Sox don't need me. Those subjects seem to provide a broad base for whichever way I decide to go after college. At this point the poli-sci/econ faculty is just starting to develop. It is an exciting time to be studying those disciplines given the turmoil that has engulfed the world. We tend to focus a lot of attention on the political and social side of communism. This leads to studying Russia, and since there is a large Asian population in California, China is key topic as well.

In my freshman year at UCLA I build a close friendship with a classmate, Raul, nick- named Bump because he's forever bumping into things. He's a local fellow and son of a contractor. His distinction is that he has coolest car I've ever seen. It's what I imagined a California guy would have—midnight blue with lacquer paint so deep it looks like you can stick your finger into it. The finish is so clear you can use it as a mirror. It is lowered, cleared of almost all chrome, and sports deep rumbling exhaust pipes. When he tromps on the gas it sounds like a jet taking off. His door opener is a single chrome button. The inside is plush with cream-colored upholstery and wood accents everywhere. I'm mesmerized by it. This machine is the envy of the school and the greatest chick magnet on the West Coast.

I spend the first term at UCLA trying to get acclimated to the wonders of this paradise. In my second year I'm feeling more comfortable, so I go out for the debate team, the newspaper, and the golf team. I'm pretty good with words and think debate would be a good development program for me. To qualify for the debate team applicants are put through a series of mock debates. I feel I've done quite well during the trials. The number of applicants is reduced gradually from about twenty-five to twelve before the last cut. At this point my old lack of self-confidence seeps back in. I can see the intensity building and how confrontational it'll be. This is a little too threatening to me and I drop out of the competition.

The newspaper is another story. In high school I had been sports editor of our rag, so I think I'm pretty good. I decide to submit a couple pieces on the sports life of the school. Steering away from the overcrowded game analysis angle, I think human interest is something I can handle. I interview a half dozen of the jocks. Then, I take what I think are the more interesting ones and write them up. I deliver them to the pretentious faculty overseer who tries to dress like his idea of a hard-bitten newspaper editor. This chain-smoking phony looks over my offerings and tells me they aren't sophisticated enough for the *UCLA Daily Bruin*. In short, my stuff is Corn Belt, sophomoric. He's probably right, but my response is, What the hell does he know? His journalist career is limited to two years as a part-time copy boy while working his way through college. Nevertheless, in class he constantly refers to "My experience in the newspaper game." No matter, it's strike two.

The last is the golf team. Here again there is a qualification round to earn a spot on the practice team. If you finish in the top ten, you qualify. The top six players will be in most of the matches with other schools. I feel confident of my game. Last summer since my victory in our city championships I'm regularly shooting in the high 70s, which isn't bad for the days before golf became the obsession it is today. I'm not feeling very well the day of the qualifier, but I have to play or give up. I start out par, birdie, par, par. Then I three putt for a bogey. Next hole is a long par three and I bogey again. I play the last three holes one over par and finish the front nine with a 38. It looks like I'm on track to break 80 and make the team. Starting the back nine I'm very tired. I don't play well, dragging myself around the course. I shoot 43, which puts me one over the 80 limit for consideration.

By the time I finish I've a fever and can hardly walk. I literally stagger to the school infirmary and am diagnosed with mononucleosis. For four days I lie in bed and enjoy a shot of penicillin in my butt delivered each morning by a nurse who must have gotten her training at a slaughterhouse. I have no appetite and drop several pounds that I can't afford to lose. When they release me a couple days later I'm told to cool it for the next sixty days, at least.

It's beginning to dawn on me that my half efforts at a random smattering of activities is getting me nowhere. The world is a very competitive, unsympathetic place. It's not like home. It's apparent that although my parents love me the world doesn't share their feelings. Second place is a lonely spot. No one remembers who finished second. It's like Mom says, "Second place is just the first loser." I've got to shape up.

* * *

My resolution on this is weakened, however, by the arrival of my first college girlfriend. Somehow, probably due to his four wheels, Bump is invited to a Sunday afternoon garden party at Mount Saint Mary's College and he drags me along. MSM is a very prestigious, expensive women's college located in the Santa Monica Mountains north of UCLA with a sweeping view of the Los Angeles Basin. As soon as we arrive the coeds surround the car. We feel like Elvis. I drop into the background so that I won't be overrun.

I watch the swarming with my usual amusement. Talk about a four-wheel personality. Then, as I'm musing over how unpolished I am, someone at my shoulder says quietly, "Lesson number one on how attract girls."

I turn and see this tall brunette staring at me with a bemused look in her eye. She is very neatly, yet casually dressed in a sweater and slacks. Her hair is pulled back and she has sun glasses perched on her head. My first reaction is Bel Air snob. Then she smiles and her warmth comes through. In my usual Joe Casual mode I stand there tongue-tied. Finally, when she sees I can't speak she asks, "Do you have a name?"

"Oh, oh, yeah. I'm Mike. Mike Still from UCLA."

"UCLA, huh? Is that where you were born?"

"Oh no, actually I'm from Illinois. I just go to school at Westwood."

"Did you come with Don Juan over there?"

"Yeah. He's my buddy."

"Does he always attract girls like this?"

"Pretty much."

"If I were you, I might be jealous of his car."

"Why? It attracts lots of girls and I get the leftovers." I laugh.

"Well, I guess that makes me a leftover, right?"

"No, no. You're too pretty for that."

"Nice recovery, Romeo. My name is Florence. Obviously, everyone calls me Flo."

"Nice to meet you, Flo. Do you have a last name also?"

"Weinberg. Yes, I'm Jewish and I know I should be at USC. I just thought I'd go see how the other half live. My dad owns a commercial window washing company. I'm an only child. I'm an Aries and my family lives in Beverly Hills. Anything else you'd like to know? What's your sign?"

"No U turn."

"So, you're a joker too? Cough it up. What's your sign?"

"I'm not into astrology. Where I come from we think it's hogwash."

"Where I come from we like to play with it. What's your birth date?"

"July 30."

"So, you're a Leo. I'll have to watch out for you. Aries and Leo are very combustible."

"What do you mean?"

"Passion and fun drive a relationship between Aries women and Leo men. Both are emotional, independent, and creative personalities. Sex is pretty wild, since these are both fire signs. The Aries woman needs to be number one and Leo likes to lead. Both signs need ego-stroking. If Leo remembers that Aries need to be first in line, then there's a chance for success. Do you think you can handle that?"

"I have no idea what you're talking about."

"Let's go for a walk and I'll explain it. Where did you say you were from, cowboy?"

"Nowhere. I'm from a small, dull town in the middle of an Illinois cornfield. We're pretty basic. We don't put much stock in anything other than enough rain for the corn and going to church on Sunday."

"Wow. You are going to be a real challenge," she says as we round a corner in the back of the garden. The next thing I know she has her arms around my neck and is kissing me like I've never been kissed before. I immediately snap to attention.

"Well, maybe you're not as backward as you act. We need to get to know each other better. Do you live in a dorm on campus?"

"Yes."

"Well, cowboy, I don't know why, but I really like you. Must be your sign. I have an apartment in Westwood. Why don't we go there and test the zodiac?"

I'm about to come apart. I've never met a woman like this before. Ten minutes after we meet she propositions me. "I don't have a car. I came with Bump."

"A boy from Nowhere with a friend called Bump. This is going to be interesting. I don't think Bump will miss you. I have a car. Say goodbye to Don Juan and we'll go. That is, unless you have something better to do this afternoon, like wash your cat."

I figure that Flo sees me as an unpretentious country bumpkin, so different from her Beverly Hills friends that I'm interesting to her. Don't know where this might lead, but what the hell do I have to lose? In twenty minutes we're back in Westwood. She has a very nice one-bedroom apartment just south of Wilshire Boulevard. It's in a small building with about a dozen units. She parks her canary yellow 1950 Chevy Bel Air in the garage underneath the building and we take the elevator up to her third floor unit. It's bright and airy with a small balcony and a view west toward the ocean. The apartment isn't high enough to see over other buildings to the beach, but it is a cheerful place. The unit looks like it came furnished so there is nothing special about it. She drops her purse and keys on a table inside the door and turns to me. She looks at me, smiles, and kisses me again. I'm beginning to get the idea that I'm just an amusement, a little diversion for her.

For the next few months Flo takes me on as a refinement project. We go to art museums where my first exposure to fine art draws me to Monet and Renoir, both very romantic. Flo steers me away from the easy charm of the impressionists to the challenges of the cubists. Her favorites are Braque, Matisse, and Picasso. "Well, country boy," she says, "you're ever so cute, but you just can't get the corn out of your representational world, can you?"

Eventually her condescension begins to get to me. At first I love learning about avant-garde art and the intricate hierarchy of proper tableware. And the sex was great. But after a while I feel uncomfortable with her little put-downs and the fact that she never introduces me to her family. Flo doesn't invite me to holiday celebrations. I'm the goy she tells her girlfriends about.

The tension between us comes to a head when I spend a weekend at her apartment. Literally, overnight everything changes. She throws a little party on Saturday night for some friends from the Bel Air/Beverly Hills area and from Mount Saint Marys, including a young man and woman who have grown up with her. Their noses are so high in the air they remind me of bird dogs. The woman asks me where I'm from since it's clear that I'm not an LA native.

"I grew up in a small town in northern Illinois. Lots of cornfields and not much else."

"Well that must account for it. For your awkwardness."

I laugh and ask, "What do you mean?"

"I usually don't have to explain myself, but in your case apparently I must. Your fashion sense is right out of the barnyard and a decade late at that. Your ideas are vintage Franklin Delano Roosevelt. And your grammar is often egregious. Is that sufficient?"

Her boyfriend laughs uproariously, and Flo laughs too. I'd like to pop the bitch, but I guess that would be too barnyard. I'm mortified and angry at the shrew's rudeness and Flo's lack of support.

I'm pissed the rest of the evening until everyone has left and then I confront Flo. "Why didn't you say something when your bitchie little friend insulted me?"

"Oh Mikie, can't you take a joke."

We clean up the apartment and go to bed, me still steaming and her still annoyed at my sulking. She goes to sleep immediately and I lie there trying to tamp down my anger and embarrassment.

In the morning, I try to get us back to normal. "What do you want to do today?"

"Actually, I've a lot of homework to do today." This is a first. Previously, for Flo, homework had never been allowed to interfere with fun. Even a bumpkin like me can take a hint. I say, "I better leave you to it then." As we stand at the door I gave her a little kiss that isn't returned. After searching her face all I can think of to say is, "You take care." She gives me a wan smile and nods. End of show.

* * *

After Flo's slam dunk I come to and see that it's time to get to work. My time at UCLA has been one long stretch of mediocrity. It's punctuated by small failures like my fruitless attempts to join the newspaper, debate, and golf teams. I realize that my accomplishments will never match my ambitions if I don't focus. I look at the calendar and note that the Selective Service System will soon have me in its sights. It's time to figure out where I'm headed and get on with it. I turn my attention back to my studies and the rest of my sophomore year is socially blank, but educationally fruitful.

Moving into upper level classes in the fall of '57 the poli sci and econ classes are challenging as well as enlightening. I'm lucky to have excellent profs in both topics. Kamalo Somayo is a bright, charming, well-built young fellow from Hawaii. He looks like an over-age beach boy. He likes to be called by his first name, and the young women love him. When he isn't working with us he's playing tennis and chasing the local talent. Somayo's well-versed in Asia Pacific politics, and he loves to pose a complex question and then sit back with a Cheshire Cat smile as we struggle to answer it. One example was, "If you were able to set up the political system for a small Asian country what form would you choose and why?"

In the econ class Ed Podatkin is quite different from Kamalo, but just as charismatic. He's a very large man, swarthy, Slavic or Russian in origin. His beard is so thick I think he must have to shave twice a day to keep it under control. If he had chosen to grow a full beard he would have looked like a great black bear. While he expects the same level of effort and performance as Kamalo, he's much less direct. His demeanor is thoughtful and kind. When he poses questions or describes some economic theory he almost always hints at the answer. Then he becomes part of the discussion group, engaging us as equals, probing our hypotheses and nudging us to see things from a different angle. His classes are not just rewarding but *fun*.

Between Somayo and Podatkin I begin to understand how the world really works. I'm not interested in political science or economics to make a career in politics. But I grasp the truth that somehow I have to use these forces to achieve my goals. Life is much more complex than I thought when I left home. Success will be a function of understanding how to use information to shape my career.

* * *

Having failed in love and grown in academia, I step back and ask myself where should I focus my extracurricular attention? Knowing I can't succeed if I spread my energy too thinly, I abandon my flirtation with debate and newspapering and concentrate on one of my earliest loves, golf. As a UCLA student I receive discounted green fees at the city golf courses. With Flo out of the picture, I'm able to play on weekends and at least one afternoon during the week.

The course I play most often is Rancho Park. It runs along the south side of Pico Boulevard between Patricia and Motor Avenues. Across the street and two blocks east is Twentieth Century Fox Studios. The course is an urban forest in the midst of concrete. It's heavily played, so anytime I go out I can get into a group. The locals like to play for money, to keep it interesting, as they say. There are a number of fellows who wager serious money. They really don't care about golf except as a gambling vehicle. They're as addicted to gambling on the golf course as someone who visits the card parlor, pool hall, or their bookie.

The standard game is built around the Nassau system. It includes optional or automatic presses. This means that at any moment whoever is down two holes or a nine hole side can request a press if they are not playing automatic presses. It makes the next hole, or even the next nine holes, count double. Under this system a person can make or lose a significant sum. To make matters even more interesting it's possible to get into a group match. This will have several teams of two people playing against all other teams in the group as well as the other team in one's foursome. At the end of the round the mathematics can be quite complex. I get involved in such a match early in my experience at the Park before I fully realize the risks. The bets are reasonable, five dollars a unit. I figure the worst I can do is lose $15 to the other team in my foursome. I'm to be educated very quickly.

We start early on a typical southern California winter Saturday morning. An absolutely clear sky, warm but not humid with a slight breeze coming in from the ocean, makes it an ideal day for golf. Rancho Park is flat with relatively tight, tree-lined fairways and small greens. It's more difficult than the typical muni course. This morning I'm paired with a forty-something Mexican named Buck. He looks me in the eye and asks pointedly, "You here for fun or money, Miguel?"

"I'd like some of both, if possible."

"Good, just watch me, do as I say and we'll clean these clowns." With that this intensely serious man goes back to smiling and joking around the group. It's clear to me at least that he has a deadly goal, which is to "kick some serious ass," as he puts it.

I'm very lucky to have Buck for my partner. He's a veteran of these matches. It turns out he's also an inveterate gambler. The higher the stakes, the better he plays. This $5 Nassau is penny ante for him. Before we tee off he says to our opponents Ed and Charles,

"How about we add a dollar a hole besides the $5 Nassau?" They look quickly at each other and nod their agreement. "Of course there are carryovers." This means that ties carry over the $1 to the next hole, making it a $2 hole and doubling from there on until someone wins the hole. They look at each other again, hesitate only a second, and nod. I learn later that Buck also has some sizeable side bets with other players in the group beyond our foursome. As we wait to tee off, he sees that I'm nervous, not about my ability but about all the bandying that was going on. He puts his large muscular arm around my shoulder and whispers, "Don't worry, chico (boy), follow my lead and we'll be fine."

Hole 1 runs alongside Pico Boulevard. It is about a 350-yard par 4. Buck said "Just play right center." My tee shot lands in the middle of the fairway, which is okay. All four of us par the hole. Hole 2 is also straight but about 60 yards longer. Again, we tie with pars. This goes on for six more holes until we came to the ninth hole. The match is still tied. I'm a little surprised at Buck. It's clear he is an excellent player, yet he misses a couple easy putts that would have won holes for us. This is the deciding hole on the Nassau front nine bet as well as everything up to this point. We tied the first eight holes, so with carryovers this added another $9 to the value of the hole. Our opponents know that Buck is a good player; still they feel confident since they've stayed with us through eight holes—perhaps a little too confident. Just as I'm about to tee off, Buck says, "Press," meaning it is now an $18 hole, plus the $5 front nine Nassau is now $10. Optional presses are the rule here and they go along with it.

This makes me a little tense because I now have $28 staring at me, which is a lot of money for a student. Buck pulls me aside and whispers, "Just make a par. I'm going to birdie it."

Nine is a 365-yard par 4. We all hit our tee shots onto the fairway. As we're coming up to our balls, Buck smiles at Ed and Charlie and says in a challenging tone designed to play to their manhood, "How about $5 on closest to the hole?" Again, they look at each other and smile, nodding their assent. Two against one are good odds. Ed hits his shot 14 feet from the hole. Charles leaves his just 10 feet away. My shot doesn't matter on the closest bet but I need to at least par for the $28 that we have on the line. My shot is 12 feet out, an easy two-putt par. Buck's drive is a few yards closer to the green so he plays last. A par will tie us for the front nine, assuming Ed and Charles get down in two, which I know they will.

Buck approaches his ball and stares at it for long minute, bending over to get a good look at how it sits in the grass. Then, he looks up at the trees for a sign of wind. There is none and he knows it. He puts his hands on his hips and shifts his weight back and forth nervously. Next, he takes his glove off, blows on his hands, dries them on his towel and wipes the glove as well. After more fidgeting he pulls a club out of his bag, looks at it and at the green, shakes his head, says something to himself, and puts it back. He takes another club out and looks at the distant green again. Finally, he stands up to the ball and takes a half dozen practice swings. Ed interrupts his routine and asks impatiently, "For Christ's sake, Buck, are you waiting for it to hatch?" Buck looks up at him and says very seriously, "This is an important shot, amigo." Looking down once more he waggles the club several times. Peering at the hole still another time he pulls the club back and swings. The shot flies up into the translucent blue sky and lands four feet from the hole. Ed yells, "Shit," and Charles notes acidly that Buck's parents were never married. As we pick up our bags and start walking toward the green Buck looks at me and winks; the hustler.

The back nine at Rancho Park is slightly shorter than the front side. Ed and Charles are more than a little upset over losing everything on the first nine. So, given their egos, they immediately ask to press the back. Buck asks me, as if it mattered, "What do you think, partner?" trying to convey a wholly false caution. We accept. He adds that the dollar a hole will continue and they nod.

Hole 10 is a short 355-yard dogleg right. We win it with two pars versus Charles's par and Ed's missed four-foot par putt. Eleven is a straight, long 411-yard par four. Buck birdies after a beautiful six iron into ten feet and one putt. I par by coming out of the right-side bunker and rolling in a six-foot putt to save par. Again, a three putt, this time by Charles, gives us the hole.

Twelve and thirteen are halved. They win fourteen when Ed's twenty-foot putt slides in. This birdie wins four holes, or skins as they are called. Now, his confidence rises. Apparently, his view is that this win sets them off on a roll. He feels that momentum had shifted. Yet one win in five holes doesn't constitute a sea change. The reality is that we've won two holes, they've won one, and two were tied. Ed declares another press for the remaining holes and we accept. It's obvious even to me that he's overly optimistic regarding his ability under stress. This now makes fifteen through eighteen worth double, two dollars a hole and the second nine is also doubled to $10. Fifteen is halved with two pars and two bogies. Buck birdies sixteen and I par it. They both par so we win two holes, doubled.

They win seventeen and press again. Now, eighteen is worth $4. Ed bogies and Charles pars out. Buck pars and I land in a greenside bunker. My shot out is a little too strong and I miss the putt coming back. Net result is we tie the last two holes. We win the 18 by virtue of winning the front and tying the back. Never satisfied with the tie on the back nine Buck suggests we go to the practice area and each hit a ball out of the bunker and putt out. The bet will be double or nothing. They can't put their machismo aside, just as Buck expected. From the bunker Buck gets up and down in two. The rest of us take three. Result: Buck and I win everything on the back side, plus the match. When we add what we won from the rest of the group I pocket $76. This is a fun game.

A few weeks later I take my six handicap into an eight-team group. This time teams are formed by a drawing for partners. Buck isn't playing this day. I draw a new fellow named Irv. I've always believed that the drawing was rigged and they set it up so that the new guy would be given to the kid. After all the preliminary banter we tee off. Irv sticks a cigar in his moth but never lights it. He doesn't remove it even to putt, just shifts it out of his line of sight. He plays pretty well in the beginning, over his head as it turns out later. We win the first six holes. The presses start and from seven through eighteen we're soundly whipped. When I come into the clubhouse most of the teams were already there ordering their first of several drinks. I walk up to the table and laying my billfold on it I plead, "Just leave the leather please."

After the usual drinks and insults I get up to leave. Buck is standing by the door with a beer in hand. Smiling at him I say ruefully, "Well Buck, I guess it's win some, lose some, isn't it?"

He puts his big arm around my shoulder and walks me out toward the parking lot. "No, Mike, not if you want to be a success. You have to go out every day determined to accept nothing less than a win. If you don't you'll be an also-ran in life like most of those jokers inside." He looks me in the eye and gives me a shake to see if I understand and accept his wisdom. In a few seconds of walking to my old car I look at him and nod. He gives me a hug and a pat on the butt. "Bueno." (Good) With a wink he's gone.

* * *

Those golf matches were an opportunity to apply my poli sci and econ learning regarding apparent versus real and risk versus reward. Buck's bet on closest to the hole was an example of apparent versus real—a fundamental political principle. Buck knew as we walked up to the fairway that his chance of placing his shot inside Ed and Charles was very good. He knew their strength and weaknesses. Without giving away his intention he casually checked weather conditions, ball positions and location of the flag on the green. With this foreknowledge he offered the bet. They had not given the situation much thought and figured that they had a good chance in two against one of being closest. Having secured the bet Buck made an apparent show of concern about his shot. The club selection, the practice swings, the seeming indecisiveness were all part of his feigning concern and difficulty. This allowed him to make a similar bet later in the match. If he made it look too easy, they would not have taken another chance. In reality, he was very confident that he could be inside their shots. The political maneuver is to show apparent concern while privately knowing the realities of the situation are in your favor.

Economics come into play with the contest of one team against the field. Before making bets against the other team in the foursome and against the other teams in the group, we must study the risk versus reward of one against several. What are the chances, with this person as my partner, of beating more than half the field? With Buck, the odds of being rewarded at the end of play were decidedly in our favor. With Irv, the new unknown partner, I let past experience, which has no bearing on the current match, plus my self-confidence from the winnings with Buck and it nearly wiped me out.

Buoyed by Buck's optimism and driven by his charge I turn a corner in my life. I set aside the negatives of my home life. I commit to expecting success. I vow to invest the energy to achieve success at school as well as other activities. With two years yet to go at UCLA I still have time to turn my record around and attain my goals.

* * *

In my junior and senior years I'm turned on. I'm pumped. Studies are number one on my list of priorities. Extracurricular activities, beyond a little golf and even less social life are given a backseat. Although I still don't know what I want to be for the first time in my life I feel truly energized and positive, as though I'm in a state of grace. It's almost a quasi-religious experience and it feels good.

The first test of my new found dedication comes in the first semester of my senior year with the appearance of Bernice. She is known familiarly as Bernie, Berney, or Bernee depending on how she feels when introduced to someone new. The better she likes you the more she chooses Bernee. I had met Bernee's older sister, Alicia, a couple months before at school. She works for one of the Hollywood studios in the public relations department. She came on a

Career Day to recruit students for the studio. Alicia is very pretty and upbeat. It's no wonder why the studio picked her to recruit. People are naturally attracted to her. Impeccably dressed, usually in dove grey with beautiful and unexpected accents she stands out. Her sister Bernee is attending UCLA studying cinematography.

Bernee and Alicia are local girls whose parents are divorced. Their father is a very successful agent and their mother is an aging actress. Dad is able to afford some heavy alimony, a large black Mercedes, as well as provide his daughters with late model cars and send Bernee to UCLA. Mom is not doing as well. Her career is limited to bit parts of middle aged women. Her dream forever behind her, she compensates with alcohol and dating aspiring young actors whom she seduces with promises of getting them into movies.

Alicia is intelligent and urbane but as unpredictable and unapologetic as a cat on ice. One Saturday afternoon we have lunch, a few drinks and are strolling down Sunset Boulevard in the perpetual sun of southern California. We're window shopping, weirdo watching, and checking out the Mercedes, Ferraris, Jags, and Alfas parading down the boulevard. Suddenly she stops and says in a loud voice, "These fucking shoes are killing me." Whereupon she takes them off, drops them into her large purse and continues strolling barefoot along the sidewalk without a care. I find her brazenness attractive and she doesn't have Flo's attitude about the hick from Nowhere.

At this point I'm still trying to focus on studying. This becomes more difficult after I meet Bernee for the first time at a party Alicia throws in her West Hollywood apartment. Bernee is a knockout, five foot six, blonde, and witty; she shows a bit of the free spirit of her big sister. And she has an appealing glimmer of sorrow just under the surface, the type of thing that makes a man want to shield and protect a woman.

I circulate during the party. It's the kind of affair you think people in Hollywood throw. There are would-be stars, aging actors, back stage pros, and hangers-on dressed in every conceivable costume. Stimulants of all types are being passed around like footballs.

Behaviors range from pseudointellectual to totally bizarro. I spend some time with both sisters and the other guests. As things begin to wind down about midnight and half the people are either out of their minds or on the way, Alicia approaches me and asks if I'm doing anything later. I say, "No." She winks at me and says in her best Mae West voice, "Come up and see me sometime, big boy." She runs her hand down my chest, but then asks if I'll give Bernee a ride home first. Being the gentleman I am, of course I agree.

Bernee and I get into what I laughingly call a car. It's a beat-up Beetle convertible with only three of the four cylinders working regularly. It leaves a trail of oil, smoke, and fumes behind wherever it goes. Surprisingly the motor starts on the first try and we take off, I should say laboriously inch along, toward Bernee's apartment. It's a cool, somewhat foggy night that lends a sensuous atmosphere to the journey. On the way we chat, flirt, and just have fun. I pull up to the apartment building in which she shares a unit with a young actress. She says, "My roommate is on location in Washington and won't be back for a week. Why don't you come in for a night cap?" I note that her sister is probably expecting me to return. To which Bernee says very simply, "Don't go!" After considering the pros and cons of this invitation for less than a second I agree with her suggestion. An hour later the phone rings in Bernee's apartment. It is Alicia. She asks Bernee if she has gotten home okay and if she knows where I am. Bernee replies "Yes" and "No" and hangs up.

The next morning after I leave, suspecting the worst, Alicia shows up at Bernee's and finds the apartment in a pronounced state of chaos. It is absolutely clear what had transpired that night. Being slightly hurt by me and much more upset with her sister she accuses Bernee of many unnamable acts. When Bernee tells me later about the confrontation she says, "I admitted nothing and promised never to do it again." I've always thought that is a perfect explanation when one is caught red-handed.

This is what Bogart called "the beginning of a beautiful friendship." It's nearing my last semester of school, and I'm entranced by Bernee. She is as sophisticated and urbane as Flo and Alicia. Like other young people in California, Bernee and Alicia grew up in a pressure pot of permissiveness and opportunity. There is so much to do in southern California and an atmosphere that encourages exploration. There are many broken families and children without guidance or a stable home they can depend on during the critical growing up years. Because the movie capital draws people from all over the world, they don't have the typical extended family to fall back on either. Bernee tells me lots of her friends' lives have imploded with drugs, alcohol, or worse due to the pressures of the area.

Bernee is different. She has Alicia's free spirit but not her wildness. She has Flo's sophistication but not her condescension. We're passionate, but we don't go off the rails. Somehow my Midwestern solid values and her freedom to think and dare make for a laugh-filled, balanced combination. And we're able to really talk about our lives. Bernee tells me she'd been a surprise baby when her mother was in her early thirties. Mom always accused Bernee of ruining her career. This lack of maternal love is something I understand. Bernee says her father is a pure hustler, obsessed with making it big time in Tinsel Town, which he does. He's committed to doing anything, I mean anything, necessary to be a big macher (Yiddish for influential person) as they say here. This upbringing probably explains why she has an appetite for adventure.

One night when Bernee's roommate is again away making a picture, several actors and probably the director, we are playing a heated game of I'll show you mine if you show me yours. Suddenly, the doorbell rings. I almost have a myocardial infarction. Bernee throws a towel around her body and walks to the door. I don't know what to do so I grab my clothes and head for the bathroom. I figure my story will be that I'm a plumber making a late call. The fact that I'm scrambling to get dressed and have no tools with me may make it less believable. In a couple minutes Bernee opens the door and says it is just her roommate's drunken boyfriend who had forgotten she was out of town. Bernee takes my hand and leads me back to the bedroom. I inform her, "I don't think I can do anything for you after that." She says she bets that with a little help I can and she is right.

An hour later the doorbell rings again. "What is this, fucking Grand Central Station?", she exclaims as she heads toward the door, stark naked. This time I don't bother to get up. I figure I might just as well die in bed as the bathroom. In a few minutes Bernee returns followed by Alicia who is clearly and totally wasted. Alicia looks at the two naked bodies and says, "Well, well. Do you mind if I join the party?" She starts to unbutton her blouse and promptly passes out on top of me. A boy from a small town isn't prepared for this.

Everything between us is not dominated by sex. Burnee and I share an intense interest in current events. We are trying to discover how the world works. What's going on behind the smoke screen of daily newspapers. We read insatiably everything across the range of the liberal arts to sports and performing arts. On weekends we like to go to the beach, but not for sun bathing. We set up an umbrella, bring a cooler for drinks and sandwiches and spend the day reading papers and magazines. We discuss what we're reading without Flo's need to put down the other's opinions. My interests center on the how and why people exercise power in an attempt to shape their world. My youthful idealism is quickly being overwhelmed by the callous realities of life. As a child brought up in the womb of the film industry Burnee is not idealistic. Although she wishes that life would not be so severe for some people she recognizes that the world is not a fair arena. I'd like to write about it some day, although I don't know how to get published. As a cinematography student Burnee dreams of creating documentaries and cinema verite films. Right now we settle for days on the beach and stimulating chats. This shared exploration is one of the most invigorating activities of my life, before and since.

A week before Christmas Bernee invites me to join her and her friend Jackie at her father's house in Palm Springs for Christmas. "We're going to stay at my Dad's house. He won't need it until New Year's Eve. You can bring your golf clubs and play golf when Jackie and I go shopping."

Bernee's logic is unassailable. She tells me to come to her place on the 22nd and we'll go down the next day to celebrate Christmas in the desert. I ask her about having Christmas with her family. She says it isn't a big deal. They just have a quick gift exchange and go their separate ways. "It's not exactly a Norman Rockwell tableau," she adds.

I induce my old Beetle to make the trip to Bernee's on the afternoon of the 22nd. We take in a movie and get back early to pack. About ten o'clock the next morning, driving Bernee's red Ford Fairlane we pick up Jackie Jeffers. I'd met her briefly once before. Jackie is a gorgeous girl with light chocolate skin, a beautiful smile, and the body of an athlete. She has that same mischievous energy that all of Bernee's friends seem to have. The three of us head east toward Palm Springs on Route 10, the San Bernardino Freeway.

December is Palm Springs coolest month with an average temperature in the 60s. The cold ocean air is blocked by the San Jacinto Mountains, which are virtually free of any vegetation except for a little mesquite tree here and there. As the sun heats the trees they give off a pungent, oily odor, which makes it great for barbeque. As we approach Bernee's dad's house we ascend from the Coachella Valley turning up to a modern house with pool and a deck that look out over the valley. The house is both minimalist and ostentatious at the same time.

After we unpack Bernee brings a bottle of cold champagne from Dad's wine cellar onto the deck. She explains that we can have anything in the house since her dad writes the whole place off as business entertainment expenses. She adds that there are a couple of good courses I can play. All I have to do is just call for a tee time and give her dad's name and it goes on his account. Eventually, we barbecue hamburgers and some bell peppers and corn on the outdoor grill; enjoying the mesquite flavor and watching the lights come on around the valley floor. Am I dreaming? This is right out of the movies. No one in Nowhere will believe it.

The next day the girls want to go up the aerial tramway to Mt. San Jacinto, where there might be snow. Snow holds no fascination for me. Its absence is one of the primary reasons I've come to southern California. The tramway is a ten by twenty carriage suspended on cables. The brochure they show me describes a "breathtaking journey up the sheer cliffs of Chino Canyon." It's only ten minutes of terror from the Valley Station at 2,643 feet elevation to the Mountain Station at 8,516 feet. I have no choice but to accompany my host and friend. With my acrophobic eyes closed most of the way we gradually make it up the mountain. The worst part is when we pass each of the towers that the cables ride on. It is an abrupt rise as we move across the tower and a short, heart-stopping drop on the other side to take up the slack. When we reach the top they have to practically carry me off. There is indeed snow. We make snow balls and angels in the snow then go inside the station for a drink and lunch at the Palm Springs Peaks Restaurant at the mountaintop lodge. It turns out to be a good dining experience featuring breathtaking views of the entire Coachella Valley. The ride back down is less terrifying because it is already getting dusk on the east side of the mountain and I can't see how far above the canyon floor I am.

After landing we take a short tour down Palm Canyon Drive, the Rodeo Drive of Palm Strings. Then we retreat to the deck for comfortable drinks and valley viewing. When the sun goes down in the desert the temperature drops like a rock. There is no humidity to hold the day's heat so it dissipates quickly. Pretty soon it is too cold to sit out on the deck even with a fire going in the fire pit. Jackie has gone to bed early again. Bernee takes my hand and says, "Let's go get warm, tiger." The next thing I know I am in bed alone and it is about eight o'clock the next morning. Presently, Bernee comes into the bedroom wearing only an oversize T-shirt. She sits on the side of the bed and asks, "Are you hungry, Michael?"

I reply, "I'm starving."

Whereupon she says, "Maybe you'ld like a taste of this" and straddles my chest. A minute later Jackie comes in and hops on board the other seat. I'm like a bicycle built for two. The girls are bouncing up and down, singing Jingle Bells at the top of their lungs and laughing so hard they are coughing and choking.

The rest of the time until we leave for home I get a chance to play a couple of rounds at two of the nicer courses. Bernee was right. I just call for a tee time, give Dad's name and all is taken care of. The morning of the 29th we head back to LA, I go to my place and collapse. Merry Freakin Christmas!

4

MAIDEN VOYAGE

I t's my senior year at UCLA. I'm becoming very fond of Bernee and despite my growing desire for her companionship, I apply myself totally to my studies. The draft is still in effect, but I've managed to get a deferment until I finish graduate school. My parents are baffled by my decision to pursue graduate studies, as their' vision has always been the traditional grow up, get a job, get married, and have kids.

Looking beyond graduate school, I've set my sights on the Navy's Officer Candidate School in Newport, Rhode Island. In grade school during the war the stories and films of naval battles appealed more to me than infantry warfare. The old slogan, "Join the navy and see the world", resonated with me. During my senior year at UCLA I'm accepted at OCS but must wait until the following spring for a class to open. This works out well, since I will be able to get in a full semester of grad work at UCLA before having to report for duty.

To survive between graduation at UCLA and my new start at OCS, I get a job at an aircraft factory in El Segundo, just south of the Los Angeles Airport. There are a number of students like me working their way through school, but most workers are folks with a high school education or less. This is my second experience of factory life and I know I want no part of it. One of the middle-age fellows who had signed up right out of high school grabs my shirt one day and tells me very directly to finish my education so I won't end up like him. There is such a hopeless tone to his words. He has already put in twenty years in this place and can only look forward to twenty-five more. He makes a far greater impression on me than anything my parents can say.

Finally, in April 1961, my turn comes to enter OCS. The program consists of three six-week periods with a short break in between. At the end I'll be commissioned as an ensign in Uncle Sam's fleet. The Navy sends me a plane ticket and travel orders specifying the day of arrival in Newport, Rhode Island. On the appointed day I report along with a group of candidates from around the country.

The first night after everyone has arrived and checked in, the chief petty officer in charge of our building calls us to attention: "Your first task here will be to engage in a Field Day. Do any of you know what that means?" No one answers the question, but it sounds like fun. "Let me help you. Field Day is the Navy's term for one of the following: One, a day for a parade. Two, a day for athletic events. Three, a day trip to an interesting place. Or four, a day of intense activity with mop and broom readying your barracks for habitation."

We know which one it will be. If you think you know how to clean a house, you don't know anything until you have had a Field Day. Starting that night and carrying on into the next day we scrub and polish the deck, the showers and the toilets. Equipped with mops, brooms, scrub brushes, rags, and polishing clothes we cover every inch of that building. We even clean the mortar in between the bathroom tiles with a toothbrush. In a precursor of what was to come, we do it all while singing, with a camaraderie and intensity that would be typical of our days together.

Lights go out at 2230 and reveille arrives at 0530. The class is a mix of two-thirds college grads and one-third senior petty officers from the fleet. The men from the fleet are called mustangs for some reason I never learn. We're housed in long, white painted, wooden barrack buildings with two sections per building. A section is thirty men. One of the petty officers from the fleet is Henry Trenton, originally from a ranch in Montana. He looks like a cowboy, lean, muscular, and tan. Our bunks are laid out alphabetically starting with "A" closest to the head and showers. Since I'm "S" and he's "T," Henry has to pass my bunk on his way to the head. I like to stay in bed as long as possible, so he's always up before me. He walks by every day with his shaving kit in one hand, a cigarette dangling from the corner of his mouth, singing, "Yank my doodle it's a dandy." I go on liberty with Henry a couple times and after a night of significant drinking he will roll out of bed and take a couple slugs of vodka right out of the bottle as an eye opener.

Another interesting fellow is Paul, a Yalie. He's very smart and fun-loving, always smiling and with a mischievous grin. He seems to be floating through this experience. Whenever we have a few days off he's picked up in a private plane and taken to Manhattan. His story is that he reads poetry to a rich old lady. One morning as we're getting ready to go to breakfast he says, "I'm going to the infirmary. I'll see you later."

I ask him if he's sick and he replies, "No, I'm getting out."

"Getting out of what?"

He says, "The Navy," and walks out.

When we get back in the afternoon after classes are over, he's cleaning out his footlocker and dressing in civies. When I ask him what happened he says, "I convinced them that I'm unfit for Navy duty" and leaves with a smile.

During the week we're busy with classes in leadership, seamanship, navigation, naval administration, naval organization, sea power, military law, military indoctrination, naval warfare, and damage control. Physical training is also part of the course with calisthenics and marching. One cold morning we're marched into a large building for what is described as a damage control exercise. What looks like a ship is housed in a large warehouse. Although full scale, it is only a simulation of half of a ship.

The officer in charge tells us, "This ship is taking on water. It's in danger of sinking. Your task is to keep that from happening. You all have been given numbers. Odd numbers are assigned below decks to stop the water coming into the ship. Even numbers are assigned on deck to handle the equipment needed by those below. Commence."

It's cold, wet, oily work. I get lucky. My job is on deck manhandling heavy wet pump hoses while others are below up to their waists in cold water battling the leaks. At the end of the exercise they look like drowned rats. I'm tired but relatively clean and dry. Actually, it was fun and a very practical thing to learn.

At one point at OCS I'm told to put my section through close order drills. Having had ROTC in high school I know how to do that. Compared with my class mates, who've never marched before, I'm world class. I have them moving smartly forward, reverse, and on the oblique. I even teach them how to hold their rifles correctly and move them on and off their shoulders in unison. After the drill Lieutenant Andersen calls me into his office.

"Still, you were quite impressive out there. Have you had military training before?"

"Yes, sir. I went to a military high school."

"Would you like to take over as section leader for the next six weeks?"

In the first six weeks I've seen what a crummy job section leader is. The school program is tough enough and the section leader catches hell for every one of thirty jerks' mistakes. You earn no credit for taking on the responsibility. So, I reply, "Sir, I have to pass on this opportunity. I need the time to study. This is a difficult program." I've passed up my first chance at leadership. I'll do my job, but I'm not ready to be a hero.

To me the high point of OCS is weekend liberty at The Moorings, a bar and restaurant down on the waterfront; at least I think they serve food. We leave on Saturday mornings after inspection, take a cab to town, register in the Viking Hotel, and drink copiously as fast as possible. On Saturday nights The Moorings is filled with salivating young ladies looking to hook a prospective naval officer. Although I participate wholeheartedly in the maneuver I manage to avoid capture. There is one harrowing escape, though, when I meet a Portuguese girl named Rugenia, about five foot two with a fire in her eyes and a smoking hot body to match. I'd always been attracted to olive-skinned brunettes, but Rugenia goes missing for a few weeks and I turn my attention to Stacey, the daughter of a local Greek fishing family and a real knockout. She raises many an OC's hopes and other parts, including mine. She's drawn to blondes so we have instant rapport. I think I'm in heaven with both girls selling hard. That is, until the night they both show up. I'm busier than a one-armed paper hanger with poison ivy that night. I run from one side of The Moorings to the other trying to keep them from comparing notes. Sure enough, late in the evening as the crowd thins out Rugenia sees me dancing with Stacey. The ladies immediately engage in hand-to-hand combat with me as the target. This ends my career at The Moorings.

At OCS I apply for flight training. I love the look of those wings and I really want to fly. I pass all the tests for flight school, except one. In the past year my eyesight has taken a beating from long hours of study in the dimly lit rooms here. I know it's a problem so I connive to see the eye chart before my turn comes. I blow right through it without a miss down to the 20-15 level. Next is an interview with the chief medical officer. This man has the last word on the flight school applications. He's a captain who reminds me of a young Lionel Barrymore. He calls me into his office and tells me to stand at ease. He then proceeds to go over my application with me, section by section. He says I've done very well, but there was one problem. Deja vu. It's Sister MF all over again.

The captain is quite pleasant as he sinks a dagger into my heart. "The bad news is that although you somehow passed the eye chart exam," he looks up at me with a knowing smile, "you failed when they dilated your pupils. It's obvious that you are nearsighted. The Navy likes pilots who can see. Here's a prescription for glasses. Take it to the lab and have them make a pair for you."

He can see the disappointment in my face. He says, "Since you've shown an interest in aviation perhaps you'd like to go to Aviation Ground Officer's School. It's the support wing for Navy Air."

No matter what it is, it's better than being assigned to a destroyer running the North Atlantic DEW (distant early warning) Line from Virginia to Iceland. I finish OCS and earn my commission, anxious to get on and gain some real experience in the fleet.

After graduation I get a two-week leave to go home. After showing off my navy blue uniform with a single gold ensign's stripe I drive down to AGO School at NAS Jacksonville. I've acquired a 1955 T-Bird. It's sea green with white-wall tires and a black convertible top. It isn't as cool as Bump's Chevy, but it's great fun to drive and since the trunk can hold my golf clubs it's functional as well. Jacksonville is notable for three reasons. First, it's a humid, boiling hot stretch of dust and swampland. Second, it's the first time I encounter Whites Only signs on public facilities. Third, the Florida belles sashay around saying things like, "Kin ah hep y'all?"

AGO School is fascinating. We're taught about the aviation arm of the Navy. This includes the mission of an AGO, planes and ships, aviation facilities and equipment, and ground support. Billets can include anything from air traffic controller to air intelligence officer. It's an interesting program about naval operations and I enjoy it. Because of the climate we start work at 5 a.m. and get off at 1 p.m. Being young men we devote our time to alcohol, sports, and women, not necessarily in that order. I manage to get out occasionally on local muni golf courses. This is the first time I play on Bermuda grass, a lumpy, gnarly grass full of horizontal rhizomes. It's not at all like the smooth, creeping bent of northern courses. By the time I leave I've learned how to play Bermuda, but my game has suffered a bit. I thought it was hot and humid in Nowhere, but this place is a steam bath.

The main topic of conversation is our preferred next duty station. AGO is a relatively short course, so we're all concerned about our future. Near the end of each tour, we're asked to list three preferred next assignments, but we never get what we ask for. We hear horror stories about people being sent to terrible duty stations like Greenland or the naval research facility in Antarctica. One of my close friends indicates no strong feelings about his next assignment. Subsequently, he's sent to NAS Argentia, Newfoundland, a short hop from the North Pole. He's never heard from again.

The choice of my next assignment is complicated by my dislike for the AGO executive officer, a bigot and a slovenly mustang who has made life miserable for me. Any onerous or time-consuming task he can come up with he gives to me, and I'm worried that this flatulent pig may influence my next duty station assignment. I don't know it at the time, but his influence is minimal. Nevertheless, he indicates to me that not only can he block my duty request, but he can block my promotion to lieutenant (junior grade) a year down the line. I do my best to placate him and not show my disgust at his blackmail attempts. Toward the end he eases up. I guess this is his way of keeping control of those in his command.

With my background in political science and economics, I lobby hard for Naval Intelligence School in Washington, D.C. To my joy I'm assigned to Air Intelligence School at the Naval Observatory also in Washington. The Observatory is located between Massachusetts and Wisconsin Avenues NW. It isn't the big Intell School but it's a move in the right direction. The next class is starting two weeks after I graduate, so I have just ten days to report in, get settled, and start school. No time to go home on leave. I drive directly from Jacksonville to Washington, D.C. At last, I hit what I aimed for, almost. Little do I know how this would lead to a very interesting career.

In January 1962, when I report into the Observatory I see a friend from my days at OCS. John Slimmer is a lanky, balding graduate of Auburn who, when he gets drunk, goes about screaming, "Wore iggle." That is Southern for War Eagle. He finds some girl who claims to be able to control his hair loss. Twice a week he pays her to pour some lotion on his head and massage it for a half hour. We never see any hair sprout, but he always comes home smiling.

It's John who tells me that our friend Kent is here as well. Kent Simmons is good-looking guy from a wealthy family and the Romeo of our group. He gets lucky more than Wilt Chamberlain. To round out the group we pick up a fourth, Pete Boudreau, a chubby-faced fun lover with a French-Canadian background from Massachusetts, and we go apartment hunting. Pete is an affable sort who likes to hang out at the local bar playing darts and just shooting the shit.

We rent a large two-bedroom apartment in Arlington just across the Potomac River, not far from the Observatory and just blocks from the famed Iwo Jima statue. We aren't in town more than a couple weeks before we've got a hot social schedule. Lots of young people work for the government, and the District is flooded with young women who work in government offices. The ratio of women to men is 7 to 1 in our favor. It's a bachelor's paradise. Liquor purchased at government commissaries is cheap, and so are the affections of some of the local ladies. There are house parties every weekend. If you get through one without making a fool of yourself, you're in the circuit and put on the invitation list for all others.

One night at a house party Kent is drunk and being obnoxious. To make him jealous his date starts making passes at me. He sees this and is outraged. He takes me outside and says, "What the hell do you think you are doing with my girl?"

"Nothing, just talking. She started the conversation because you were hitting on that redhead with the big maracas."

"You never mind what I am doing. You just stay away from my date or I'll pound you into the deck. Do you understand?"

Kent is a strong fellow, bigger than me and in excellent condition. I try to explain what happened but he isn't buying it. For the rest of our time in D.C. he shuns me in the apartment and at school.

Despite the drinking and playing, we work hard at Air Intelligence School. AIS trains pilots as well as other line and staff officers. The curriculum consists of intelligence briefings on the military status of the USSR, Japan, China, and our European allies. We study the ships and aircraft of each and can quote their specifications. A fun but intense exercise is ship and plane spotting. The silhouette of a ship or plane is flashed on the screen at 1/60th of a second and we have to identify it. We add some competition to the lesson by making the fellow with the lowest score throw ten dollars into the pot for the graduation party; the one with the highest cumulative score wins a dollar from everyone in the class. I finish second to one of the pilots, which carries no prize.

Near the end of AIS we apply for our next duty stations. I request Naval Intelligence School again as a natural follow-up to AIO. Even my master's work doesn't help. The Navy decides that I've had enough schooling and need to go to work. I'm assigned to the headquarters of the Fleet Air Detachment (FAD) at NAS Barber's Point, Hawaii. Not my goal, but not a bad second place.

Before leaving, I visit my parents and brother Bob. There's no news there although Bob doesn't seem to be too happy. I can understand that. When the time comes, I launch my drive to San Diego for my flight to Hawaii. Taking off in early March, the first night from home I sleep in a little motel along the highway in southern Missouri. I hit Amarillo, Texas, about noon the second day and stop for lunch. When I come out it's snowing. Heading west across the flat land of northern Texas, the wind has picked up and the snow is blowing so hard that I can't see more than twenty feet in front of the car. By the time I decide to turn back to Amarillo the snow is covering the road and turning it into a skating rink. I come down into a shallow but slippery defile and skid into a snow bank. There I am, in a convertible Thunderbird with snow up to the door and no warm clothes. Why would I have a coat? I'm going to Hawaii. The only comfort I have is a bottle of whisky to keep me from freezing.

After about two hours a large black Buick stops. The driver waves to me to get in. The driver, whose name is Jerry, is a thirty-something from Wisconsin. When I close the door he introduces himself and claims, "I thought the southern route would avoid any storms. I guess I was wrong. Where did you come from?"

"I started not too far from you in northern Illinois. I thought this route would be clear too."

We drive very slowly for only a few miles before we get stuck. The sun is blotted out by the storm clouds and it's getting dark. We realize we have to stay put. We'll freeze to death within a hundred yards if we decide to walk out. Just as the light begins to disappear a yellow state highway dump truck stops and motions us to get in. There are already two men in the truck. It's a very tight fit, but no one is complaining except a big man who is the passenger on the window side. He's generous, though, sharing his bottle of whisky. I'm jammed in between the driver and Mr. Buick. We drive ahead slowly trying to keep the big truck on the road. Between the whisky and the close quarters I began to drift off. Suddenly we stop. Now we're stuck again. It's pitch black outside, and the wind is piling up snow around the truck. The truck's two-way radio gives out static but no contacts. The driver keeps the motor going so that the heater will keep us from freezing. We spend the night there packed in like sardines. At dawn the blizzard finally begins to let up a little bit. Now it's just snowing. By 0900 the big man begins to throw up. I'm feeling rather nauseous myself. The driver slips in and out of consciousness and Mr. Buick is okay except for some vomit on his pants from the big man.

By now the snowdrifts around the truck have trapped the exhaust from the motor and let it seep into the cab. We're slowly being asphyxiated. I tell the driver, "Open the window. We're suffocating."

Because he is on the lee side when he opens the window a bit we get some fresh air. But now the gaseous air is replaced with an icy wind that still swirls around us. We sit there through the day and into the second night. Although the storm finally eases we still can't leave the truck and no one can get to us.

Early the next morning we hear the sound of a snow plow ramming its way through the snow. The snow has stopped during the night. The plow comes from a highway station near the county seat about ten miles to the west. Behind it is a yellow school bus. They're picking people out of vehicles just like us. There must be a couple dozen in the bus when we board. A short while later we meet a snow plow coming from Amarillo and leading another school bus. The snow plow clears a place to turn the bus around and head west. As we head back I see my Bird half off the road. In about an hour we pull into a cluster of buildings sticking up from the snowy prairie. It's the county courthouse. Once inside we see several dozen refugees like us. There is food being served and lots of people sleeping on cots.

By mid-afternoon it's warming up and we're taken back to our vehicles, which are strung all along the road. When I find the Bird I discover I've blown a tire while trying to get out. One of our rescuers helps me put on a spare and shoves me out of the ditch. I drive into a gas station just the other side of the county seat to have my tire repaired. The garage man tells me, "Mister, you better spend the night at the county building because the highway west of here is only partly cleared."

I'm glad to do it because I'm still feeling the effects of my truck adventure and I'm exhausted. Early the next morning I climb into the Bird and, stopping only for gas and food, drive 1,000 miles straight through to the port in San Diego. Along the way I'm on a flat stretch of road in northern New Mexico. The sun is bright and the air clear as a crystal. No cars are in sight. In fact, nothing alive is in sight. I've never had the Bird above 80 mph and want to see what it can do. I gun it and gradually get it up to 100. Then, it starts to float. The suspension isn't stiff enough to keep the tires on the road at that speed. I'm losing contact with the surface. I don't have control. I'm afraid that if I try to steer, the Bird will take off into a snow-filled ditch. I take my foot off the accelerator pedal and try to hold the steering wheel absolutely straight. To my relief rather quickly the Bird slows down. For the second time in a couple of days I almost meet my maker.

When I arrive in Dago I'm handed surprise orders to Atomic, Biological, and Chemical Warfare Defense School on Treasure Island in San Francisco Bay. Not a bad diversion. Mark Twain allegedly said that the coldest winter he ever spent was a summer in San Francisco. He got it right. The reason it's cold in the summer is that the huge Central Valley heats up, thereby lowering its air pressure. The cold, higher pressure ocean air is drawn inland through the narrow Golden Gate. It rushes across the Bay, swamping Treasure Island with cool moist air as it rushes up the Sacramento River to the Central Valley. Along with the wind is the fog. In midafternoon you can stand on Telegraph Hill and watch the fog almost dash eastward.

ABCWD School turns out to be a fascinating education. The instruction focuses on atomic radiation, germ warfare, and chemistry. We're drilled in using masks, making or finding shelter, taking cover, preparing for an attack and dealing with aftereffects. One day, to simulate a response to a nerve gas attack, we have to roll our pants up over our thigh and stab ourselves with a glycerin solution that is a simulated nerve gas antidote. The notion of doing it is much worse that the actual act. One fellow passes out at the thought. I discover that once I penetrate the skin there is no further pain.

That program is followed by still another training exercise at NAS Alameda. Alameda is across from San Francisco, on the southwest side of Oakland. The program here is a duplication of AIS school in D.C., but it's devoted to Asia Pacific operations. The course is too short to spend much time in San Francisco, but a couple buddies and I do manage to make a foray or two into The City. Somewhat reluctantly, when the course is over I turn my car in at the port of Oakland and catch a plane to Honolulu.

* * *

When I step out of the plane the scent of flowers is so strong I can almost bite into it. The air is also deliciously warm and fresh. On the driveway out of the airport there are small bamboo stands where Polynesian women sell flower and sea shell leis, plants and bouquets of plumeria, hibiscus, kukui and many other native flowers. This is the paradise I dreamed of back in Nowhere.

NAS Barber's Point is about twenty minutes west of the airport on the leeward corner of Oahu. It's quite warm and relatively dry since the rain typically comes from the northeast and loses much of its moisture as it crosses the island. The station is not very big, hosting only a small number of patrol and fighter squadrons. It boasts a new two story BOQ that is air conditioned and well appointed. I'm assigned a large room a few steps from the back parking lot. FAD HQ is less than a mile away across a dusty, barren stretch. As soon as I arrive I drop my gear in my room, take a shower and dress in my tropical tan, short sleeve uniform. No jackets here. It's too hot. My Bird will be here in a couple weeks. In the meantime there are people headed back and forth to the HQ all day and night so getting a ride is no problem.

Arriving at FAD HQ I report to the executive officer, lieutenant commander Ulrich who is tanned, droopy eyed and has a prominent chin supporting a collection of large teeth and a slight lisp that turns into a free shower occasionally. He tells me, "Still, your job here is to brief pilots going out to WestPac and debrief them when they return from their tour. In addition you will maintain an intel library and an archive of classified documents. Most of the flying here is patrol aircraft. A typical example is the VP-6 squadron in the next hangar. They're flying Lockheed P2V Neptunes and will soon have P3V Orions. We fly cover when necessary with F-6s. We also support a small ground to ground missile unit housed at the west end of the base. They have a practice range south of Kauai."

During this period the Neptune is used in several ways. It performs as a gunship, an antisubmarine chaser, overland reconnaissance and sensor deployment aircraft, and in its traditional role as a maritime patrol aircraft. The Neptune is also based at Cam Ranh Bay in South Vietnam, as an electronic "ferret" aircraft intercepting low-powered tactical voice and Morse code radio signals. One of their missions is the sowing of seismic and acoustic sensors over the Ho Chi Minh Trail.

My role is to read intelligence publications, write up summaries of key points, and give them to the Fleet Air Detachment CO (commanding officer) Ed Callahan. I personally brief the CO and XO to keep them apprised of the status of Asia Pacific activities. I also brief various personages who pass through and have a need to know what is happening across the Pacific. One essential duty is to keep an organized classified library in case someone wants more information or needs to go into the archives. It's administrative tedium —something I'm not good at. Sometimes I feel more like a librarian than an intelligence officer.

Callahan is an aviator and is a commander on his last assignment. Ed only flies now and then, just enough to keep his flight pay. He'll retire when he leaves FAD. As a result he doesn't see any reason to be a hard ass. So long as we keep him out of trouble, he's content. Ed is an avid golfer and we get off on the right foot as soon as he learns I hold a single-digit handicap. One day we're playing the Marine Corps base course at Kaneohe on the windward side. Kaneohe Bay is the threshold leading up to the huge lava-ridged mountains that run up the eastern coast of Oahu. It lives up to its name of being windy. The breeze comes in off the Pacific across the course and slams into the volcanic ridge that shelters Honolulu. In the morning the rising sun gradually paints the ridge with gold and emerald green. In the afternoon as the sun crosses the range's peaks the sharp vertical ridges fall into shadow. But the light dancing off the ocean creates a moving, mottled panorama across the mountainside. The sight is breathtaking.

Being on the windward side of Oahu means that the coastal plain receives a lot of rain. Much of it is drained from the clouds before they can cool and water the leeward side. We're late getting off and by the time we reach the last par 3 we can hardly see the green, much less the hole. We just aim at what looks like a waving flag. When we walk up to the green we can't find Ed's ball. My ball is on the fringe but his is nowhere to be seen. Finally, I say, "Captain, you better look in the hole." In the Navy the commanding officer is always addressed as captain no matter his rank.

Ed laughs as he walks across the green and then lets out a "Wahoo!" when he sees his ball in the bottom of the cup. From then on he views me as his lucky charm, and I let him.

My duties are interesting but not overwhelming and with Ed's passion for golf we often leave right at 1700 to get in a round before

71

dark. When Ed isn't available I play with whoever shows up. All in all, being single and with no entanglements, I play about five days a week. Before I leave FAD my handicap drops to 4. This leads to captaining our golf team. We have two other single-digit players and three average ones. We win the base championship in a walk away and then get slaughtered in the armed forces island tournament won by the Marines from Kaneohe.

When Callahan leaves we get a new CO who can't be more unlikeable. He tries to ingratiate himself to the pilots, but he is just a natural-born, forty-pound-overweight putz. I don't know how he can get into the cockpit of our F-6 fighter planes. One time he gets on my case because I can't find a particular intelligence bulletin he wants to see. He's right. It's my failure. From then on I'm on his shit list. When it comes time for me to go to my next duty station he puts in my record that I don't seem to be committed to a naval career. At that point he could be right.

One Saturday night I'm invited to a party at the home of Louis and Celia Cravano. Lou is a lieutenant and pilot assigned to FAD. They're a wild couple in their late thirties. To give you a taste of their style, one evening we're at a party together and it is time to go. Lou and I are on the front lawn chatting with another couple for several minutes. Finally, he turns toward the house and yells, "Celia, are you coming?" To which she yells back, "Hell no, I'm not even breathing hard."

The party at their house is a large affair of about twenty-five people. We mingle, eat, drink, and just have a relaxing, fun night playing Charades. There I meet Grace Danielski. Despite the last name she is a Chinese girl in her mid-twenties, a neighbor of the Cravanos. She has a certain presence that is difficult to describe, but quite compelling. She's pretty with skin like porcelain and is tall and willowy. Even when she's standing at ease she gives the impression of being very attentive. Rather than casting her gaze around the room when Grace talks to someone she gives them her full concentration. At the same time, I'm certain she isn't missing anything going on in the room. She's soft spoken but direct. Although it is obvious that she's quite intelligent she's also very approachable. Her smile envelops you like sunshine in the morning. Grace seems to know many of the people in the room and they are attracted to her, as am I, despite the red flowered muumuu that hides her slim figure. She tells me, "Danielski is my husband's name and I'm here alone because his unit is deployed to WestPac. My Chinese family name is Liu and my given name is Chan-juan." She laughs deliciously when she explains that it means graceful in Chinese, hence the English translation, "although I'm not sure I live up to it." I find her to be very knowledgeable about Asian matters, witty and a naturally authentic person.

After the games are over and we have a chance to talk more, there is instant rapport between us. Rather quickly our conversation goes beyond the typical where are you from, what do you do stage. I ask her, "What is your interest in Asian Pacific matters?" I assume she will say that it is because of her Chinese background or because her husband is flying patrol off the coast of China and over Vietnam.

She surprises me with her answer: "My father, General Liu, was on Chiang Kai-shek's staff. When the Nationalists lost the mainland to the Communists we escaped to Taiwan and helped form what is called the Republic of China. After we emigrated to Hawaii my parents sent me to Stanford where I completed my bachelor's in the political economics of Asia Pacific in three years. It wasn't that hard since I grew up in the middle of it. I would have stayed on to finish my master's, but my father suddenly became quite ill. I have no siblings, so I came home to help my mother."

What a surprise to find someone outside of the intel community who knows so much about the region. Plus, her knowledge is from the inside. Grace tells me her father eventually had a falling out with Chiang over his abusive rule of Taiwan. General Liu applied for a visa and led his family in another move, this time to Hawaii. Since her father was a former general with extensive knowledge of China's military capabilities, he and his family were welcomed and given citizenship quickly. In the polyglot society of Hawaii Grace quickly learned English.

The rest of the evening I fend off other people and try to keep her to myself. When she says she has to leave I am more than disappointed. I want, no, I need to spend more time with this extraordinary creature. Celia has introduced Grace as a neighbor who lives just a few doors away. Not wanting the evening to end I offer to walk her home and she doesn't refuse. We say our goodnights and walk out to a gorgeous tropical night. The air carries the scent of hibiscus, gardenia, orchids, and lilies. The sounds of the night are soft, mystical, and exquisite and so is she. Some unknown night birds chirp in the trees. A bright three-quarters moon lights the sky and casts soft shadows along our path.

I'm in heaven with this woman. I'm breathless. Never have I met anyone remotely like her. I walk as slowly as I can without being too obvious. I want this evening to go on forever. As we reach her house I try to find some way to keep the conversation going that doesn't sound totally stupid or maudlin. Eventually, I have to say goodnight in a way that is sincere and won't be a cliché. I don't hint at coming in and she doesn't offer. Finally, I just say, "It's been a delightful evening talking to you. You're an extraordinary woman. I hope we have a chance to meet again. I would ask you out, but you are married and in my old-fashioned way that makes it impossible."

She listens to me without a word and then reaches out her hand. I take it not knowing what to do next. After a second I expect her to pull it away but she holds on for a moment and looks right into me. Without thinking I pull her hand up and kiss it. She smiles with the look she has that covers some pain somewhere inside. Then, she says, "It's not about me. It's about you." She turns and walks up the path to her house.

I'm mesmerized. What does she mean? I wait until she reaches the screen door. She turns and waves before opening the door and entering. I stand there transfixed. How I want her to come back out, but she doesn't.

Finally, I turn and walk toward the Bird. Wow. My first reaction is that this woman is either a tease or a great actress. She can't be genuine. Then, I get my head on straight and stop denying the obvious. "Don't be stupid Michael. She's real." So real I shudder to think of her. When I get into the car I sit there taking deep breaths and waiting for my blood pressure to come down. My mind is the center of a vortex, a whirlpool, a cyclone. I'm paralyzed by this woman. After several minutes, when I stop shaking and gather some semblance of self-control, I start the engine and drive back to the base. Once inside my room in the BOQ I take a long cool shower. I don't sleep that night or for the next couple either.

There is that one major problem. Grace is married and showing no signs of not wanting to be. Later, Celia tells me that she had seen how well we were getting along and reaffirms that Grace is a special person. Furthermore, her husband is a real jerk. He flies P2Vs in patrol squadron VP-6. He is forever flirting and maybe more with the base wives. A week later I receive my orders and soon leave Hawaii without saying goodbye to Grace. I want very much to call, but it seems inappropriate. I have to write it off as a wonderful night but an impossible situation. Very close, but not quite again. This one really hurts.

5

HOME PORT

The last year at FAD I continue to press the issue of Naval Intelligence School wherever and whenever possible. Ed Callahan pushes for me through his contacts before he leaves. Despite the current CO's admonition regarding my career plans, it works. When my tour with FAD ends I receive orders to proceed to the Naval Intelligence Training Center, Anacostia, Washington, D.C. By now I've been promoted to lieutenant with special commendations from my golf buddy Ed. Like they say, it's who you know that counts. In the military that is absolutely true. Almost all career officers are excellent, especially those in the upper ranks. There are also always more qualified people than there are billets. Knowing someone who supports you can be the tiebreaker when your file comes before the promotion board. However, if you ever have an enemy on the board, you're a dead man.

Ever since my time in D.C. at AIS I have been in love with our nation's capital. It's like a home port for me. It's a model of what a nation's capital should look like. Its broad avenues, monuments, parks, and museums proclaim *capital*. The National Mall running from the Lincoln Memorial over the Reflecting Pool to the Washington Monument and culminating at the congressional building on Capitol Hill is breathtaking. The greatest monument in the city is the Lincoln Memorial, a commemoration of peace and humanity rather than war or triumph.

I arrive for my assignment in September 1964 and settle in Alexandria, Virginia. Alexandria is six miles directly south of the center of the District and just south of the Pentagon. It is west of Anacostia Naval Station, which is on the Anacostia River across from Fort McNair and the Navy Yard. Anacostia's history goes back as far as 1608 when John Smith sailed up what he thought was the eastern branch of the Potomac. There he met the Anacostian Indians.

Alexandria is a great place to live. It's a historic area with loads of character, filled with colonial-style brick buildings dating back almost two hundred years. Plaques adorn many buildings and describe people and events as far back as 1812. The historic center of Alexandria's Old Town is a concentration of boutiques, restaurants, antique shops, and theaters. Old Town and many Alexandria neighborhoods are compact and walkable. It's also close to some of the better public golf courses in the D.C. area. Two of the best are Army Navy Country Club and East Potomac, both within a thirty-minute drive. Put together, the aura of the capital, the ambiance of Alexandria, and the proximity to great golf makes it home for me.

Intelligence School is a rigorous program of general considerations and daily data gathering. I've always loved history and geography. That, along with my poli sci and econ degrees, make this assignment bread and butter for me. I don't have the same appetite for partying now that I did four years before. By now I'm a lieutenant, which makes me feel like I'm no longer in diapers.

The first week in class it hits me. This is it. This is what I was meant to do. I'm in the center of this world of data—verbal and nonverbal knowledge. It is an endless library. The Navy is going to teach me how to find the data, sort it, organize it, turn it into intelligence, and inform my world with it. And they are going to pay me to do it. It's my epiphany. At last, I have a direction and a goal.

The study program combines rigorous academics that test mental acuity as well as commitment. This is actually a spy school. We learn everything about espionage from how to pick a lock to data management and interrogation to escape and evasion. The curriculum is an advanced and broader version of the AIS program with more emphasis on command issues and on how America has to play the game. Given that we are averse to bribery, we try first to turn an asset by offering something more valuable than money to them. Sometimes it is just the opportunity to get revenge for something going on in their country. Yet, in the end, money is nearly always the lubrication that loosens assets' jaws. The basic idea behind intelligence is gathering information that is not accessible through other means. The lucky ones get to do it while on embassy duty. The rest of us slug it out ashore or at sea. It is intriguing, exciting, and dangerous some of the time. Other times it is tedious administrative work. Either way, at least for me, it's what I was meant to do.

At Anacostia, again a low golf handicap makes me appealing to the commanding officer and the executive officer. Both the CO and the XO are avid golfers. Because of their rank and position as heads of the school we're able to play some of the better private clubs in the area. One time, through a senator on the Appropriations Committee, we are invited to play the prestigious Congressional Country Club. It's northwest of the Capital on River Road in Bethesda, Maryland. Congressional has two courses, the Blue and the White. The Blue is where they host the U.S. Open and the PGA championships about every ten years. The course is long. From the Black championship tees the course is over 7,500 yards. In the course of a four-day tournament, that adds up to about 90,000 feet, or seventeen miles, of walking. We play from the Gold tees, which still requires over 6,700 yards. We have caddies and a cart.

Senator Blank, we'll call him to note his value, is a classic pot-belly, pat-on-the-back, kiss-the-baby, old, smoky back room politician. He believes that he is the next Lyndon Johnson. He isn't in the same league, but this doesn't stop him from acting like a pompous ass. He claims to have a 15 handicap although it's not apparent once we're on the course. Whenever he has a chance he improves the lie of his ball. I feel like offering him a tee when he lands in one of the many bunkers he visits. The decision is made that the senator and I will team against my CO and XO. They claim handicaps of 14 and 12 and I have a 6. The bet is $10 with automatic presses.

The match is fairly even since I'm on my way to breaking 80 while my partner is a nonentity. The only thing he contributes is a blue streak as he misses shot after shot. The front nine ends in a tie so we double the bet or the back side. We reach the eighteenth green trailing by one shot. Three of us are on the green and the senator has picked up after a half dozen strokes and a water ball. The CO and XO par the hole and I have a 12-foot side hill putt for a birdie. The senator "helps" me line up the putt and stands so close by I can smell his whiskey breath. The CO and XO game me by commenting in several ways how difficult the putt is.

As I stand over the ball I'm thinking about what's at stake here, and it's a lot more than $20. In my mind I am saying, "If I make it we tie. If I miss it we lose." What would either result mean? The putt is not as difficult as the decision. I seem to be caught on the horns of a dilemma. Finally, I take a deep breath to steady and relax myself. I strike the ball, not knowing what to pray for. It rides the curve on the side hill nicely and keeps the right speed. It dips perfectly toward the hole and in the last six inches it hits an invisible small dent in the green and lips out. I tap it in and the match is history. Based on Senator Blank's anger you would have thought that we were playing for the national debt.

As we walk toward the locker room, he asks if I'm sure I didn't give that last putt my best effort. He says that if I had played a higher line as he had suggested the putt would have gone in. Actually, if I did, the ball would have rolled off the green. What he's really saying was that by missing the putt I am kissing up to my senior officers. I'm ready to throw the bastard into the lake, but obviously I can't. If I don't kiss his backside he will probably see to it that I never get promoted. Given his position he might have been able to do that by trading favors with officers on the promotion board. Remember, it is who you know that counts. As we sit in the nineteenth hole and my seniors pay for the drinks, Blank says pointedly, "Charlie [the

CO], aren't you boys coming to the Hill soon for an appropriation for some new equipment?" The CO answers affirmatively. Blank replies, "Well, you know, Charlie, funds are tight these days but I'll see what I can do." That is the bastard's last comment as we are going out the door. What a son-of-a-bitch. Now, the seniors are pissed at me for missing the putt as well. If they could send the prick home happy he would have passed their appropriation.

Fortunately, I play other matches with the boss and other senior politicians. I have ample opportunity to spend some time with them afterward. The golf is secondary to what I learn from being around these powerful people. I observe how they carry themselves and how they express themselves. I hear and see how they deal with friends as well as enemies. I overhear stories about how they set someone up and then pull the rug out from under him. I witness how they develop protégés. This was a graduate course in leadership. It is a master class in political science that I could never have afforded.

Between the studying and golf, I have very little time for socializing. For the academic year I am basically a monk. Because I am so focused and committed throughout the course of the program, I manage to handle both the academic and physical challenges. Guess where I finish in the class ranking? First loser.

I want to round out my training by going to the language school in Monterey, California. My passion for Asia Pacific is obvious to anyone who knows me. When we have assignments in school to apply our training to specific cases, mine is always about that region. As time comes to express our career interests I'm lucky enough to coordinate my graduation from NIS with the opening of a Chinese language class at Monterey. I point this out to the officers in charge of recommending next duty stations. Fortunately, the CO and XO have forgiven me for missing the putt in the match with Senator Blank, and I'm assigned to the fall term of the Chinese language class. For the next eighteen months I will be on the Monterey Peninsula. It's just a fortuitous coincidence that it's the home of Pebble Beach and other great golf courses. As we shake hands at graduation they point this out to me with knowing grins. I can never thank those two men enough for their guidance, support, and friendship. Wouldn't it be nice to have senior officers like them throughout my career?

Before heading to Monterey I have time to stop at home. I'm looking forward to seeing my family and friends again. Bob is going into his junior year in high school and is generating a place for himself that will later lead to promotion to captain and commanding officer of the precision drill team. I'm very proud of him. He's worked very hard to distinguish himself. Mom and Dad's marriage has gone on the rocks. Mom is as viperous as before, and Dad is hitting the bottle and complaining about his ulcer. There is nothing I or anyone can do about it. But it breaks my heart to see my family falling apart and Bob caught in the middle. I am hoping that it will hold together long enough for him to get out and into college.

I drive to Monterey in a 1958 Porsche Speedster I bought just before leaving D.C. It's seen better days, but the price is right. I've wanted a Porsche since I saw my first one three years ago. This little car really isn't designed for extensive freeway travel, but I make it home safely if I drive very slowly. Mom and Dad can't get excited about this toy, as they call it. They have grown up on Detroit monsters and this is too far off the track for them to appreciate.

Monterey is enjoying beautiful fall weather when I arrive. People are coming in from all over to attend the Navy's postgraduate schools' offerings. There are a couple of receptions in nearby private homes for the newbies. One is overlooking the course at Pebble Beach. I don't get to see much, as it's dusk when we arrive. Still, I catch the ambiance with the sound of the waves breaking on the rocky shore, tall cypress, fir, and eucalyptus trees each adding their scent to that of the sea. It is magical and I am most anxious to play there.

Pebble is a public course. In the spring it's windy, sometimes rainy, but absolutely gorgeous. Anyone who can afford the high green fees can play. The only downside is that the course attracts tourists who should never have been allowed to pick up a club. They hit and miss balls over the course and the woods while just having a grand time. Taking the pro's advice I beat the horde by teeing off alone at 0730. The first three holes give me a chance to warm up for the ocean side journey that is to come. I play them in par. On the 327-yard fourth I cut my drive and have to scramble to get a par with a fifteen-foot putt. This is where I get my first sight of the ocean. Five and six are dog legs and gradually rise to a promontory. I go par bogey shooting to a hidden pin on six. The seventh is the most scenic. It is on top of a cliff with the ocean on two sides. Seven is only 107 yards, all downhill with ocean right and long. I take a short iron and pray that I don't get wet. The less adventurous route is simply to pitch a short shot down the hill and let it run to the green. The only problem is that a bunker protects the whole front of the green. I figure I didn't come here to lay up, so I punch a nine iron and pray. The wind coming in from the ocean on the right holds the shot and I have two putts from twenty feet for my par. The eighth hole is a monster requiring a drive to the top of a promontory followed by a 200-yard shot off the cliff and over an inlet several hundred feet below. If you hit one over the bluff you don't go looking for it. I miss the postage stamp green and make my second bogey. From the eleventh through the sixteenth the course winds over hills and through the forest. They are a good test but don't offer the ocean view. To compensate for that there is almost no wind. I par the simple twelfth and bogey the thirteenth, which is a dog leg with a second shot to a small, very sharply defined green. I hit the green but can't hold it and end up in a collection area to the left. Sixteen is a short, easy dog leg right with the second shot over a ravine tightened by trees on both sides. I get careless and cut the shot right of the green. Two putts and I've earned another bogey. The seventeenth is a 209-yard hole directly into the wind with ocean on the left side. I hit a three iron and come up short in the front bunker. On in two and down in four for another bogey. I'm really upset with myself. I have a very good round going through eleven but I'm sloppy and let it get away from me. Seventeen is followed by the famous 548 par-5 closing hole along the rock-covered ocean beach that everyone has seen on television. For anyone with a handicap over 8 it is a long day. I'm happy to par in for a 78.

Despite being surrounded by world-class golf courses, sooner or later I have to concentrate on why I'm here. Chinese is one of the more complicated languages for a Westerner to grasp. First, you have to learn the calligraphy. There are thousands of these pictographs, some freestanding and some combinations of others. To read a newspaper you need to recognize at least a thousand. In addition to this, pronunciation is critical. You can say one thing with a certain intonation and if you emphasize the same word a different way you find you have said something quite different. For me, although I love the process, it is very difficult.

One of the receptions for new students is held at the home of the wealthy Arbuckle family on 17-Mile Drive. Their money comes from the Watson steamship line that a great grandfather founded. They are still the principal stockholders. The Watson Lines work the Pacific from as far north as Alaska to as far south as Melbourne. The father, Wilfred, commonly called Fred, is chairman emeritus of the line. The family alternates living between San Francisco and Carmel. They have two houses, one in San Francisco's Sea Cliff and the other a huge, beautiful property on 17-Mile Drive in the woods on the north side of Carmel. The Drive starts in Pacific Grove and winds south along the coast past the toney Monterey Peninsula Country Club, the ultra-exclusive Cypress Point Golf Club, and Pebble Beach before dipping into Carmel, then turning north and looping back through the Del Monte Forest returning eventually to Pacific Grove.

The Arbuckles reek of old money but are very cordial. The mother, Betsy, has a silly streak that makes the whole family enjoyable to be with. Fred is a big fellow, about 6'3" and 250 pounds, with a hearty laugh and an immense capacity for vodka martinis. Every night he will work his way through a pitcher full. Although he is mellow I never see him drunk. Fred is perhaps the best-liked man on the Peninsula. Few people pass without stopping to talk with him. He is friendly with everyone from the gardener and housekeeper to store clerks, waitresses, and business executives. Golf is his passion followed closely by barbequing. Saturdays and Sundays or any other day barbequed beef, chicken, or fish is the entrée. They have an outdoor cooking patio facility that would make most four star chefs jealous. When all the fixings are ready Betsy will lean over the railing from the first floor and call down, "Freddie, we're ready." To which Fred will reply, "Just a couple more minutes, Betsy," as he works through the pitcher and chars the meat.

They have three children; Jennifer is nearly twenty-eight, Paul is almost twenty-seven, and Lynda is twenty-six. She's very animated, energetic and a lot of fun to be around. She's tall and thin with long brown hair that she likes to wear in a ponytail. Lynda is clearly well educated and turns out to be an alumna of one of the major women's colleges back east. She dresses quite well in expensive by unpretentious clothes. In time I ask her for a date. I enjoy being with Lynda because her light-heartedness is a welcome relief from the pressures of school. Jennifer is an aspiring singer who has no ear for music. Brother Paul is supposed to be working at the family company. However, it is a casual position, theoretically managing their south valley freight forwarding company. Their small fleet of trucks picks up the produce of the Salinas Valley, canned fruits and vegetables, and barrels of wine and olive oil and delivers them to the docks in San Francisco. When Paul feels the need to show productivity he'll drop in at the office. Mostly, he engages in dressage with the family's stable of horses and goes to competitions wherever they might occur. He's never won because he won't put in the effort needed to be competitive. Just about any excuse will take him away from the training.

For some reason the family takes a liking to me. They give me an open invitation to come to dinner on any weekend. Fred's handicap is in the high teens. He loves taking me to Monterey Peninsula Country Club, where he is a member, and getting big money matches with his buddies. About once a month or so we play Cypress Point where he is also a member. He keeps a membership just to play a half dozen times a year. The ultraconservative atmosphere bothers him. He refers to the place as the Stuffed Shirts Home.

Cypress is very exclusive. It hosted a famous impromptu match in 1957 between the two best professionals, Ben Hogan and Byron Nelson, and the two best amateurs at the time, Ken Venturi and Harvie Ward. It has gone down in golf lore as "The Match." If you are invited to play there, at the end of the match you cannot shower or go to the nineteenth hole. When the game is over, so are you.

Cypress is not a long course. It is an intricate ocean setup designed by Alister MacKenzie in the late 1920s. The front nine takes off inland through the Del Monte Forest. On the back side it emerges and flows toward the Pacific. Holes fifteen through seventeen are regarded as among the finest in the country. Sixteen is a par-3, 220-yard carry over a corner of the Pacific Ocean to a small green. You just hit and pray. All members are quite wealthy and play big money matches. I'm very uncomfortable having hundreds and occasionally a thousand dollars riding on a match, but Fred assures me that if we lose he will cover it. If we win he always gives me my share and usually some "pocket money" along with it. When we win or I shoot a low round, he announces it at dinner with many details and great gusto. Paul doesn't like this.

One Friday, Lynda and I are planning an early movie and a late dinner. I leave school about 4:00 and head to her house on 17-Mile Drive in the Porsche. When I enter the gate the attendant recognizes me and the little car. "How you doing, lieutenant"? "Wonderfully well, John," I reply. He waves me through the gate and five minutes later I am pulling up in front of the Arbuckle place, as they call it. I call it a mansion. It has about twenty rooms, eight of which are bedroom suites. There is a large living room and an even larger dining room that can accommodate at least forty people. There is the main kitchen that is fit for a castle. Sitting rooms, a library, verandas, a game room, a movie room, and a gym make up most of the rest. I ring the doorbell and Paul answers. "Come in, sport. Lynda is shopping with Mother and called to say she will be late.

You know women, once they get into shopping nothing else matters. I thought we could kill some time at the stables. You've never been there, have you?"

"No, I haven't. Do we have time for it?"

"We won't be long, sport. I think you will enjoy seeing the horses. They are gorgeous. We'll take the cart and be there in two minutes."

They have a well-appointed electric cart that can hold six to eight people. It has a radio phone in case you need to call someone. The cart is painted blue and white, the colors of the ships in the Watson fleet. We get in and Paul takes off like he's driving Le Mans. I have the feeling he's trying to scare me. He's not far from it. Within two minutes flat we screech to a halt at the horse barn.

Paul takes me around introducing me to people and to horses. It is truly an impressive facility. I've never seen horses such as these. They live better than most people. There is only the faintest smell of manure and it actually smells a bit sweet. When I was a wee tyke I remember seeing and smelling the few farm horses that were still around. But they were heavyweights bred to pull farm equipment. We step out into the paddock and there is a groom walking a huge gray and black stallion. When he comes by us Paul takes the reins and introduces him. "His name is Khan. Hop on board, sport," he says.

"I'm not much for horses," I reply. "I've never ridden more than a couple times."

"Don't sweat it, sport. I'll hold the reins and you can just sit on him. It's a great feeling to have something this majestic and strong under you. I'll give you a leg up."

Reluctantly, I put my foot in this hand and as I throw a leg over the back of the horse he snorts and sidles away.

"Don't worry, sport. I've got him."

I sit there a few seconds enjoying the view and feeling the power of the huge animal under me. All of a sudden I hear a whistle and this monster does a 360 spin before he takes off across the area where they have set up jumps for dressage training. Paul drops the reins and jumps back. I'm on top of this locomotive with no reins. This is an

English saddle so there is no pommel to hold on to. I grab has mane but it's not much use. We approach a small jump and Khan goes over it, and fortunately I go with him. Next, he turns toward a double rail jump. As he approaches it with no rider to guide him he undershoots the jump and goes down, throwing me several yards away into the sandy soil. I land on my left shoulder and roll out of the way of Khan. Someone comes running up and grabs the reins. Paul arrives with a false worried look and asks, "Are you alright, sport?"

"I think my shoulder is dislocated or broken. Better get me to the hospital."

"I'll take you," Paul says.

"No thanks. You've done enough for me already. Just go back to the house and tell Lynda that I'm okay but on my way to the hospital."

One of the grooms drives me and an hour later I'm in bed at Community Hospital in the forest above Monterey. The ER doctor has confirmed a hyperextended shoulder and popped it back in place. She tells me I will be in a sling for a few days and can forget about golf for at least two weeks. After hearing how it happened, she wants to keep me overnight to check for a concussion. Two hours later Lynda arrives. She is a mess. She's crying. I tell her I'm okay but she has a hard time accepting it. Paul told her that I fell off a horse without including any salient facts about how. By Monday I'm cleared to attend classes again, albeit with my arm in a sling for a few more days.

Two weeks later I'm invited to a Saturday night party at the Arbuckles. It's formal, so I'm wearing my dress uniform. There are several captains, a general, and an admiral in attendance. My puny two stripes make me look like hired help in this crowd.

Paul is there and he greets me with, "How are you, old sport? I'm really sorry about the stable incident. No hard feelings, I hope?"

I nod and go looking for Lynda. The evening goes well for a couple hours until I am walking back from the bar with drinks for Lynda and myself. Suddenly, I trip and go flying into the stern of the admiral's wife. I pick myself up and try to brush her off.

"That's quite enough, lieutenant. We'll take care of it," he exclaims.

Lynda comes over and asks what happened.

"Someone tripped me."

"No one here would do that."

"Maybe not, but I didn't just slip."

The rest of the evening goes well so long as I stay away from the admiral and spouse. She has a wet derriere and rightfully blames it on me. As I'm talking with Lynda and another couple Paul shows up and makes a joke about my flying into the admiral's beloved. As he turns to go, his drink hand hits me and his drink goes all over my shirt, tie, and coat.

"Oh my god," He exclaims. "Here is a napkin to clean yourself with, sport."

Lynda isn't looking at the time of the spill and thinks I am the klutz. I'm thinking to myself, what else can happen? The party drags on. People are into heavy debates concerning the state of the political scene. You might imagine that there aren't a lot of Democrats in the room. With Kennedy as president and Reagan the new governor of California, the night is filled with obscenities. Kennedy is gradually sending more troops to Vietnam and on that the room is divided, although antiwar marches and race riots have no support in the room. These people are steeped in politics because it has a major effect on their fortunes. Sometime after midnight I'm thinking it is time to get my soiled uniform out of here with me in it. Lynda and Paul, of all people, accompany me to the door. The valet brings my old Porsche around. Next to the Cadillacs and Mercedes are a Ferrari, a Maserati Quattroporte, and a couple Rolls-Royces. My small, old Porsche looks like a toy. Paul looks at it and chuckles, "How do you get in that thing, sport, with a shoe horn?"

Lynda and I ignore him. I give her a little kiss, take off my damp coat, and go down with my shoe horn to get in the car.

Paul says, "Take the ocean side of the Drive. The moon is full and the sight is something special." As I head off in that direction, both of them wave.

It's a gorgeous night. There's a nearly full moon bouncing its silver beams off the ocean. A stiff onshore breeze is chasing white caps toward the rocky beach. Five minutes later I'm just approaching one of the scenic turnouts where the Monterey Peninsula Golf Course meets the ocean. Unknown to me earlier in the evening someone called the gate pretending to be a resident and cleared two men through. I see a car parked in the turnout with the hood up and two men with flashlights. When they see me one of them steps out into the road and waves for me to stop. I pull up and he walks toward me. I'm not certain what is happening here, so I keep my left foot depressing the clutch and the right gently on the accelerator. I can see through my head lights the man is smiling and I relax for a second. I roll down the window and am staring into the muzzle of an Army issue 45 mm pistol. It is too late to take off. He says, "Pull over slowly next to my car."

Not having any alternative, I comply. When he orders me out I slide around and stand up. Something hits my back at the kidney level and I go down. For the next few minutes they use me for a punching and kicking bag. I pass out briefly until I feel myself being picked up by the arms and legs and carried toward the ocean. "He ought to like this touch," one of them says. They swing me once, twice and then I'm airborne. I crash onto the rocks just above the surf and pass out again.

It is just getting light when I feel someone shaking me and asking, "Are you alright?" Then another person gasps, "He's all beat up. Call an ambulance. This guy looks real bad."

I drift in and out of consciousness the next couple of hours. I can tell that I'm off the beach and in the hospital because it's warm, quiet and doesn't smell like seaweed. Someone is working on me, but I can't do anything but sleep. When I finally wake up Lynda is here and she is crying, almost sobbing, as though I am dead. In fact, due to the pain in my ribs, back, and head I am tempted to take that option. I try to speak to her and can only mutter and give her the OK sign.

Soon a couple of doctors and a nurse come in. They check me over by pushing on painful parts. One of the doctors says, "You've had a rough night, lieutenant. Can you tell us now you ended up on the rocks?"

I give them the best description I can. I never saw one of the men, the one who gave me a kidney shot. I only have a dim view of the one who pulled me over. The second doctor says, "Well, you have a broken rib, bruised kidney, broken nose, possible concussion, and assorted lacerations." The first doctor says he's a surgeon and that he has already given me an admiral's nose. Other than that, they claim I'm in no danger and after a little healing time I should be fine. But they recommend that I find new playmates. What a couple of kidders.

Next, two cops, one plainclothes and one in uniform, join the party and ask if I feel good enough to answer some questions. I tell them I'll try. All this time Lynda is hanging on to my hand like I'm falling off another cliff. I tell them what little I know and they leave. I see a reflection of myself in Lynda's compact mirror and realize why she is so upset. For the next several days I'm getting up and taking short walks in the hallway with my mobile IV unit.

Meanwhile, the guard John at the 17-Mile Drive gate had been suspicious of the two men who had come through earlier. Even though they had been cleared to one of the properties in Carmel he had written down their license number and alerted his shift replacement to keep an eye out for anything unusual. Sure enough, about an hour after midnight their car had come out the gate followed by my little Porsche. Everyone knows the Porsche and the guard can see I'm not the driver. The bad guys take my car out so Security won't find it and be suspicious. Immediately, the guard calls the police and private security force and tells the cops to look out for my car. During the night the security force cruises the Drive and finds nothing because I'm over the cliff unconscious. By dawn the police have found my car just a few blocks away on a street in Pacific Grove, the city on the north end of the Drive. In the car is my soiled uniform jacket with my billfold still inside the breast pocket. That rules out robbery as the motive. There are also bloody fingerprints on the door. Immediately, it's clear that this is an amateur job. The police trace their car through the license number John gives them and find it belongs to a local fellow who has a history of assault. The fingerprints lead them to the gun man, who it turns out is an army deserter from Fort Ord, just ten miles north of Carmel. This is where the story gets thick.

Earlier, Perp Number One is contacted by another man who tells him he has a wealthy client who needs some work done. Perp One then talks to Perp Two who is hiding out at his house. He is the deserter and needs some money to disappear. They drive to 17-Mile Drive before midnight and wait in one of the pull-offs. At the appointed hour they get a call from someone who tells them I'm coming down the ocean side of the Drive. They're ready for me and do the deed.

The detectives on the case persuade Perp One to give them the contactor's name. They pick him up and then persuade him that it would be in his best interests to finger the person who put out the contract. Imagine everyone's surprise, but mine, when they identify Paul. He's arrested and charged with conspiracy to commit a felony, assault and battery, plus sundry related crimes.

On Monday afternoon, Lt. Cdr. Ling from the language school comes in to visit me. He says he just heard about my situation. "Michael," he begins, "this is the second time within two weeks that you've gone venturing. Don't you think you've had enough?"

"I agree with you. The doctors say I'll be in their hotel for about a week, barring any complications.

Ling continues, "We'll have to work out something so you don't fall behind the class. After a couple days rest I'll send one of the instructors to help you."

The MDs tell me it'll take at least a month to heal sufficiently to return to active duty. Good to his word, Ling sends me a tutor who helps me keep up with the class. He is an older Chinese man who is quite pleasant but also a workhorse. When I eventually get back to school I jump right back into the curriculum.

In time, the incident blows over, the justice system swings into motion, and Paul is out on bail pending trial. The grand jury orders him bound over and the judge sets bail at $500,000 and takes his passport. Fred orders him out of the house. I don't know where he's staying, but I suspect it is somewhere on the Peninsula with a friend. Throughout this family upset, Lynda and I keep dating. She is a great gal but a bit nervous. We're all a little off the mark. I'm thinking that nerves are not a trait that will take her out of the running for a wife. Besides I believe that getting her out of here will calm her down. So, at a Fourth of July picnic the following summer I propose to her. She says yes and we plan a wedding to coincide with my graduation in late Fall.

Along about September I see that Lynda is having problems. She can't seem to make up her mind about the details of the wedding. Betsy is no help. She is constantly asking Fred and Lynda what they think and then ignoring their suggestions. From the looks of it she intends to invite most of northern California. They are native Californians and she feels that anyone west of the Rockies who is not invited will be upset. Not being a wedding expert, I figure this is what goes on with young women as they approach a major event of their lives. One minute Lynda is flying high and the next she is depressed. I decide it is time we have a talk. My questions for her are simple.

Number 1: Do you love me?
Number 2: Do you want to marry me?
Number 3: Are you scared?
Number 4: Are you sick?
Number 5: What is upsetting you?

The answer to the first three is yes. The answer to numbers 4 and 5 is I don't know. So I try the big one. What would happen if we broke off the engagement and didn't get married?

At this I see her go into a shell. She says, "I'd have to leave here. I couldn't stand what people would say."

I tell her to think it over and we will talk again soon. In a week we sit down to talk. This time Lynda says, "I'm sorry I caused you to doubt me. It is just such a confusing, hectic time. I do love you and want to marry you."

This takes some of the doubt out of my mind, but leaves a lingering question: "I truly love her, but can I help her level out later?" When you're young and stupid you think you can solve any problem. With some concern we go on with the plans and she seems back to her old self again. I can see that part of the problem is her mother, who can't make up her mind on invitees, flowers, caterer, or anything else. She stresses everyone around her. I feel guilty about suggesting we break the engagement, and I figure that once we are away together we can make it work. With that we move ahead and the week after Thanksgiving in 1967, we get married in a very big wedding. There is a huge guest list obviously very wealthy. Probably enough money in the room to buy Nowhere and throw it away.

6

SHIPPING OUT

Shortly after the wedding I receive orders to report to CINCPACFLT (Commander in Chief Pacific Fleet) in Honolulu no later than 15 January 1968. Lynda is quite happy with that and off we go. We arrive on January 10 and settle into a house that Fred has bought for us in Alewa Heights. This is an upscale neighborhood between Nuuanu and Kalihi Valleys overlooking Waikiki. The house has four bedrooms and two baths, of course a small swimming pool, and a gorgeous view of the city, Diamond Head, and the Pacific Ocean. It comes with his and her new cars: a Chevy Impala for her and a Chevy convertible for me. I thank Fred profusely, but tell him, "Fred, this is way too much money to spend on us. I'll pay you back at least for the cars." On a lieutenant's pay I have no idea how I'll do it or how long it will take.

Fred responds, "Michael, don't fret. I make this much money every week without even paying attention. Besides, you've given me a pleasure that far exceeds this by kicking those stuffed shirts at Cypress. Basically they paid for the house. You didn't know it because I didn't want you to be nervous, but I had side bets on our games that you won for me at Cypress and Monterey totaling about a hundred K."

All goes well as we newlyweds move in and settle into our tropical paradise. Three weeks after we arrive, the Vietnamese Communists launch the Tet Offensive with 80,000 Communist troops striking more than 100 towns and cities, including provincial capitals, and district centers. They even carry out some raids in the capital city of Saigon. The offensive is the largest military operation conducted by either side up to that point in the war.

The initial attacks stun the U.S. and South Vietnamese armies and cause them to temporarily lose control of many sections of the country. They quickly regroup and with superior American fire power they beat back the attacks, inflicting massive casualties on Viet Cong (VC) forces. Overall, the offensive is a military defeat for the Communists. However, it has a profound effect on the U.S. government and the military. It shocks the American people, who've been led to believe that the Communists are incapable of launching such a massive attack.

CINCPACFLT reacts as though it is another attack on Pearl Harbor. For the six months after the Tet Offensive we are working twenty hours a day digging for evidence regarding how we didn't see this coming. The CINCPACFLT CO, Admiral Bacon, has some very uncomplimentary words for American intel. "Clearly, the VC had better intel than we did. How is that possible with all the personnel and equipment we've dedicated to this? This is a major embarrassment as well as a deadly mistake for our troops. We desperately need accurate and timely intelligence to guide our response and build a strategic battle plan. And we will have it or else."

Lynda hasn't been feeling well and unknown to me goes to a doctor about two months after we arrive in Honolulu. One evening we're sitting on our lanai looking at the lights of Honolulu when Lynda turns to me and says very directly, "Michael, I'm pregnant." I'm ecstatic. She's somewhat ambivalent about it probably due to the uncertainty of our situation and being away from home for the first time since college. I'm not home very much during this time, and it causes her great anxiety. In June a new strategic plan is finalized and the pressure drops. Now I'm working regular hours and can spend time with Lynda. I get a week's leave and we fly to Kauai for a mini vacation at Poipu Bay. This is a quiet resort on the southern corner of the island. The big tourist buildup is just starting on Kauai, but Poipu is still relatively quiet.

The weather is quite warm, but the constant ocean breezes make it comfortable. We're in a beautiful suite that overlooks the beach. We enjoy sitting on the lanai sipping pina coladas and watching the gorgeous tropical sunsets. We spend time on the beach, go shopping and sightseeing, and generally catch up on our relationship. It's much needed since things have been tense between us. Lynda is away from her family for the first time, she's had trouble connecting with the other wives. I never saw a shyness in her in Monterey. Perhaps that was because she was in the bosom of her family and friends where everything was familiar and she felt very protected there. Although Hawaii is a very benign, secure place Lynda can't seem to embrace it. She's lived away from home when attending college in the east. I didn't know it until I questioned her about it now, but she hated being away from home. She felt very fearful of the people and the place even though it was as secure as could be and filled with girls of her age and economic background. To add to her angst is the fact she is going to have a baby without the support of her mother and Carmen. I can understand the need for love; the love she had in abundance at home. What I don't understand is why she can't adjust. It's not like she's alone in an alien place. It frustrates me to see her upset and not trying to work her way through it. My suggestions about taking some kind of classes or joining the Navy wives group or a bridge club or volunteering or anything to feel more alive are rejected. I know what it feels like to be alone, but she isn't alone. I may be busy, but I'm home every night now and most weekend days. I guess my frustration or impatience or lack of sensitivity is something I need to deal with if I'm going to be happily married. The little holiday and the lighter work load seem to improve our situation. Lynda slowly seems to relax and open her eyes to possibilities.

Then, it hits us. In October I'm given orders to report aboard the USS *Ranger*, which is patrolling the coast of Vietnam and launching aircraft to support operations in Vietnam. It's to be a six-month assignment provided everything goes well, which it seldom does in times like these.

When I come home and give her the bad news Lynda comes apart. "I thought we were going to have a normal life. Now the Navy takes you away from me when I need you the most. It isn't fair. It's just not fair."

In a week after she gets over the shock we discuss various scenarios for the next three to four months. It makes sense that she should return to Monterey and have the baby there during my absence. I'm heartbroken that I won't be home when the baby arrives sometime in January 1969. I feel like turning in my commission and leaving the Navy. That doesn't seem to be a practical solution on several levels. All I can do is hope to be back soon after the event. Arrangements are made and Lynda leaves a week before I ship out. Our parting is with many tears on both sides. We rent the house for twelve months to an Air Force family on TAD (Temporary Additional Duty) to Hawaii and leave it in the hands of a property manager to oversee. We lend the cars to some people on the staff who can use them.

In November 1968 I arrive onboard the *Ranger*, a Forrestal class ship. The Forrestal class is the first class of super carriers in the Navy. They are called that because of their extraordinarily high tonnage, full integration of the angled deck, and extremely strong air wing, capable of handling eighty to a hundred jet aircraft. The Forrestals are a stable and comfortable aircraft platform even in very rough weather.

I report to Commander Cedric Johnson, CO of the intelligence unit. It is a small unit. I'm the only one on board who has been through intel school. We have two noncoms who speak Vietnamese and Chinese. Johnson is a nervous man who knows that he's in over his head. He's constantly changing orders so we don't know what to expect minute to minute. He jumps at the least movement. When Captain Skovill, commanding officer of the ship, wants to talk to Johnson or me, Johnson almost pees in his skivvies. About once a week he orders us to go through a Field Day drill. Instead of monitoring radio communications between VCs and Chinese, we are devoting precious time to housekeeping.

Johnson doesn't like me because I'm clearly smarter and better suited for this mission. Whenever possible he overrides my recommendations or takes them to the XO indicating that he had provided guidance and oversight to the report. In truth, he only knows what I choose to let him know. On the other hand, I've a career to think of, so I have to do what I can to make his tour successful. The two NCOs see that I'm a buffer between them and Johnson and wholeheartedly support me.

Two months after coming on board and putting out to sea, I can see we're wasting our time and adding no value. I inform Johnson that the three of us will monitor VC radio 24-7. There are teams, often led by warrant officers with the appropriate ethnic backgrounds, who go behind enemy lines and bring out pieces of their electronic equipment to be analyzed in one of our labs in Hawaii or Washington, D.C. Through these means, we learn what radio frequencies their crystals were set for so we can monitor them.

Johnson is uncertain about this arrangement. He really has no idea what the mission of our unit is and is afraid to tip his hand by asking someone about it. Johnson is further concerned when I tell him I'll take the midnight to 0800 watch because, knowing the Chinese habits, that is the time during which they are most likely to pass critical information. He likes to spend hours taking to me and "briefing me" on what intelligence is all about. This is his way to pick my brain. He asks what I think about something and then agrees with me by adding some superfluous point or useless opinion. The midnight shift gives me an excuse not to have to deal with him until I awake after noon.

While I'm off the coast of Vietnam my son Davey is born in Monterey in January 1969. I'm a very proud father, happy beyond words. I'm also angry because I missed his birth. In her letters Lynda writes about how time consuming it is to take care of a new baby. She doesn't seem to be as over the top as I am. Obviously, it is difficult to deal with a newborn even with help. Not having a husband around for psychological and physical support just makes the matter worse. I can't blame her for not being as excited as I am.

Throughout CINCPAC there is great concern that the Communists will try another attack around the Tet anniversary since the first one has been so successful. Our unit is on full alert 24-7 to make sure we don't miss anything. The VC surprise us by not attacking on Tet but waiting until it's passed and our forces have presumably relaxed. Four nights after Tet, about 0200 I'm monitoring several frequencies switching back and forth as my light board picks up any signals. When one lights up I tune it in and hear an animated conversation just starting. I know it was only beginning because they're using standard greetings. It's between a Chinese and a Viet-speaking Chinese. I rouse the Vietnamese speaking NCO who would have the 0800 to 1600 shift. I didn't know how long this will last but it sounds very intense and they may resort to Vietnamese at any time. He stumbles in five minutes later and puts on his headphones. I tell him, "If they start speaking Vietnamese, it will be up to you to tape record and translate."

Turning back to the Chinese conversation it is clear that this is an important issue. The speakers switch back and forth between conversational and military jargon. In time it starts to make sense. They are discussing a plan to move an unusually large component of munitions and troops into Vietnam from China. There is a long border between the two countries and the shipment can come across anywhere. The movement will be tomorrow night starting at midnight, twenty-two hours from now. The unanswered central question is, where will it take place?

They obviously have spent a long time planning the transfer so they don't have to talk about it. Just as clearly they have staged the munitions just inside the Chinese border and are making preparations on the VC side. They don't want to take chances that it will be discovered. With the U.S. and the South Vietnamese army flying recon constantly, the danger of discovery is substantial. The NCO and I work up a detailed report of what we hear. At 0700 I leave the watch to the NCO and wake up Johnson. "Sir, this is a transcription that we intercepted early this morning. I believe it is very important and needs to go topside ASAP."

He can hardly believe what I hand him. I think he is frightened by the gravity of the intelligence that he holds in his hand. It is a career-determining moment. I try to not only reassure him of its truth and gravity but urge him to take it immediately to the XO.

He says, "I'll look this over. If it's warranted I will take it topside. In the meantime you get some sleep."

He doesn't have a clue about the implications of what I've shown him. I know his game. He'll take my report to the executive officer, possibly with some inconsequential changes he'll throw in. But I also know he can't answer any questions that the CO or XO might have and they're sure to have a lot of them. Clearly, this information needs to be acted on immediately. We've only sixteen hours before the munitions and troops start to cross the border. If they make it uncontested, many South Vietnamese and American troops will suffer. The Vietnam–Chinese border is several hundred miles long. My report gives a list of possible transfer coordinates as best it could without any local knowledge support. So, taking Johnson's order directly I go to my room and lay on the bunk fully clothed. I know that once the captain sees the report and discovers that Johnson is unclear about the details I'll be called to his quarters behind the bridge.

Sure enough, at 0830 Johnson gets up his nerve to deliver the report. I'm summoned to the Combat Information Center (CIC). When I arrive Johnson starts to explain how we put the report together, but Captain Skovill cuts him off and focuses his steel-blue eyes on me. His questions are pointed and rapid. Am I the one who personally heard the conversation? How clear was the transmission? Am I certain of the details? Specifically, where do I believe the move will take place? The most critical questions are, when and where? It must be precise. I have a good answer for each one including the time, but admittedly have some uncertainty about the place. Here I need someone with local ground knowledge of the border area. Something this heavy will have to have a significant well-paved road on which to travel. There are a couple of possibilities. The captain turns to his XO and tells him to find someone, somehow, whom I can talk with to pinpoint the move.

Then he asks both of us what we recommend. Out of courtesy to rank I let Johnson go first. He has no ideas and mumbles some vague generalities, so the captain turns to me to go over the key points in the report that indicated the possible transfer points. After some hard grilling he dismisses us and tells me that as soon as they find the person with local knowledge he wants to see me in CIC. He doesn't say anything to Johnson.

Johnson and I leave his quarters and as soon as we are out of sight and hearing Johnson starts to chew me out for insubordination. He almost threatens to have me keel-hauled. I take it because no matter what he says I've won the day already. He tells me to return to my quarters and stay there until he summons me.

I lay down on my bunk still fully clothed. I am in the middle between being exhausted and wanting to know what the captain will do with my intel. Within an hour the level of activity on the ship picks up. You can just feel the intensity, an energy and urgency rolls throughout the ship. We are several hundred miles south of the latitude of the shipment. The ship shudders and leans to port as the captain turns the *Ranger* around and starts steaming north at flank speed. By now it is coming up on 1300. Communications are streaming out to the strategic commander of the South Vietnamese command in Saigon. This will lead to a squadron of fighter bombers preparing to strike the point I claim is the target. If I prove to be wrong the United States will have spent millions on a false alarm and my career will be over. Johnson knows that his will be also. I know he is in his room in a catatonic state or else bouncing off the walls like a handball.

About 1500 I'm called by the XO to report to the CIC. When I arrive Johnson is standing at the big planning table making vague suggestions. The XO says he has a local expert on a secure frequency ashore ready to discuss the terrain and roads. The XO motions me to the table and tells Johnson to step back. I go over the key elements with the local expert. I repeat the magnitude of what is going to cross the border. At the end of our discussion we decide that the enemy will split the move into two parts for safety and speed. The part with the munitions will take the well-paved eastern highway because they need to get the arms undercover ASAP. The other part will come down the western road, which is smaller but will be easy for troop trucks to navigate. We select the two points on the map where we believe the transfer will take place. I pass our decision to the XO. After a long pause he steps back, looks very hard at me and asks, "Are you absolutely positive that this information is accurate, son?"

"Sir, the info is accurate and the only risk is that it's a set-up. If we have time we can do a high altitude recon to find evidence of the buildup. However, throughout the overheard discussion last night the tone and words being used suggests it is genuine. I feel extremely confident that it is not a ruse."

The XO says that he has run the intel through HQ in Saigon and the consensus is that it is legit. The only question is where it will happen. "Okay, lieutenant," he says, "We are committing a large portion of our fire power to this based on your word. You damn well better be right. Dismissed!"

I return to my quarters and lay down once more. This time exhaustion takes over and I fall asleep. Six hours later I wake with a start as the ship lurches. We are launching aircraft, probably reconnaissance to look for any evidence of a buildup in the target area confirming my report. I check with my men in the intel center. They are very excited and more than a little apprehensive. They understand the magnitude of the operation. They also hear an increase in traffic indicating that something is happening on shore.

I take a shower and go to the officer's ward room. I've not eaten for about twenty hours. The ship is buzzing. Preparations are underway for a launch of fighter bombers. Of course, Chinese radar will pick up the planes coming north and east from the carrier. They probably will scramble MIG-21s from the closest Chinese air field. So long as we don't get too close to the border, they most likely will not fire on us. The plan is to let the transfer start unimpeded to ensure that everything is across the border and into Vietnamese territory. This will avoid a provocation with China. Low-level fighters will drop napalm that will light up the place. Then, fighter bombers will saturate the target area with high explosives followed by strafing runs from both types of aircraft. Now it occurs to me that if anything goes wrong and China retaliates I might be responsible to starting World War III.

About 0400 the XO calls me to CIC. He is there with Captain Skovill and they are all smiles. Everything turned out just as I had predicted. They wiped out the shipment. "Well done," says the captain. "This won't hurt your career." I shake hands with them as well as with the ops officer. I also learn that on the way north, a flight of six air force fighters see several MIG-21s taking off from a previously unknown air strip. It's probably a maintenance base. Three of the fighters peel off and attack the MIGs as they begin to climb out. The score is four MIGs bagged without so much as a single bullet hole in our side. Now, the Air Force is happy too.

A month later the *Ranger* heads back to port in South Vietnam for refueling and rearming. The XO calls me to his quarters. "Lieutenant, I've received orders for you that on our arriving in port you're to brief the joint command in Saigon. Immediately afterwards you're to fly to Hong Kong and brief our consul general there."

On arrival in port I disembark and head to CINC Vietnam HQ. After a week of waiting for the brass and the intel section to find the time, I carry out the two days of briefing. Then I take off for Hong Kong. The flight takes about two hours. I'm told that after I complete my mission there I will receive further orders.

Once aboard the plane I open my orders that confirm I am to provide a complete briefing to the Hong Kong consul general. Hong Kong is part of the British Commonwealth. I'm also to brief the CO and staff of the Royal Navy on the events leading up to the raid on the raid as well as the intelligence we have on the result to date.

On arrival I go directly to the U.S. Consulate on Garden Road, Hong Kong side, to be assigned quarters and then prepare to debrief the consul general and staff. I work with the AV staff to set up the graphics I employed in the joint command briefing in Saigon. The interrogations are long and sometimes confrontational, especially with the economic officer who is clearly a CIA agent.

After two days of grilling and discussion I make an appointment to sing the same song to the Royal Navy Command. We finish that grueling examination in one day. At this time since the UK still controls Hong Kong it likes to think it also controls the waters in that part of the world. The atmosphere clears as they realize the Americans have no intent of upstaging them. Being essentially good fellows, the Brits invite me for drinks at the Royal Navy Fleet Club.

The next night I have off so I decide to treat myself to dinner at the Empress Hotel. I'm pretty full of myself. How many lieutenants provide the intel to launch a massive strike? After dinner I go for a walk hoping to find a tobacco shop that sells good cigars. It's unlikely that I'll find a shop on the main street since this is the area of high-end stores. In a couple blocks I look down a side street and see a small tobacco shop wedged in between a sushi restaurant and a brightly lit record store. As I push open the door the noise is behind me and I encounter the odor of decades of tobacco and smoke. This would knock a nonsmoker out. But for me it's delicious. The shop walls seem to shine with the oils of the tobacco. In one corner are two easy chairs and a small elephant-base table with an ashtray. There's a yellowish light that illuminates an elderly Chinese man in a smock standing with his hands on the counter facing me. His fingers are stained from years of handling and smoking tobacco products. Although I speak Mandarin Chinese he probably speaks Cantonese, so I try English. Being a crown colony of the British Commonwealth all educated people speak English. "Good evening sir."

He replies in kind and with a slight bow asks how I am this beautiful evening. "How may I help you?" he asks.

"I'm looking for a good cigar to celebrate an event."

"Wonderful, sir. Do you have a favorite brand?"

"I'd like Monte Cristo, if you have it."

"Of course sir, one of the best cigars in the world. They're over here. How many would you like?"

I know enough to ask the price before purchasing. If an American asks about the cost they don't think you have a lot of money and may state a lower price than if you don't ask. "What is the price?"

"US Dollar 15. Hong Kong dollar HKD 77".

"I'll take two."

"Very good sir. May I show you a recent arrival of a new cigar?"

"Certainly."

"Do you like a mild cigar or a full-bodied one?"

"I prefer mild."

He moves to the right side of the counter and reaches in to pull out a box. "These are a new brand. They are very mild, handmade of course. The maker has given us a very good introductory price. Here. You can smell the mildness. They are from the Philippines. The filler and binder are grown in Tagaytay on the slopes of the old volcano at 2,000 feet above sea level and overlooking Lake Taal. They use only long seco fillers for light, smooth, consistent burning. It has a beautiful ash also."

Machine-made cigars take chopped up tobacco leaves, sometimes including stems, and wrap them in paper made from tobacco leaves. Aficionados call these, derisively, sweepings. Machine-made cigars are cheaper and sometimes burn unevenly or have plugs through which the smoke can't travel.

He continues, "The tobacco farm is not very large, so the production is limited at this time. The wrapper is shade grown in Baguio. Because Baguio is at 5,000 feet elevation the temperature is relatively cool. This makes the wrapper very mild." He hands me a cigar. "What do you think of the aroma?"

I pick up the cigar. It's a corona about five and a half inches long and two-thirds of an inch in width. Thickness is determined by what is called ring gauge. In this case the cigar is a 42 ring gauge. "It's slightly sweet, very light with some sense of leather and toast," I say.

"Would you like to try one? They are only USD10 because of the introductory offer. That is HKD 51. You can take it with you or smoke it here." He gestures toward the two easy chairs.

"Yes, it sounds interesting. I'll try it here. If I like it I'll take a few with me."

The old tobacconist gives me the cigar and a box of wooden matches. I relax into the easy chair, light up, and begin to enjoy a truly mild but flavorful smoke. The shop is quiet due to the late hour so the old man lights one and joins me. The cigar burns evenly but quickly.

I tell the old man that I speak Mandarin. This immediately changes our relationship. We chat about how business is in Hong Kong, what the influence of the PRC is here, and what he thinks the long term holds for the region. In about thirty minutes I finish the cigar. There is a lingering aroma of cherry and coffee. There is no heavy aftertaste. Actually, there is a very slight, pleasant sweetness. It might be too light for people who like full-bodied maduros, but it is very good for me. I buy three of the Filipinos.

Once I'm back on the side street I start to enjoy the spring air when something hits my head very hard from behind. I sense that I'm being picked up and tossed into something hard. I drift in and out of consciousness feeling that I'm being roughly handled. The next thing I know I'm in a dimly lit room, tied to a chair, stripped of my uniform, blindfolded, and surrounded by what sounds like three or four Chinese men and, I think, one woman. There is a strong odor that I recognize but can't put a finger on. The room is very stuffy and the odor almost makes me vomit. I can't tell exactly how many people there are because I'm blindfolded. Someone grabs my hair and starts asking questions about our strategy, plans, and arms level in VN. The bastard is smoking one of my cigars and blowing smoke in my face. He is too stupid to pick the Monte Cristo and is puffing on the Filipino. I tell him or her that I'm a lowly lieutenant who is not involved in discussions at that level. In the background I hear a man repeatedly cursing with what must have been his favorite expression, Ngo dill kau kui, Ngo dill kui lo mo (an expression regarding your mother that is too filthy to render in English).

Next, I take two hard blows with something heavy that feels like a baseball or more likely a cricket bat on each of my knee caps. Their question is repeated and so is my answer. Then, I'm dumped out of the chair and make a three point landing on my knees and my nose. Someone once told me that the knees are a very sensitive part of the body. They're right. I pass out from the pain. When I come to in a few seconds, they yank me back into the chair and threaten to kill me if I don't talk. My answers don't change. Someone is alternatively punching me in the stomach and banging on my sore legs. After about an hour, I guess, there is no progress. It is evident that they are not professionals at interrogation, thank god. If they were they could make it much more painful. They are very frustrated and seemingly tired of this game. They break off the grilling and gag me so that I can't make any sounds. For a while I don't hear anything so I guess they are on a break. I'm still tied to the chair and blindfolded. Although I am exhausted, the pain won't let me sleep. I'm in a twilight zone. Periodically, I fade in and out. When I come to there is still no one in the room. I've no sense of time passing. The blindfold doesn't let me see even a sliver of light. It seems like time is suspended. After what seems like forever the faint sounds from the street die away. It must be very late.

Eventually, they return. I hear them talking about food, so I guess its morning. The process starts again. Their breath is foul. I try to show no reaction to their blows. Finally, someone loses his patience. When I don't reply to his questions I get punched in my mouth. I feel my jawbone break. Then, someone yells in Chinese,

"You fool; now he can't talk." After much heated discussion and yelling back and forth they decide to move me, but don't want to do it in daylight. They leave me to sit through the day, still bound and leaking urine. No sense in putting the gag back on. I couldn't yell if I wanted to.

Still blindfolded, they untie me and dress me roughly in my uniform. Two men grab me under each arm and drag me down some stairs. My knees are very sore, throbbing and my legs won't hold me. On the first floor the uniquely foul smell that I think is cooking durian almost makes me vomit. I can tell its dark out again, so I have been in their custody for about twenty-four hours. Since this is a weekend no one knows I'm missing. If they notice that I've not returned to my room last night they might guess that I'm running around with one of the nightclub girls. Once on the street they throw me into a car. We drive around making lots of turns so I won't be able to lead anyone back to their building. The cursing man pokes me painfully on my knees and laughs in a high-pitched, hyena-like howl, continually repeating his obscene mantra in my face with his foul-smelling breath. Finally, they toss me out onto the sidewalk of a side street and quickly drive away.

In just a few seconds I am surrounded by a group of people who are remarking on how badly I look. At first they think I am drunk. I convince them I'm not by showing me my broken jaw. I try to tell them through my shattered teeth to get the police. Soon the police and an ambulance arrive and take me to a hospital. I don't remember much until early afternoon when I wake up.

I'm in considerable pain. Several MDs and nurses are around my bed talking and gesturing vigorously. After the chair above the durian restaurant, the fresh cool bed feels great and the hospital smell is a relief. They've given me a sponge bath so I don't stink anymore. I thank god that the terrible odor of the restaurant and the grilling room are gone. The lights are bright and the conversation animated. I understand the Chinese but I don't get some of the medical terms. With all these people talking and pointing I feel like a sideshow freak. There's more than enough pain in my legs and mouth. It reminds me of the beach party in Monterey. I decide I'm really not ready for a chat, but I gesture that I'm in pain. They give me a shot and, since I won't be dancing tonight, I decide to go back to sleep.

The next time I wake up a nurse notices, gets up, and leaves the room. Shortly thereafter she returns with two doctors. They introduce themselves in English before she tells them I also speak Chinese. With a conversation in medical Chinglish they tell me I have a broken nose, which they have already repaired. My nose has had a tough life the last year or so. They inform me that the patellar bones on both my knees have vertical fractures. The patella, commonly called the knee cap, is a small bone located in front of the knee joint. It protects the knee and connects the muscles in the front of the thigh to the tibia, the shin. Surgery to repair this is necessary and it will take about six to eight weeks to heal. *Heal* meaning being able to stand and wobble. Even then full use will require an extensive period in physical and cardio therapy. The final note is I'm told I can expect to have arthritis in both knees the rest of my life. I ask them to keep that news to themselves. If the Navy finds out my career might be over.

Then, they give me more good news. My jaw is broken and a couple of my teeth are missing. Next, comes the really good news. Due to the hole where my broken teeth were removed they can feed me while my jaw is wired shut. After the jaw heals the dentist will build a bridge to fill the open space. Thanks for small favors. I take a little liquid nourishment, although I am not hungry and I hurt all over. After my "dinner" they reload my IV with some painkillers and I'm out again.

The next day the U.S. delegation is in attendance peopled by the consul general and a couple of the so-called political and economic officers. After the CG asks me how I'm feeling he tells me that within a few days when I get stronger I will be evacuated to Letterman Army Medical Center in San Francisco. Then, the officers jump in and start pumping me about the experience. I tell them about the odor and the fellow who kept yelling those swear words. I remember that he has a high-pitched voice as well. Shortly, they run out of questions and I run out of energy.

Four days later, I'm feeling reasonably well. Now they come back at me with questions and suggestions regarding the smell and the cursing man. They offer a number of odors until I identify one. There is no question about it—this is the smell. It is durian, a large fruit grown in this part of the world. The odor is from a shop that processes it. It has a distinctive smell that foreigners find unpleasant. It has been described in many foul terms, such as garbage, dirty socks, rotten onions, turpentine, and raw sewage. Perhaps one of the least offensive is, "It smells like hell but tastes like heaven." The restaurant must specialize in cooking durian dishes for the smell to be that pervasive. This narrows the search considerably because there are only a couple restaurants and food stands that specialize in it. The police choose two restaurants and stake them out. Surveillance reveals an unusually large number of men repeatedly coming and going up the stairs above the durian restaurant on the east side of town near the harbor. A raid uncovers Communist documents and captures several men with previous arrest records for petty crimes. After some interrogation they tell me they believe the high-pitched hyena cursing man is a U.S. consular employee.

The police ask me if they can bring him to my room so I can positively ID him by sound. I'm more than happy to find the bastard who did this to me, but I've never seen him. We devise a plan where they will cover my eyes and bring in two men. As they talk I'm to let them know if one of them is the man. In the morning the nurse wraps a gauge bandage around my head. The suspects think I can't talk well due to my broken jaw. The plan is that the cops will get a conversation going with one man on each side of my bed.

In they come. They tell the suspects I'm not able to talk much because of my jaw. They can see its wired shut and one of the mugs snickers. The dialogue starts and the cops make prejudicial remarks about white men to get the men agitated. In a few seconds one of them responds with an oath that is not what I heard but is definitely *who* I heard. He talks some more. I open my eyes. One of the men is surprised and then smiles wickedly. He is the one with the same voice. I tell him through clenched teeth in Chinese that he is an asshole and when I get out of here I am going to beat the shit out of him. That does it. He lets loose a string of curses with "Ngo dill kau kui" being the leading epithet. That completes the ID and he is hauled off, very angry that I've spotted him. Back at the consulate the staff verifies that when he is upset his favorite curse words are "Ngo dill kau kui." After some additional work on him and testimony from consulate people, it turns out that he is a Communist agent put in the Consulate to spy. After another week in the hospital, under guard, I am evacuated to the States.

7

BEACHED

It's a very long flight from Hong Kong to Travis Air Force Base outside of Sacramento, California. There is a refueling stop along the way. Needless to say I don't get off and walk around. I can't tell which tropical paradise we land at since there are no windows in this first-class section and I am not invited out nor offered a mai tai. On April 11 I'm back home in America. Travis is the main port of entry for injured or wounded military personnel. From there I'm driven with two others in an ambulance to Letterman hospital in San Francisco.

The hospital is in the middle of San Francisco at the west end of Lombard Street. It was built in 1898 and rebuilt in the 1960s to become the Letterman Army Medical Center and now includes the Letterman Army Institute of Research. If you're lucky you get a bed in the tower with a view of the Bay and Golden Gate Bridge. If not, on the east side you have a view of Lombard and Union Streets populated with small shops and restaurants. On the south and west sides you look into a conifer forest.

The Letterman staff is first class. They've treated just about every wound or injury there is. I present no problems for them. The ENT specialists inspect the work on my nose and jaw. "First-class work," she says. It should heal nicely in about four or five weeks."

The orthopedist and rheumatologist have a different story for me. The condition of my knees concern them. X-rays show the full extent of the damage. They take turns explaining it to me. "The patellas are clearly fractured," the orthopedist states, "but the ligaments that connect the thigh to the shin bones aren't ruptured. There is fluid buildup that I know is painful and will get worse, so we'll put a drain in each leg. The prognosis in Hong Kong is correct. You won't be playing volleyball for several months."

The rheumatologist continues, "Normal healing time is six weeks. That will be followed by physical therapy to help the leg muscles function again after a long rest in a cast. That is just to get you to a walking state. One thing you can count on for sure is that you will have arthritis in both knees the rest of your life."

The sunshine around this cloud is that soon I'm going to meet my son for the first time. Davey is only four months old, but I'm told he already shows the blue eyes and wisps of blonde hair of his dad. One sparklingly beautiful San Francisco morning Fred and Betsy Arbuckle arrive with Lynda and Davey. Lynda comes running into the room and is about to throw her arms around me when she sees my face and the casts on my legs. She lets out a cry, but quickly recovers and gives me a gentle little hug.

"Don't worry sweetheart. I'm bent, but not broken yet."

Lynda holds onto my hand and steps aside for a moment to let Betsy come over to my bed. She gives me a motherly kiss on the cheek and asks, "Michael, does it hurt much?" Her eyes are misty and her breathing a little rapid, but she handles my sight, showing her inner toughness.

"Michael", Lynda says somewhat strained but cheerfully, "We have someone for you to meet. He's been wondering where his daddy is."

Fred is carrying a bundle in a blue playsuit as though it is a couple dozen eggs. He brings it over to me and puts it in my arms. It's my son, my boy. I'm a father at last. This is a thrill that I never forget so long as I'm alive. He's obviously the most beautiful baby in history. Fred is smiling so hard that he is squeezing tears out of his eyes. "Congratulations, Mike, you have a wondrous son." Now it is my turn to tear up.

We talk for a while bringing each other up to date on our respective adventures. I want to hear all about Davey's birth and how Lynda came through it. Lynda leans over and hugs me tenderly, afraid of hurting me. I tell her I'm not in danger and it is just a matter to healing, which will take several months. We lighten up the mood by talking about Davey.

Lynda says, "He didn't want to come out. I was in labor for sixteen hours. Finally, they took him by caesarian. It took me a couple weeks to recover. Now, thanks to mom and Carmen, we are both doing fine. I'm so happy that you finally get a chance to meet your son."

About this time Davey signals that he's in need of a fresh diaper. Lynda and Betsy leave with him to find a place where he can be handled. For the first time Fred brings up Paul. He says Paul has been convicted of conspiracy to commit a crime and assault. He is now serving ten to twelve years at Folsom State Prison in Folsom, California. Perp One received a similar sentence to be served at San Quentin across the Bay from San Francisco. Since Perp Two is a deserter, he's handed over to the army for trial as a deserter and for participating in conspiracy and assault. Subsequently, he's given a dishonorable discharge and sentenced to fifteen years at the U.S. Disciplinary Barracks, Leavenworth, Kansas. Although the name does not sound too severe USDB is a maximum security prison. Actually, he is lucky. Desertion in time of war can be punished by death. Fifteen years in a military prison might be worse than death. The military does not believe in making prison life a pleasant experience.

Fred is incredulous that Paul would be part of such a heinous act. He tells me that Betsy is having a very difficult time with it. She cries herself to sleep many nights. The only hope is that time will lessen the pain.

In four weeks, after they have done everything they can to prepare my knees for therapy, I'm transferred to Letterman's Inpatient Rehabilitation Center. IRC is located in the basement and is referred to as the dungeon. Rehab is like a junior hospital without the smell of people in great pain. Paradoxically, as the initial pain lessens rehabilitation brings up a new level of discomfort. I can't feel sorry for myself when I see some of the terrible injuries to others. Young men stumble about on crutches or in wheel chairs, mostly cheerful through the soreness of rehab exercises. One fellow is wrapped in some strange body braces. He jerks along trying to get his balance and move with some semblance of normalcy. Others are not as lucky. They've lost limbs, have been horribly disfigured and some are even blind. After a couple days of resettling me and monitoring my vitals to ensure that fundamentally all is well, one morning a pretty young physical therapist comes in at 0730 and introduces herself as Sandy Hong. "It is time to get up, lazy bones. We have a lot of work to do with you."

I reply, "No therapy before 0900."

"Our routine starts at 0730. You can't lie in bed all day and expect to walk again."

"I respect your routine, but I can't function well that early in the morning."

After debating our opposing points of view Sandy leaves to return at 0900. She's a real doll. Her attitude and approach is very refreshing. It almost makes me want to get into therapy. The first thing she does is roll me onto my stomach and start massaging my thighs and calves. After I'm warmed up a little she tries to teach me how to get out of bed. This is no small accomplishment with casts on both knees. Besides the pain of moving there is the fear of falling. Sandy assures me that she will not let me lose my balance and crash.

"First you let your legs droop over the side of the bed as you sit up. Then, you grab the handle bars on this walker. Lean forward as far as you can and slowly push up. When you get your chest upright your legs will follow"

"Easier said than done."

"Come on, don't be a sissy." Sandy prods while she and another therapist manhandle me into a wheelchair. There is considerable pain despite the medication. They wheel me into the hallway and head for a therapy room. I'm quite a sight going down the hall with two ramrods leading the way. I look like an old war machine.

The physical therapy regimen is designed to build up the muscles that begin to atrophy as early as two weeks in casts. We start by riding in a wheelchair and learning how to stand up. Over the next few weeks I graduate to moving awkwardly, slowly and very painfully with a walker. Lying in bed most of the day causes me to sleep several hours when they are not taking daily blood samples at 0700 or giving me shots for various purposes. In all, I count forty punctures including IVs and blood samplings during the first three weeks after arriving in Letterman. When they come by to check vital signs or stab me they always ask what my pain level is on a scale of 1 to 10. I learn that any point up to and including a 7 does not earn me pain killers. Accordingly, my pain level increases to 8 or 9.

In six weeks the casts finally come off and it's time to learn how to walk again. The therapy continues now with stretching the leg muscles that have been immobile for over a month. This is no fun as the legs prefer to remain straight. Stretching, resistance, massaging, and hobbling on a walker, crutches, and then canes manage to keep the pain level up. The goal is to walk around the corridors of the rehab center first without a walker, then without crutches, and then with two canes. Each day I am supposed to extend the distance. Walking with or without assistance is still quite painful, but it must be attempted. No matter what, standing compresses everything in the knee joint that was traumatized by the blows to the patellas. By the end of the fourth week I am tottering along with a minimum of discomfort but by no means stable. I shuffle along more than walk. Sliding my feet rather than picking them up helps keep the pain down but doesn't help my rehab. Quick turns result on wobbles, staggers, and occasional falls if the therapist is not close by. It is embarrassing to lie on the floor and not be able to get up unassisted. But, again, I cannot complain because my wounds are nothing compared to people back from Vietnam who will never be able to function like they did when they headed west across the Pacific.

Although the physical therapy will continue for months, we move to what is called occupational therapy. This is self-help practice. It covers my ability to take care of myself at home. I have to demonstrate that I can make a simple meal, wash the dishes, take a shower, go to the bathroom, and dress myself. Up till now, I'd only had sponge baths, so my first shower thanks to OT is one of the greatest feelings ever. The nurse's assistant who helps me shower is a stocky, middle-aged, Mexican lady, Senora Angelica Flores. As I'm rubbing the dead skin off my abdomen and thighs, she says, "Don't forget the balloons." I laugh so hard I have to sit down again. She is a doll and we become good friends.

Most of the staff are very sensitive to my struggle to walk unaided again. They do have a mean streak, though. They deliberately drop things on the floor to see if I can pick them up. There are little therapeutic games we play to test coordination, strength, comprehension, and other motor skills. Tasks I have taken for granted since I was six years old have to be relearned. The last check is to determine if the blows to my jaw and head caused any permanent brain damage. There are tests of comprehension, expression, hand-eye coordination and speech. These I pass with no problems.

My jaw is wired shut for three weeks and meals come through a straw. This makes it hard to ingest enough calories to put back some of the weight I've lost or to build stamina. By the time I'm released I will have dropped about twenty pounds. Four weeks after arriving at Letterman the wires come out of my jaw. The fracture is relatively minor.

For the first few weeks at Letterman hospital and then the rehab center, the Arbuckles visit me regularly. They've moved to their house in Seacliff, which is on the northwest point of San Francisco only a few miles from Letterman. Houses in the Sea Cliff neighborhood are multimillion dollar mansions and come with impressive views of the Pacific Ocean, the Golden Gate Bridge, the Farallon Islands, and/or the Marin Headlands. A small public beach named China Beach is a couple hundred feet below at the water's edge. The fresh smell off the sea is very therapeutic. Eventually, as it becomes clear that I am healing well they return to Monterey. Lynda goes with them so they can help her with Davey.

On June 30, 1969, I read a page one story in the *San Francisco Chronicle* reporting that two navy patrol planes have collided off the coast of San Diego. One was based in Moffett Field just 25 miles south of San Francisco. No survivors. This was an exchange exercise where one plane flew in from Hawaii to be fitted with the latest surveillance gear while the other, which had already been reconfigured, flew out of San Diego to Hawaii. The flight plans assured that there would be plenty of separation. However, a rainstorm off the coast of California combining with the late departure of the San Diego flight apparently obscured the flight paths. It is a terrible shock to lose two planes and crews in a noncombat accident. A couple days later in a follow up piece the names of the pilot and crew are listed. The pilot of the inbound plane is Lt. Raymond Danielski, Grace's husband. Frankly, I feel ashamed that I have mixed emotions. I hate to hear about anyone dying and especially naval personnel being killed in the line of duty. But realizing that Grace was now a widow brought possibilities to my mind that I had not allowed myself for a long time.

* * *

After being in the hospital or rehab for months, in June I'm finally allowed to go home, though I'll still have physical and cardiopulmonary therapy three days a week at the Navy's health facility at the Presidio in Monterey. This means more pain, but I'm happy beyond words to be out of these institutions. It's like getting out of prison—except I have to go back for more outpatient therapy, which makes it more like being on probation.

I call the Arbuckles' house in Monterey home because it's where my little family lives—with or without me. The sights, sounds, and smells are just as I remember them only eighteen months ago: the fragrance of the eucalyptus, fir and redwoods, the sound of the surf and the fog horns, and the chatter of the birds flying through the forest; what a beautiful place. It's wonderful to go to Pebble Beach and to Monterey Peninsula Country Club just to be in the golf environment. All I can do is putt a little until my back and knees give out. The knees can't bear too much weight yet, and bending over puts a lot of strain on my back. My core muscles are very weak from the long layoff and can't support my back.

Cardiopulmonary therapy is designed to rebuild stamina and strength through exercises that include walking and weight lifting. I contact the facility and am assigned a trainer who will guide me through the process. His name is Albrecht Bohrman, called Al for short or, on a bad day, "the Nazi trainer." When I arrive for my first session three sensors are attached to my chest and lead to a monitor attached to my belt. They record my heart rate and blood pressure before, during, and after the exercises. My program is three times a week for fourteen weeks. Ramon, will take me back and forth. We start with an initial blood pressure (BP) and heart rate scoring. Then, there is a five-minute stretching routine that loosens muscles before stressing them. The weights are customized to the patient starting at two and a half pounds and lifting time starting usually at two or three minutes. As I progress the weights and time will increase. Next is the treadmill for five minutes, one mile per hour and one percent grade incline. This will be increased until I can do at least two miles at a three percent grade. The idea is to build muscle and stamina by gradually increasing the variables every other visit. The therapy is tough not only physically but psychologically; I feel embarrassed to be so weak.

At home, I'm both happy to be with my family and in the environment I love so much, but I'm worried as well. It's obvious that Lynda is struggling. Clearly, there are things that are troubling her. I need to find out what they are, if I'm one of them and what we can do to fix it. She's despondent and increasingly withdrawn. The happy girl I met three years ago is missing.

One night we finally have the opportunity to go out to dinner together, something we have not been able to do for months, since I left for Vietnam. She is subdued, and the conversation is stilted.

After dinner we drive down to the ocean and park at a vista point. We get out of the car and walk along the edge looking at and listening to the surf breaking on the rocks below. The air is filled with gulls looking for their dinner. They screech as they race through the air diving through the water or scavenging on the beach. When we first met we would walk holding hands in this place and talk about our ideas, hopes, and plans for the future. It is a far cry from where we are now. We can't seem to connect, and our bond is weakening. I don't understand what is behind it. I ask her what's bothering her.

"Lynda, I'm concerned. The joy we had in the beginning seems to be slipping away. I don't know the reason or reasons for it, but it scares me. I need you to know how important you are to me. When I met you I didn't have a clear goal in mind for myself yet. I was over thirty and just kind of floating like a ship that didn't have a rudder. Somehow, being around you calmed me, comforted me, gave me hope that I would find myself. I miss you. Whenever things are difficult I think about you and it makes me feel better. In the last year with my being gone and you having to have a baby without me to support you must have been very hard on you. It was on me too. I wanted so much to be with you when Davey arrived. I felt it was unfair to all three of us that we couldn't share the moment of his birth. Now that we've moved along some I don't see my smiling girl anymore and I miss her. I need her."

"Michael, those things have made life a struggle for me. To make it even worse I have a baby to care for. I was hardly ready to be a wife and then all of a sudden I'm a mother. I wasn't ready to be a mother. No one taught me about how to deal with this tiny, demanding child. I see Carmen and Josepha handling it so smoothly. I wish someone had prepared me for this. There should be classes on how to be a mother. On the one side I feel like such a failure and on the other I almost resent having to deal with a baby. What married woman doesn't want to have a baby and be a mother? This is a dreadful thought. I'm ashamed of myself for it, but I can't seem to drop it. Some of my girlfriends have babies and it's all they can talk about.

I'm just not as devoted to Davey as my girlfriends are to their babies, and I feel terrible for it."

"Do you think that this is a result of all the upset in the family in the past two years?

"I suppose that has a lot to do with it. But it eats at me every day and every time I see Davey. I should be better. I want to be a better mother, but I just can't seem to do it."

"Sweetheart, don't feel guilty about your feelings. Feelings are true and legitimate no matter how negative they might be. We have to find out why you have them and how to exchange them for positive and pleasant feelings."

"That's easy to say, but not so easy to do. On top of it all that I can't get over Paul's attack on you. Setting you up for a beating that could have killed you still bothers me greatly. I can't put it aside. Whenever there is a spare moment or when I see or hear something I think about that horrible night. He's my brother and he plotted to have my husband beaten and maybe killed. I see all the little things he did to pick at you; the stables, the party. He never gave up. I can't reconcile those things. I've missed you too. I feel like my cornerstone is gone. I'm floundering. I don't seem to be able to move ahead because of that. Dad's talking to me about seeing a counselor to help me cope with it."

"Lynda, since I woke up in the hospital in Hong Kong you've been the light at the end of my tunnel of pain. It scares me to think of why Paul would do this. I agree that it was a horrific experience. For you it has the extra dimension of where it came from. I've had a lot of time to think about us, you, me, and Davey, while I've been in rehab. Why do you think he did it? Was he jealous of me or mad at me for some reason? Did he see me as a disruptive force in your family? I don't get it. Tell me where Jennifer is in all this. Why is your mother so disconsolate?"

"Jen has always been withdrawn and a little crazy. She's a would-be singer. Her artistic side pulled her into another place. She never wanted to take part in family gatherings, I guess because she thought we weren't interested or supportive. If we questioned her choices she always got angry. She has a quick temper, you know. I don't know what she thinks or feels about Paul. She's living in LA and hasn't been involved. When we told her about the beating she just asked if you were going to be okay. When Paul was caught and went to trial we told her and she didn't even reply. She and Paul were never close so I guess she's just ignoring his situation.

As for Mom, I think she sees some of her family traits in Paul's behavior. Her family history is not very healthy. She had an uncle who was a drunk and an abuser. Another uncle committed suicide. An aunt ended up in a psychiatric hospital. When Mom was in high school her mother died of cancer and her father had a debilitating stroke. He spent the last half dozen years of this life in a home for stroke victims. He couldn't function except to mumble. Mom went to work right out of high school. She was a waitress on one of Daddy's ships. That's where they met. Nearly everything on her side of the family is a disaster for one reason or another. I'm wondering if we're cursed."

"Wow, that's quite a story. I can see why you might feel that way. Add to that you've had a rough time with me. First, the beating and then my absence and the Hong Kong kidnapping and beating. I haven't had much chance to be a good husband. But things are looking up. I'm here now and I know I won't be shipped off again for a while."

"I hope you're right. I just feel like such a failure."

"Don't worry, honey. You're no failure. We're together now and it's going to get better. Trust me."

After our talk on the beach I'm not truly comforted. She's identifying with her tragic family history along with trying to reconcile what has happened the past couple years. That would affect anyone. Despite my reassurance of Lynda I wonder just how strong her psyche might be.

The best part of life in Monterey is playing with Davey. I'm with him every minute I can be. He is such a joy. Why do children have to grow up and learn about the real world? They are so much happier in the innocence of their infancy. Davey and I are together every minute that he is awake and I'm not in therapy. It's such a rush to be with my son who is a bubbling bundle of joy. We play simple games like rolling around on the floor together or sitting him in my lap and making believe we are driving something. It doesn't matter what we do. It's just sheer fun. When he finally goes down for a nap I sit by his crib and just look at him. I don't care if I'm a doting father. I've a lot of time to make up. After the last six months I feel entitled. I know that in a few months I will be separated from him again.

* * *

A month or two after coming home to Monterey, when I've become strong enough to handle daily life on my own, I get orders for my next assignment. I'm to report at the Naval Intelligence School in Washington, D.C. This is great news, since Lynda and Davey and I can be together, and we will be moving to a city I love. I'm looking forward to settling back in Alexandria, and I'm certain Lynda will love it as much as I did.

I go to Alexandria ahead of Lynda in order to look for an apartment for us. Shortly after I arrive something happens that throws all our plans into disarray. Lynda's father Fred calls me from Monterey to explain.

Lynda was home in Monterey when her mother Betsy called from a store in Carmel. Betsy says, "Hi. honey. Will you do me a favor?"

"Of course, Mom, what is it?

"Go into my office and look in my desk for the folder on Pittman's Pens. I'm there now and I want to return that pretty gold Monte Grappa pen I bought your father and get another one instead. They will do it, but I don't have the receipt or my account number. Just look in the bottom left drawer for a folder marked Luther. My account material is in there. Just give me the account number."

"Mom, why do you have the Pittman account filed under Luther instead of Pittman?"

"Because that is the salesman's name that I deal with all the time, honey."

"Mom, what if Luther dies or quits the store? How will you ever find the Pittman account?"

"Oh, if that happens they'll tell me the name of the new sales clerk. Just get me the account number please. The drawer is locked but the key is in the center drawer. I don't know why I lock it; no one except Carmen and Josefa ever go in there. I'll wait on the phone."

"Okay, hang on." Lynda ran up the stairs to her mother's office, which is right next to mine. Betsy has a beautiful blonde mahogany desk always with papers covering it. Lynda found the key and opened the drawer. There were a number of file folders marked alphabetically. Thumbing through the "L" folders she finds, Laura, Leona, Linden. Who is Linden? Lynda pulled out a thick file and opened it. It is filled with copies of letters on Betsy's personal stationary, written in Betsy's style. Sticking out of the back she sees a certificate of birth. She scans it and sees her name at the top. How nice she thinks, Mom keeps my birth certificate in her desk. Then, Lynda sees on the line "Mother's Name": Lizabeth Linden. She looks at the date and baby's name again, and it is her birth certificate.

Lynda is shaken. She picks up the phone and asks Betsy who Lizabeth Linden is.

"Oh my god! I can explain everything, darling. I'll be right home."

"Mom!" Lynda yells into the phone, but her mother has already hung up.

As soon as Betsy had hung up the phone, she picked it back up and dialed the number of the Monterey Peninsula Country Club. She told the receptionist, "I need to talk to Fred Arbuckle right away. It's an emergency. Please get him quickly. He's probably in bar at The 19th Hole." After a very long sixty seconds, Fred answered. "Oh Fred, she's found out. Come home right away."

Fred ran directly to his locker without an explanation to his domino partners, grabbed his jacket and keys, and bolted out the door. When he arrived at the house, he found a scene that was even worse than he had anticipated. Lynda is screaming and throwing Betsy's collection of Lladro against the walls. Fred tries to grab his daughter, but she pulls away.

"Daddy, how could you keep this from me all these years? How could you? When were you and Mom going to tell me? Ever? Never?"

"Calm down, Lynda. Let us explain."

"How can you explain something like this? Mom, why all these letters to Beth Linden? Were you sending her money to keep her mouth shut?" Lynda shook the letters in her mother's face. "This is humiliating. For nearly twenty years I've been going to Beth to have my hair done and she knew all along that she was my natural mother. I always wondered why she took such great care of me. Now I know. Everyone knows the terrible secret but me."

Another Lladro hit the wall before Fred could grab his daughter. "Honey, calm down, calm down. We'll tell you the whole story." He guided her to a couch and sat beside her. Betsy paced in front of Lynda, trembling as Fred began to tell the story.

"Twenty-six years ago Beth was a young girl with no money and no family. Betsy met her at the salon where she was doing the odd jobs that are necessary in such a place. She was a dear little girl, always smiling, always cheerful even with the most demanding customers. We fell in love with her. We had her over for dinner a couple times and gave her some money to help with her expenses. In time it was obvious that she was pregnant and without a husband. Beth was going to have the baby and then she didn't know what she would do. We felt very sorry for her, that we should have so much and she should have nothing. Your mother and I thought . . ."

"Don't call her my mother. My mother works in a beauty salon in Pacific Grove."

"Don't say that to your mother. Betsy has loved you and cared for you since you were born. We knew that if we adopted you we could provide for you when Beth couldn't. Also, Jennifer would have a little sister to grow up with and everyone would come out a winner. Betsy knew at the time that she couldn't have another baby. Clearly, we could afford it and Beth would have help when she most needed it."

"But why didn't you tell me? Why did you keep this a secret?"

Betsy speaks up, "Honey, we were very afraid. No one but Beth knows what happened. Jennifer was less than three years old and just happy to have a baby sister. We should have had the courage to tell you, but you were so young and we were too afraid that you would be terribly distraught. We were afraid of what you might do."

Fred moved to put his hand on Lynda's shoulder, but she pulled away. "I'm going to my room and then I'm going out. I have to get out of this place and away from you." Ten minutes later Lynda had dried her tears, picked up her purse, and left the house. She decided to lose herself on Cannery Row and picked the first bar she comes to. Hopping on a bar stool she ordered a drink and gulped it down. In one corner there was a group of young people laughing and having a good time. The music was loud and brassy. Soon one of the girls in the group stood up and came over to Lynda. "Hi, I'm Jessica. It looks like you are all alone and maybe could use a friend. Would you like to join us?'

Lynda considered it for a moment, then nodded and followed Jessica. After introductions one of the men named Ronnie asked, "What are you drinking?"

Lynda replied, "Scotch on the rocks."

"Whoa, this lady knows what she's doing." He orders two drinks for Lynda saying, "This saves time and the waitress's legs." The night is full of laughter, drinks, and snacks. Someone suggested they go find a restaurant while they're still able to walk. Everyone roars and agrees. Once in the cool damp air with clouds covering the moon and a light breeze blowing in from Monterey Bay, Lynda felt refreshed and ready for more fun with the group. She especially liked the look of Ronnie. The group wove their way down the street laughing and talking loudly. They picked a seafood place and tumbled in. A couple hours later the party started to break up. Lynda couldn't stand the thought of going home and she couldn't remember where she parked her car. She accepted Ronnie's invitation to go somewhere for a night cap and then look for her car. Not finding a bar still open Ronnie suggested they stop at his place, which is just a couple blocks off The Row. He says, "I'll put on a pot of coffee and maybe you will be sober enough to remember where you parked your car." They laughed over the silly scene and drove over to Ronnie's. His apartment had a view of the Bay and they settled in waiting for the coffee to brew.

In the morning Lynda woke up in a strange bed. Her head ached and she felt like she would throw up. From somewhere she smells coffee and heads toward it. "Hi, sunshine. Sleep okay?"

"Not really. Where am I?"

"In Ronnie's Rancho. You were superior last night. Did you have fun?"

"I don't remember, but I have to go. Where are my clothes?"

"I picked them up and folded them on the couch, in there. Would you like a little breakfast before we go find your car?"

Thirty minutes later Lynda in her car and headed for 17-Mile Drive. When she turns into her familiar driveway she sees a police car, the local security patrol, and her father talking very animatedly. She pulls up and her father rushes over to the driver's side. He pulls open the door and asks frantically, "Are you okay? Where have you been? We've had half of Monterey County looking for you. Your mother is going crazy. I had to have Dr. Busch come over. He gave her a strong sedative. Carmen and I put her to bed."

"Sorry, daddy. I just had to get away." Trembling from head to toe she blurts out, "I still can't believe that you didn't tell me one of the most important things of my life, who I am. What were you thinking I would do, kill myself, leave you and mom, what?"

The policeman and guard move discreetly to their vehicles and drive off while Fred walks her into the house.

In time, the shock wears off and discussions replace shouting. She begins to come to terms with this new knowledge, but her relationship with her parents remains strained. Lynda is so upset that she makes excuses about coming to Alexandria with Davey. In the end she never moves to Alexandria.

8

THE STORM

In February 1970 I report to Naval Intelligence School.
"Welcome aboard, Lieutenant Commander Still. Your promotion came through late last week. We assumed you were on your way so we saved it for today. We're happy to have you at NIS." The speaker is Captain James Barton, the commanding officer of the school.

"Thank you, sir. The last year has been rather hectic. I'd forgotten about the promotion board meeting."

"Have you settled in yet? How are your legs?"

"The legs are coming along. Thank you. Just need to use a cane for stability and confidence. It keeps people from running me over. So long as you don't make me go out for volleyball, I'll be alright. It will not affect my performance. As for being settled, just temporarily, sir. My wife and son will follow as soon as I find a suitable place."

"Commander Still, I have a copy of your orders here from ONI [Office of Naval Intelligence] and I'm a bit confused by them. It says you're to update the Asia Pacific curriculum. I wasn't aware that it needed updating, are you?"

"No sir, I've not seen the curriculum or any of the study materials. My job is to be confined to Asia Pacific curriculum exclusively."

"Then, how do you expect to update something you haven't seen?"

"Sir, I expect that the current material will be available for review."

"Well, I don't know what ONI has in mind or who gave them the idea this program needed updating. In the two years I've had this command no one has suggested that it was deficient in any regard."

"If the captain will give me access to the materials and instructor, I'll do my best to turn out a product of which you can be proud."

"Very well, report to the XO, Commander Height, and he'll give you access to whatever you need. But I don't think you will find much room for improvement. Also, you should talk with Mr. Feng before you start any changes. He's been a lecturer and advisor to the school on Far East matters for nearly twenty years. There's one more thing. We have a tradition here where we contribute a few dollars each month to the Navy Kids Foundation. The money goes to a variety of needs that children of naval personnel have. It's voluntary so you can make up your own mind. The amount is not great, typically about $10–15 a month."

"Thank you, sir. You can count on me for that. And I'll be certain to check with Mr. Feng."

What a way to start. I'm in trouble with him if I recommend anything new and in trouble with ONI if I don't.

NIS puts officers through a five-month basic course of instruction wherein they receive training in electronic, antisubmarine, surface, and air warfare; counterintelligence; strategic intelligence; air defense analysis; and combat mission planning. From there intel officers are assigned to an aviation squadron, air wing, aircraft carrier, amphibious command ship, or an admiral's staff. That is how I ended up on the Ranger off Vietnam. The lucky ones draw embassy duty.

The executive officer is Commander Gregory Height. I knock on his door unannounced because I'm certain that Barton has let him know I'm coming and to resist any wild schemes I might have for change. He calls me in and congratulates me on my recent promotion. "Have a seat and take a load off your knees. That must have been a very painful experience. Will you need any special accommodations as you continue to recuperate?" This fellow is the opposite of Barton.

He's genuinely sympathetic and an advocate for upgrades. I wouldn't be surprised if he went through back channels to recommend changes.

"I've reviewed your folder. Your recent adventure made very interesting reading. Maybe if we just cut you loose we won't have to worry about China." He says it with a wide grin and watches for my reaction. I wonder if he's testing me and he certainly is. Everything in the military services is a test. It goes back to the fundamental truth that I learned the hard way long ago: it's not only what you know but who you know that counts. I'll have to be careful with this one. He says he'll show me around. Rather unusual, I'm thinking. It could be there are some issues with Barton and no one wants to take them head on. Hell, it could be anything.

Height shows me the classrooms, offices, and study areas. He gives me information in a way that makes it clear he's trying to determine who, why, and what I am doing here. He winds up the tour with a note about Mr. Feng. "You'll need to watch out for Mr. Feng. He's a personal friend of the skipper and as such will pass on anything that you indicate to him you are planning on doing. Feng was with Chiang in China and came over here after the Nationalists lost the war to the Communists in 1949. His information may be accurate but it is pretty old, I think. You'll have a chance to sit in his lecture in a few days. Then, you can make up your own mind. A word to the wise; move cautiously. There are mines in these waters." That is undoubtedly the truth. The unknown is, who is laying them?

I go to the office labeled Instructional Materials. It's not a big place, but there is evidence of modern learning technology with various audiovisual reproduction equipment and projectors. Inside I meet a middle-aged, smiling, chubby civilian who says his name is Eddie Swanson. He directs this unit. He's very friendly and I don't feel any hidden agendas here. Eddie has a master's degree in instructional technology and obviously several years of experience. He's been at NIS almost ten years, he says, and has two civilian assistants named Barbara and Ruth who have some training experience from industry as well as a young navy NCO, Maria, who is learning the trade.

Eddie describes the two types of intelligence officers that NIS turns out. One is the URL (unrestricted line officer) who's eligible to command air or sea units and other offices in any designator. For them, the training is to enhance their performance as a warfighter. They may engage in clandestine operations as needed. On the other side are the intelligence specialists who support the warfighters. These are designated as RLs (restricted line officers). They can only hold command billets within their area of specialization and cannot command a deep draft vessel or aircraft unit. RLs are given intense specialized training to help them understand social dynamics, tribal politics, cultural mores, philosophies, and religious influences. Eddie classifies the former as spooks and the latter as librarians, although I doubt that the RLs would care for that label.

"Eddie, I'd like to prep myself with the curriculum, class schedules, and the materials currently in use for the Asia Pacific region. I presume these are available somewhere."

"Right you are, Commander. I'll assemble a package and have it on your desk in the morning. I don't know how experienced you are with learning technology. If you have any questions about theories, practices, and materials, please feel free to call on me. That is what the Navy pays me this exorbitant salary to do."

He's a funny fellow, very relaxed and down to earth. I thank him and go to my office. It's nothing special. Just the typical gray steel desk and chair, a typewriter, writing materials, a book shelf, and the ubiquitous unit-monogrammed coffee cup. Of course it has the standard green walls. The fellow who sells green paint must be a great salesman. He's covered the Navy with it. There is a small library in one corner containing unclassified periodicals and miscellaneous publications that should be of interest to intelligence personnel. There's also a two-feet-by-three-feet-by-four feet safe in which to keep classified materials. Finally, in the passageway there is a small galley where one can find a drink and a refrigerator.

In the morning Commander Height calls a brief meeting to introduce me to the staff and each person's responsibilities. Afterward,

Eddie introduces me to his staff and shows me the equipment that they use to organize and produce class material. I spend the day studying the materials and make a list of questions for Eddie.

The next morning I hear a knock on my open door and look up to see a small, elderly, Asian man. He says, "My name is Feng. I teach the Asia Pacific region."

"Mr. Feng, please come in. I've heard good things about you. I'm very happy to meet you. Have a seat." I motion him to one of the two chairs in front of my desk and I take the other facing him. "I understand you've been teaching here for some number of years."

"Yes, almost twenty years."

"There must have seen many changes during that time. What do you think have been the major ones?"

"Technology is the most noticeable. We receive more information, faster than before. The media provide additional information, although it is very general and politically driven. Technology has given us the ability to easily make draft copies of what we need and give them to Mr. Swanson for professional preparation."

"Yes, but what about the region? Surely with the changes in the mainland PRC there must be much to discuss."

"Yes, with the death of Lin Biao in a plane crash the threat of revolt against Mao has stopped. But the failure of the Great Leap Forward and the confusion of the Cultural Revolution have spawned much distress. In my opinion, China has become more militaristic with the development of its H-bomb, commissioning of nuclear submarines and launching of the first satellite."

Feng added, "Washington is softening its line regarding China. This is very good because China and America must reach some agreement or we could see another war. If we are to get along, the Americans must realize that they are more direct than the Chinese. Chinese people will take longer than Americans think to substantially improve Sino-American relations."

"I can see that you are very up to date on the China situation. Do you talk about it in your class?"

"Not as much as I would like. I have been advised to focus on intelligence techniques on both sides, which I believe are not the important issues."

"Who has given you that directive?"

"Captain Barton."

"This has been a most enlightening discussion. I'm very pleased to meet you and I look forward to working with you. With your permission I'll sit in on your class tomorrow. Thank you for coming to visit me."

After Feng leaves, my opinion of him changes radically. I think he has a lot of true information about intelligence to offer and for some reason Barton is not supporting that. I pay Eddie a visit and ask him to have lunch with me. He readily agrees and I suggest we do it inside. I don't want anyone thinking that we're plotting a coup. He laughs and says he can order in. That, he thinks, will not look threatening because we have to work together on any new materials. "If there are going to be any." He chuckles and watches my reaction.

I must be getting paranoid. Where is this guy coming from? Is he a pawn of Barton or Height? Or maybe he's the type of intellectual who makes chronic jokes about management. Anyway it works here; I'll have to proceed cautiously. I'm not even certain what ONI wants. I had a very short briefing on my mission here. I don't want to be a sacrificial lamb that will be swept aside if there are major changes. Then, too, there could be other people here to observe and report.

At lunch the next day in my office, I ask Eddie, "Please describe the organization and the school activity as you see it. As a civilian you probably have a different perspective. You can speak freely. Not being a naval officer you don't have to worry about your career."

Eddie volunteers his opinion: "Many of the instructors are smart and committed to their career, this assignment and how this assignment will affect those careers. I'm certain that is something that you need to be aware of also."

He's spot on. Sometimes people at my level—and even commanders—find this is their last job and they are encouraged to retire before reaching the normal retirement point. When it comes to curriculum organization and class delivery, Eddie sees a clear strategy carried out through a wide variety of skills and knowledge. No one here is a professional trainer, although all URLs have training as an important part of their command responsibility. Military personnel are either shooting at someone or training to improve their aim when the time comes.

In the afternoon I sit in on Mr. Feng's class. It's pretty much as he said. He talks about the fall of the Nationalists more from a military than a political standpoint. Then he describes how the Americans, British, and even Soviets are practicing spy operations around and inside China. The Chinese recognize what is happening and try to keep it in check. Intelligence gathering is an ancient and never-ending game played between nations. Until just a few years ago many Americans thought that the U.S. was above such chicanery. Naively, they believed that there must be some Marquis of Queensbury rules somewhere that would preclude such activity. But intelligence, or spying as it's rightfully called, goes back at least as far as pre-Christian times. Alexander the Great succeeded in part by his ability to know his enemy's strengths and weaknesses before a battle. Genghis Khan employed a large number of men on fast horses whose job was to rapidly spread intelligence throughout his armies. Spying is not going away, only becoming more sophisticated. Everyone must know that the CIA is a spy organization. What many don't know is that the people who work in embassies and consulates are really spies, not agricultural, economics, military or political delegates. Everyone on both sides is aware of this arrangement. I have to ask myself, am I supposed to be ONI's spy or do I have a legitimate analytic job to do?

I spend a good part of my time sitting in on classes, followed by many informal discussions with the instructors. I try to convince everyone that I'm here solely to look at curriculum, not individuals. Still, some are concerned that I'm a spy and are very guarded, just reiterating the party line. I feel like they're quoting the NIS brochure to me. Others are more forthright and share with me their honest views of the strengths and weaknesses of the program. Eddie Swanson is outspoken. As a civilian he does not fear the consequences that can some to a member of the armed forces. Swanson has definite opinions on the shortcomings of the curriculum. Seeing how materials are put together, he claims, "Much of the material is almost adolescent in its level. The students are being shortchanged. They could get much more out of the program if the maturity level was increased."

I also build a relationship with Feng. I don't believe he is Barton's spy. On the contrary, based on not-too-subtle comments, I get the notion he really doesn't like Barton. But I have to be careful. He might just be trying to befriend me to learn what I think of Barton and then go back to tell him.

By the fourth month of this five-month program I have a pretty clear view of the nature of the NIS experience, not only in the Asia section but across the school. No matter what I think about the program overall, I must confine my report to the Asian topics. Nevertheless, I believe I can write the report in such a way that an astute reader can see between the lines if they want to. Many times in business, government, and the military, studies like mine are commissioned with no intent of making changes. I don't want my study to end like that.

Naval intelligence officers are responsible for handling classified documents and converting data into critical intelligence information. They collect classified data from military and spy reports and satellite images and also work in coding and decoding. They may also participate in special operations as needed. During their training, most of what they learn is tactical or technical— the mechanics of computer programming, air traffic control, antisubmarine warfare, anti-air, and electronics. But I believe strongly that there needs to be a strategic background to the material. For instance, Mr. Feng knows a great deal about the personalities and thought processes of China's leaders. But he's delivering his material without describing the antecedents and motivation behind their behavior. It's like a college professor whose only contact with his subject comes from books. Being Chinese Feng understands the philosophy, religion, and economic bases for leadership behavior. He should be sharing this with us. It's what would allow the intel officers to make sense of the data they collect. My job is to convince the NIS of this.

By the end of the summer the class is graduating and I have to prepare my report. I'm very aware that Captain Barton won't like it. He made his position very clear at our first meeting. He seldom talks to me and when he does he's very guarded. His questions are phrased in a strange, almost sinister manner. As examples, one time Barton asked me offhandedly, "How are things going?" His words were casual but his body language was aggressive and indicated that he wanted a thorough response. Other times his question will be stated with a negative undertone such as, "Have you found any problems yet, Mr. Still?"

Barton isn't about to accept an overhaul of the curriculum. No matter how much I soft peddle it, the report is going to recommend that more time and thought should be given to the strategic side. My concern is that he will do damage to my career directly or indirectly. Even if he writes a neutral report on me, by the time I am up for promotion to commander and especially captain, if I last that long, the report will be in my file and I will not be competitive before the promotion board.

Nevertheless, I have to turn in an honest report to ONI. Naturally, I send Barton a copy and request a date and time to discuss it. I expect that there will be an immediate explosion or a long wait while he formulates his reply. Either way my career is on the line.

In the meantime I receive a call from the assistant to my commanding officer at ONI asking how I am coming with my report. I tell him it's ready and will be sent to Captain Barton that afternoon. He asks about the general tone and sample recommendations. I give him the condensed version. After a pause he says, "Send me a copy of your original report, before Barton has a chance to change it. Tell him I called you on behalf of ONI and ordered you to send it. ONI assigned you this duty, so of course you report to ONI." The "of course" has a clear meaning; Don't forget who you're serving.

"Yes, sir. I'll have it sent by courier tonight." Now, I really am a spy. Frankly, I don't like what amounts to criticizing my CO. The only way I can justify it is that ONI is actually my commanding officer, as he reminded me.

Two days later I get a call to Barton's office. It's D-Day. This is going to be ugly. I hope I survive it. I knock on his door at 1100 and he calls me in. I see immediately that this is not going to be pleasant.

He doesn't ask me to sit down, so I stand more or less at attention. "This is quite a report, Mr. Still." He looks up expecting a reply but I just say, "These are my conclusions, sir."

"I see this as very nearly insubordination, Mr. Still."

I start to reply but he cuts me off. "What made you put together such a report?"

Once more I try to speak and he cuts me off.

"What the hell am I supposed to do with this? Turn the place upside down to respond to your obviously biased and erroneous conclusions? —No, not conclusions, I'd call them accusations. What do you think ONI is going to do to my command when they see this? Have they seen it?"

"Sir, I received an order the night before last to send it to them."

If he was mad before, now he's apoplectic. He's so angry he can't even speak. He jumps up from his desk, grabs the report, comes around to my side, puts his face six inches from mine, and, spitting mad, says menacingly, "Just as I thought. You are a fucking spy. How does it feel to crucify your commanding officer, Mr. Still? Are you getting pleasure out of this? Do you realize that this will terminate an exemplary twenty-six year career?

There is nothing I can say.

"You stay right here. I'm not done with you, Still."

With that he leaves the room with me standing in front of his desk. I wait fifteen minutes, then thirty minutes, still standing in front of his empty desk. What I didn't know was that when he went storming out of the office, he grabbed his hat, obviously intending to leave the building. I'm left standing there wondering what to do if he doesn't come back in a reasonable amount of time. What are my choices? Where does the Navy stand on standing in place for hours? If I leave for the head, will that be considered mutiny? I don't think so because I'm not trying to take over his command. I remember that Article 93, I think it is, of the Uniform Code of Military Justice forbids cruelty or maltreatment. Is it cruel if an officer ends up soiling his uniform? Is it cruel to make me stand an unreasonably long time, given my injured knees? My mind flashes back to an incident at FAD where the CO brought in the ops officer and gave him a royal chewing out for some alleged omission. Then, in his final report he recommended the officer be sent to the aviation parking lot of old planes in Arizona, which effectively ended his career. At that time the man was a lieutenant commander just like me. Finally, I decide to leave the room and go to my office to await the outcome. While I am there I write up the incident in detail for my protection.

Meanwhile Barton decides to go to ONI and refute the report. The man's anger and fear makes him lose perspective. He barges into the anteroom of Captain McKay, the deputy director of ONI without an appointment. When he is brought inside I understand he begins a rant, accusing me of everything from insubordination to spying and malfeasance. He sputters about the report, claiming section by section that it is deliberately inaccurate. After being surprisingly patient in listening to the tirade the director tells him he will send his aide, Captain Henry Samson, back to NIS to investigate the matter.

Barton suddenly realizes he's made a strategic mistake. He has no evidence to contradict the report and, worse, he's invited an investigation into his office. This is the worst possible outcome for him. Not only will his career be over because of his wild and false accusations but the investigator will likely discover his most closely guarded secret: that the Navy Kids operation is a scam. At all costs he must keep Samson out of his desk until he can come up with an explanation of its legitimacy or remove the Navy Kids file from his desk.

Upon arriving at NIS Samson says to Barton, "Jim, why don't you go home, have a stiff drink and relax. You know how these things work."

"Okay Henry. But first I'd like to take ten minutes to get my desk ship shape. I left in a hurry and it's not in its usual orderly condition."

"Jim, don't worry about it. I understand. You just go home and relax. Come in tomorrow and we'll talk this over. I'll need the keys to your desk."

Barton has no choice but to leave quietly so as not to look like he is covering up for something. In the meanwhile Samson will talk to me and others involved in the report. Being an experienced senior officer as well as a smart man, Samson senses that there is more to this than just a conflict between Barton and a subordinate officer. This is Barton's worst fear. He knows that Samson will find the Navy Kids file. Yet he may still have a chance. He has filed a 501(c)(3) claiming Navy Kids to be a not-for-profit corporation. That means he has to file a tax return each year showing the officers of the corporation and all revenue and expenses. He made himself the director. His aged and senile father-in-law, whose name is different than Barton's, is unknowingly listed as the secretary and treasurer. This small corporation, he hoped, would not attract attention of the IRS.

When Barton returns to the office the next morning, Captain Samson is there and has been interviewing me, Swanson, and Feng. Mr. Feng has not only agreed with my conclusions but alerted Samson to Barton's extraction of "voluntary" contributions to Navy Kids. When Barton arrives, the Navy Kids file is on the desk in front of Samson. Barton tries to explain that it's a non-profit for children of navy personnel who need financial assistance. He is hoping that Samson will accept that and not dig deeper, but Samson isn't buying it. "Jim, that is a good thing you're doing. You're to be commended for your sensitivity and willingness to help others who need help. Tell me where the money comes from."

"It comes from various sources such as my church, a social club I belong to, and miscellaneous donations from friends and voluntary contributions from some of the NIS staff."

"Can you give me some examples of where the money is being spent?"

"Certainly, Henry. Here is my log of cash disbursements. I have to keep this for tax purposes."

Samson pauses and prepares to return to the report. That's when Barton sees his opening. "Henry, perhaps I've been too hasty in my response to Still's report. I guess I'm getting old and stuck in my ways. I've been thinking of retiring anyway. Under the circumstances, for the good of the Navy, I'd like to turn in my commission and retire six months early."

"Jim, if that is what you want to do, I'm certain it can be arranged." With that Samson leaves for the day and reports to the deputy director what he's found.

When Samson returns to deputy director McKay, they put their heads together. They agree that Barton's reaction to the report was excessive and irrational. They can't understand why a man in this last command before retirement would make such a fuss. He was going to retire in six months with the typical commendations, gratitude, and parties. Samson says, "Sir, there must be something else that led Barton to go off. I recommend that, just to be certain everything is legitimate, the foundation be checked."

A short time after that JAG (Judge Advocate General) staff investigates the foundation and the fraud is uncovered. Upon questioning Barton admits that he used the funds for gambling. Barton is quickly and quietly court-martialed, dishonorably discharged, forfeiting his retirement pay and benefits, and remanded to the naval prison near Portsmouth, Maine.

* * *

In the end my report is presented, read, and accepted and I receive orders to return to ONI headquarters. I learn that I am being assigned as acting curriculum director at NIS to oversee the program upgrading along the lines of my earlier report. ONI will reassign Commander Height as well and bring in a new CO and XO.

Two weeks later when I return to NIS, I report to Commander Height. The first thing I have to do is talk with all the instructors. I request that Commander Height call a meeting to tell everyone what's happening. The staff knows that Captain Barton has left, but they don't know the full story behind it. The place is filled with rumors. Height describes in the softest terms possible what has happened. Then we proceed. I know that no one is listening because they are all trying to digest what they just heard. Nevertheless, being professionals they snap back to the issue at hand.

I prepare an unclassified synopsis of the report for everyone to read. It focuses on school matters, not on Barton. At the meeting there are many questions. The ones that come up about Barton Commander Height handles. Then I attempt to explain how the Asia curriculum will be changed with an emphasis on strategic issues. The staff seems excited about the changes. I suggest that the instructors think ahead to how the strategic orientation might be introduced into their work. These are smart people. They can read between the lines and know that they need to react quickly and decisively to rework their materials. Ed Swanson is more than happy to help them. They can do this freely knowing this is what ONI really wants.

Over the next few months Mr. Feng and I work on the Asia section with Eddie's AV support. Feng is delighted to delve into the cultural issues that affect Chinese strategy and U.S. responses. Swanson is also happy because he gets to design materials of greater interest and, we all expect, greater impact. In the meantime Commander Height leaves for his next duty station and is thankfully not tarred with Barton's brush. Being a URL officer rather than a career intel officer, he is made executive officer of a newly commissioned destroyer out of Newport. A new commanding officer and executive officer arrive at NIS. They have been briefed on the Barton incident and told to support the reorganization of NIS. They do and the work goes well. By the end of our six-month assignment we have not only totally revamped the Asia section but have helped some of the instructors start redesigning their sections for the next class in the Fall.

I'm happy to have weathered that storm—and ready to cope with whatever the next one has to bring.

9

RIP TIDE

The temporary assignment at NIS ends in December 1970. I'm expecting to be assigned somewhere in WestPac. I'm wrong. Instead, I receive orders to report to the newly forming office for Defense Investigative Services, formerly an NIS function. On my arrival the XO, Commander Robinson, calls me to his office.

He's a Type A personality who doesn't waste time on pleasantries. Immediately upon my entry he asks, "Commander Still, how are your legs? Have you fully recovered from your problem in Hong Kong?"

"Yes, sir. I still have some discomfort at times, but nothing that stands in the way of performing my duties."

"Good. You've shown a marked aptitude for investigation both on the Forrestal and lately at NIS. We've been given a new form of intelligence, criminal investigation, formerly part of NIS. You'll be one of the early agents. The program will be different from the standard NIS curriculum that you completed in '66. This focuses on criminal activity. The course will cover criminal acts, criminal intelligence, forensic sciences, information systems, and computer crimes. There will be both naval officers and civilians in the class. This training will enhance what appear to be your inherent investigative talents. Report to Commander Richard Coon in Room 139 for your materials and schedule. You and your classmates will help us develop this into a very valuable ongoing service. Good luck. Dismissed"

I'm surprised and intrigued by this development. I've heard of the Defense Investigative Services, but didn't know much about it. It may be an interesting opportunity to learn more about solving complex situations. When I join my fellow trainees the next morning I find a different set of characters than I've been used to in the Navy. There are a number of people with law enforcement backgrounds; policemen, lawyers, accountants, military police, and state troopers—they're a tough bunch. It's apparent that this is a very serious program, but I'm puzzled at its function. Is it a duplicate FBI or CIA operation? And I'm wondering about my place in it. What does this mean to my naval career?

Over the next months we're put through an intense course in criminology. The law enforcement veterans plow straight ahead. For me, it's a struggle. At NIS I learned about interrogation and information technology, but forensic science is an entirely new world. A great deal of time is directed toward criminal investigation procedures—building a case through interviewing, developing sources, working undercover, and counterintelligence. By the end of the program my mind is a whirl. I get the material, but I'll have to learn how to apply it in the field. Hopefully, when I get my first assignment, there'll be experienced people to help me get acclimated.

No such luck. Right out of the box I'm ordered to report to ONI on July 15 for special assignment. When I arrive I'm ushered into the office of the deputy director, Captain McKay again. This is unusual. I smell a skunk in the woodpile.

We immediately engage in what I call a listen-and-nod exercise: He talks; I listen and nod. "Commander Still, there is a major problem in San Diego that you will solve. Someone at NAS North Island (NASNI) is going around shooting at people. He, presumably a man, is not trying to kill anyone. He just wants to wound them. To date, he has taken his shots about twice a month. This is now in its third month. Your job is to find him and bring him in."

This is strange to me on so many different levels. I've never heard of a serial shooter just trying to wound people. And I don't know why they picked me for this serious assignment. I'm a naval intelligence officer, but my investigative experience is limited. All the smart boys must be on assignments elsewhere. It could be that they expect the FBI or CIA will solve the case and I'm just there to get forensic experience.

The boss continues. "You're going in undercover as a public relations man. The cover story is that the chief of staff is angry over the way military personnel are being treated because of their service in Vietnam. He wants to put out a favorable story about the Navy and its personnel. Your apparent job is to tour the base looking for positive stories. You'll have an assistant, a lieutenant (jg) who is an expert photographer. She'll meet you at the BOQ in San Diego. After you introduce yourselves to Captain McMurray the CO of NASNI you're on your own. Your orders are waiting for you on my assistant's desk outside. You're to report no later than 20 August 1971. If there are no questions, you'd better get started."

San Diego is a gorgeous place. It offers ideal weather, a casual yet cosmopolitan atmosphere, and access to Mexico just thirty minutes south. NAS North Island, where I'll be conducting the investigation, is the largest naval air base on the West Coast. The total on base population is over 20,000 military and civilian personnel. Although I'm anxious about tackling such an important job, it's exciting to be working at North Island. The evening of my arrival I put in a call to my partner, Lt. (jg) Jeanette Hendry, who is also staying in the BOQ. We agree to meet in the dining area for breakfast at 0800. After a six-hour flight my knees are stiff, so I wobble a bit as I maneuver across the dining room the next morning. I hope no one thinks I'm hung over. There are a small number of people still having breakfast and I look around for female officers. I finally spot her, and she stands up and greets me with, "Good morning sir, I'm Lt. (jg) Jeanette Hendry. Everyone calls me Jenny." She's about five foot seven with an athletic presence. I slowly ease myself into the chair across from her, and we start to get acquainted. "Did you arrive yesterday?" I ask.

"No, I came in two days ago. I finished my last assignment and had nowhere to go, so I decided to come here and relax in the sun. I was communications officer at NAS Whidbey Island for the last year. It's a bit damp there, so I'm drying out."

"Is it as wet as Seattle?"

"A bit more. They're just coming into the major rainy season, which will last about four or five months. The weather isn't so bad, but there isn't much entertainment there for a single person."

"I just arrived from D.C. last night. There's plenty to do there and a large single population."

"I see from your left hand, sir, that you're married. Is your wife here with you?" This gal moves quickly and in this case a bit indiscreetly at such an early stage. I'll have to watch that she doesn't talk too much during the course of our investigation.

"No, my wife is in Monterey. She's not well, so she and my son won't be joining me here."

"I'm sorry to hear that. From what I gather about this assignment there probably won't be much time for family life anyway."

"You could be right. What have you been told about what's going on here?"

Jenny reiterates the story, almost word for word, that I was given.

"It looks like after we report to the base commander we're pretty much on our own, that is unless he wants to muck about in the case."

"Have you handled cases like this before? I certainly have not. I'm here supposedly as a photographer. I went through AIO School in D.C., as I understand you did as well, but this is new territory. I've heard about your exploits in Vietnam and Hong Kong. I think they gave me this job because they believe a woman is not as threatening and won't arouse suspicion if she goes around poking her nose into other people's business."

I note that she researched my background for this assignment. That's a good trait; be prepared. But I'm thinking, Michael, she's aggressive. Better watch that and focus it since she doesn't have any investigative experience. "I've been involved in intel work of various types and have taken criminal investigative training, but this is a new angle for me. We'll have to start by familiarizing ourselves with the base and its operations. I'll be very surprised if the FBI and maybe CIA are not already here stirring up the pot. Do you have experience as a photographer?"

"Yes, sir. I'm an amateur, but I've been at it since high school. I've won a few local and regional photo awards. Where do we start, sir?"

"We start with an appointment to talk to the base commander. Undoubtedly, he knows we're coming. I'd like to know what ONI told him about our purpose. I'll call his office this morning and we'll go from there. If you stay in your room, I'll call and let you know the answer."

"Aye aye, sir.", she says respectfully but with a smile.

I like this officer. Although this is a new world for her, she moves like she knows where she's going. She seems fearless—which she'll need to be before this thing is finished. I go back to my room, call the CO's office, and request a meeting at his convenience. An hour later I take a call back and am told to meet Captain McMurray at 1300. I let Jenny know to meet me in the BOQ lobby at 1230.

Promptly at 1245 we walk into the Captain's anteroom and give our names to the receptionist. In a command as big as this the CO has a number of sections under him and several persons in his immediate office staff. Exactly at 1300 we're escorted into the boss's office and stand at attention five feet from his desk.

He sizes us up for a moment, then says, "At ease." We assume the parade rest position. "I've been informed that you two are here to work undercover on the shooting case we have. I presume you've looked at the file."

"No, sir. Neither of us has been privileged to see the file as yet. We've sealed orders and a packet of documents with orders not to open them until we see you."

He looks amazed, pauses, and says, "I hope you're a quick study. I'm tired of having interlopers from the FBI and CIA poking around here. The rumor mill is operating at flank speed and people are very nervous. The worst fear is fear of the unknown, and that's where we are. We haven't a clue as to who this idiot is, what he's planning or why. So far the shootings have been confined to North Island. Hopefully, they won't spread southward. I've arranged an office for you on Level One. I suggest you get down there immediately and respond according to your orders. I want to know everything you find and know it before anyone else does. Do you understand? This shooter is already making my security people look bad. They've been instructed to let you have the run of the base provided you don't get in the way of operations. They believe that you are here to write some positive stories about the base. My security chief, Steve Prince, knows the real story, but he won't share it with anyone. We'll keep it at that. If you have problems with anyone, let me know. Report to me once a week with a one-page confidential memo until you find out who is doing this. I expect that won't take too long. Dismissed."

With that we're given maps by the receptionist to find our office and a packet to learn about the base. Once we settle in our office, we open our orders. The case is this: Three months ago someone shot a petty officer in the leg. No one could tell where the shot came from, but the slug was from a .22 caliber target pistol. This is the first clue. He's using a target pistol because of its accuracy of up to 150 yards or more. Neither base security nor the local police have been able to come up with a motive or any clues beyond the bullet. Given that it was fired from a training pistol, the shooter was either fairly close to the victim or an excellent marksman. With planes taking off and landing all the time the jet noise could muffle the sound of a small caliber weapon. Since then, there have been two more attacks. The most recent was three weeks ago. Given the pattern, that suggests that we may have another incident shortly.

Our first stop is with the head of security, Lt. Cdr. Steven Prince. Prince is what you would expect from a professional security type: large, friendly, but brusque and to the point. The shooter is making big problems for him. If the fellow isn't caught very soon, he will look very bad.

Prince starts giving us his thoughts. "I believe that it's an outsider. We have many people coming and going through here. Someone with a grudge against the military could get a kick out of playing this game with us. The strange thing is that he shoots people only in the leg, nowhere else."

"The incidents always take place during the workday. How could anyone fire a weapon in midday without someone hearing it? Also, it's windy here so he can't get too far from his victim and still be accurate."

"He could have a suppressor on it that would muffle the sound and cover most of the muzzle flash. Distance is a good question. He'd have to be firing from a stable platform to be as accurate as he's been."

"I think your suspicion of an outsider gives us someplace to start. Are there people other than employees who come and go on a regular basis?"

"Sure, vendors. We have suppliers going to the commissary with everything from skate boards to food. There are maintenance crews from the utility and telephone companies. There are delivery people like FedEx and UPS. The list is pretty long."

"Do you check them through the gate?"

"Of course. We usually know they're coming and we log them in and out."

"You don't log the drivers, do you?"

"No, just the company. The company would know who the driver was on a given delivery day if we need to know that."

"This seems like a good place to start. If your office can get the company driver records on the days of the shooting, it might provide some leads. Some vendors probably come only on specific days and go to specific sites. Others, like FedEx or UPS, make several stops at the base mail center, HQ and other points. Once we have the list of potential suspects the vendors must let us know when those individuals will be coming in again. This will make stake outs more efficient and hopefully more productive. I know it's a big haystack, but we have to find the needle and do it quickly."

"Consider it done. We'll push the vendors to cooperate and do it quickly and discreetly."

Jenny and I go back to our office to develop a plan. We agree that obtaining driver records on the day of the shootings might give us a manageable list of suspects to start with. Then, we can go to the places where those identified drivers make stops—for instance the commissary—and stake them out while doing our cover story interviews. Due to the urgency of solving this case, we'll have to separate and cover two sites at the same time. Jenny suggests that Prince might be able to release a man or two to help us cover the ground. "He's on the hot seat big time and I think he'll cooperate as much as he can without giving away our cover."

That afternoon we review the list of vendors with Prince. It seems thorough and includes the names and times of entry. We spend several hours going over and over the list and together develop a schedule of stakeouts for the first four days. At that point we'll get together again and review our progress.

Every morning Jenny and I make it a point to rendezvous for breakfast in the BOQ dining room at 0730 to review progress and plan the day. In a couple of days we've established a productive and pleasant routine. One morning Jenny asks, "Can you tell me about your family, your wife and children?"

I'm a bit taken aback because up to now our time together has not included any personal information. There has been no reason to avoid it. We've simply been too focused on the case to talk about anything else. I answer, "This assignment is too short to relocate my family. I have a son, Davey, who is nearly a year old. They both live with my in-laws in Monterey. What about you?"

"I was born in New York, but spent most of my life in Colorado after my parents separated when I was three. I don't have any siblings. I left home to go to college and never went back. After graduating I went to work and studied law at night. When I finished law school four years later I went directly into OCS in Newport. I had a short tour in D.C. at JAG, but asked to be sent into the fleet. That's how I got to Whidbey Island."

"Sounds like a lot of hard work."

"It was, but I had nothing to go back to so I just kept charging ahead. I learned, for me at least, that some problems can only be solved by hard work. You can't sit there and complain about how bad your life is or how cruel the world is. The world can be cruel, but it's also filled with opportunity. You just have to make a decision of which way to handle it."

"I agree. Hard work is a great palliative. But you do feel alone at times, don't you?"

"Sure, it gets a bit lonely at times. I would like to find someone, but in this business who has time for romance or family?"

"Along the way didn't you ever meet someone who really touched your heart?"

"Yes, in my senior year in college I met a young man who was a petroleum engineer. I was crazy about him. But he loved the oil business. His company sent him to work their oil patch near Lake Maracaibo in Venezuela. It's pretty wild country and I couldn't go with him. After a year of letter writing it was clear that he loved oil more than me. That realization broke my heart. It drove me to stop waiting for someone and to make my own way. That's when I decided on law school. I liked the investigative side of the law business. It's what made this assignment so intriguing for me."

"I know what you mean about meeting someone and then losing them. It happened to me on my first duty station. The circumstances denied us any future. I had to move on, but I never forgot her. A few years later I met my wife. We had a baby when I was at sea and I've only seen them a few months out of the past year. It would be nice to have someplace to call home. Actually, I do. It's Monterey, but I'm not there with them."

"That must be very hard for you. When we finish here, do you think you will be able to be with them for a while?"

"Yes, for a short time. But I expect I'll be sent somewhere in the Far East given my language ability and interests over there. I won't be able to take my wife and son to my next duty station. Fortunately, they are well off with my in-laws. My son will have everything he could want, maybe someday a father too."

After two weeks of fruitless stakeouts we're very frustrated. Then, late one afternoon Jenny and I decide to go for a walk around the base to see if anything speaks to us. We're talking about what to do next when we have to stop at a corner to wait for a large garbage truck to pass. Suddenly, I realize we've not considered the trash people who roam the base every day picking up waste material. When we get back to our office, I call Prince: "Steve, we've missed the trash company."

"My god, you're right. I'll get on that immediately."

Over the next week, while we're waiting for the waste management info, we go over records of all the vendor drivers once more to see if we can find anything suspicious. There is nothing much there; petty indiscretions, mostly lids stuff. No reason to closely check on any of them. I file my weekly confidential with the CO and try to stay away from him. I'm not solving his case and I know he is getting upset by it.

Then, we receive the waste management company data. There is so much trash that the company has three trucks working full time to keep the base clean. There are four regular drivers and one young relief driver. The first thing that hits me is that the relief man was on the base on every shooting day. Two days later he drives into the base and we are ready to follow him. There is nothing suspicious about his behavior except that he spends a lot of time talking to people on his stops. When Prince's men follow up, the people tell them that he asks a lot of questions about the base and the way it operates—more than one would expect. Prince calls the trash company and tells them he is going to detain the man for questioning. Naturally, they are concerned and insist that we wait until their lawyer and human resources person arrive. The fellow's name is Manuel Torres. He's twenty years old and has been working for the company for almost two years, right out of high school. While we wait, we get him a cold drink and make small talk. He tells us he is working to save money to go to college.

He wants to be a detective someday. That's why he's always asking questions. Soon the lawyer and human resources chief arrive.

We tell Manuel that this is a random search and today we picked him up to learn if he has heard anything back at the company that might relate to the shootings. "Maybe Manuel," I suggest, "one of the drivers has made negative remarks about the Navy, the military or our country."

"No sir," he replies. "All of the men seem to be proud to be working here."

Just then Prince is called out of the room. We wait and one minute later he comes back in with a pistol in his hand. He says, "Manuel, is this yours? What's this doing in your truck?"

He begins to deny it, but quickly see's he's caught and admits it's his. "I can explain. Where I live you have to be prepared to defend yourself day or night, man. Two of my friends were kilt last month when someone thought they were in a rival gang. They weren't. They weren't gangbangers, but they got shot anyway. I carry it on my way to work and way home for pertection."

Prince asks him very threateningly, "Don't you know it's a federal offense to carry a gun on to a military base?"

"No, man. I din't know. I'm jist tryin to pertect myself man."

The lawyer says, "Manuel, don't say another word." Then, he turns to Prince and me and asks, "Can we talk in private?"

We go into a room next door and the lawyer opens up with, "Did you really get this out of Manuel's truck or is this just a cheap trick to scare the kid?"

Prince replies, "One of my men found it in a small gym bag under the seat."

"Does it match the type of gun that the shooter used?"

"It's a .22 caliber. We'll have to have ballistics check it. In the meantime I'm going to hold him."

"You're wasting your time. I can have him out of here in an hour. Let's be smart about this. I want you to catch the shooter too. But I'm sure, and I think you are too, that this is not your man."

153

"Maybe not, but I can't tell the boss I let a suspect go before I had a chance to run the gun. I'll hold him overnight and get SDPD ballistics to do a rush test. He may not be the man, but we've checked almost every vendor who came on the base during the shootings and he was here every time. Besides, we have four more of your men to check, and after a night in the brig he might remember something he overheard or saw."

"Let him go and I'll ensure he shows up tomorrow."

"Not a chance. You go find a judge who will release a suspect we haven't had much time to interrogate. I don't think you can do it in an hour or eight hours. If he's clean in the morning you can have him."

Back in the interrogation room the lawyer explains to Manuel that we have to hold him until ballistics checks the gun. He nods and says they'll find it isn't the gun that shot anyone.

The next morning we talk to Manuel again while we wait for the ballistics report. After an hour it is clear that he hasn't heard or seen anything that would be helpful. In the afternoon the report shows this was not the shooter's gun. Manuel is released to the lawyer while the Navy decides whether or not to press charges for bringing the gun on base.

Now we turn our attention to the other four drivers. Three of them were on base the days of the shootings. The fourth was on sick leave during one of the incidents. We run the three men's records through the FBI. When the reports come in Jenny and I go to Security to look at the reports. The first two don't reveal any past problems. The third, on a man named Paul Trammel, is a surprise.

Prince says, "I've heard about this man. He was a hero in Vietnam. The story I heard is that he was a gunnery sergeant, E-7, in a company of Marines deployed north of Khe Sanh. The North Vietnamese launched an attack in his area and the company took heavy losses. The platoon leader was wounded, and Trammel took over the platoon and led a counter attack. I don't know all the details, but apparently he singlehandedly wiped out a large number of the enemy, also captured a large number, and led the platoon to safety.

Then he went back and personally carried out a number of wounded. He was badly wounded in the leg and by the end of the encounter could barely stumble, much less walk. He was given the Navy Cross, our highest award next to the Medal of Honor. After he recovered from his leg wounds it was confirmed that he could no longer perform the full duties of an active Marine. He was discharged with honors. I remember stories of his prodigious strength. He's a big guy. His nickname is Bull."

I say, "I don't think this man could be the shooter, but I'd like to meet him and thank him for this service if nothing else."

Jenny and Steve agree so we jump into Steve's patrol car and head out in search of Bull. It's mid-afternoon when we see his truck just pulling into a pickup station. Steve stops in front of the truck, must be instinct, and we get out. Trammel turns to see us and has a quizzical look on his face. Steve starts, "Good afternoon Mr. Trammel, how's it going?"

Trammel nods and still wondering why we are here answers, "Never better. What can I do for you?"

"We've heard about your service in Vietnam and wanted to shake the hand of a true hero."

Trammel replies, "Thanks, but that's past history."

I offer my hand and pull it back checking for broken fingers. Jenny shakes his hand and he is gentle with her.

"Mr. Trammel, do you mind if we ask you a few questions about the shootings that have taken place here the past couple months? You get around the base and may have seen something."

"No problem."

"According to your company's records you were on base the day of every incident. Do you recall anything, anything at all, that might shed some light on this? Did you see or hear anything that might help?"

"I don't remember anything out of the ordinary if that's what you mean. There's always lots of noise of planes taking off and landing. Sometimes I can't even hear myself think. It reminds me of Nam."

155

Pointing to the truck, Jenny asks, "These things have always fascinated me, so big and powerful. Would you mind if I got in the cab to see what it's like?"

"I don't mind, but it's against company policy for anyone to get into the truck except the driver. We don't want anyone to get hurt."

Steve speaks up, "We'll take responsibility for anything Lt. Hendry might do. Go ahead lieutenant; have a look."

Trammel starts to protest but sees it's useless. He's continually shifting his weight back and forth from one leg to another with a small grimace.

I ask him, "I heard that you received serious wounds in your leg in Nam. Do they still bother you?"

"Not much. I can still do a job, even though the Marines didn't think so."

"Did they discharge you for being unfit for duty?"

"Yes, that was their reason and it's ridiculous. I can do anything any man can do and do it better and faster except for running. I can bench-press a locomotive. Did the record show that I was the best marksman the Marines ever had? I blew the top of the chart off with every hand gun, rifle, and machine gun." At this he checks himself; he realizes it wasn't a good thing to mention.

To make him think I missed the implication and can understand his resentment, I tell him I had my legs smashed also. Fortunately, they didn't dump me. Was the discharge all because you can't run?"

"I can run, but not very fast or for long distances."

"That doesn't seem to me to make you unfit for duty."

"You're damned right, sir."

Jenny calls down from the cab, "Mr. Trammel, what is this tripod behind the seat for?"

He hesitates for just a second and then replies, "I'm a photography bug. I keep it handy in case I see something I want to shoot, I mean photograph. Little slip of the tongue," he says and laughs.

Steve and I laugh with him, "Yes, not a good word to use around here these days."

Jenny calls down, "I love photography too. Where is your camera?"

"I forgot it this morning."

"What do you have?"

"Ah, a Leica."

"Is it a SLR?"

"A what?"

"Single lens reflex."

"Oh yes. It only has one lens."

Jenny looks at me while Steve takes Trammel around the truck asking about the lift mechanism. "Mike, he doesn't know what a SLR is. He's no photography fan. Everyone knows what a SLR is. There's something wrong here."

"I agree. He's quite nervous—and he's angry with the Navy for ruling him unfit for duty. Take my handkerchief and wipe down the tripod and both window sills. We might find gun powder residue."

Shortly, Trammel and Prince come around to the front of the truck. After the wipe-down Jenny talks to Trammel about photography. Steve and I go back around the truck to talk out of ear shot. "Steve, we've got a circumstantial case, at least. Do you want to detain him like we did with Torres?"

"Definitely. I'll have the office call the company and tell them we're holding him. They can send someone to pick up the truck and continue the route. I'll tell him we want to take him in for questioning. I don't think he'll fight it. If he does it'll make him look guilty."

At first Trammel is angry. "What is this? I'm just here doing my job. Why do you want to hassle me? What are you going to do with my truck?" Once he sees it's futile, being a Marine, *once a Marine always a Marine*, he knows about authority and taking orders. So, he pulls the truck out of the way and shuts the motor off. Then he gets into Prince's car in the back seat with me.

Of course, the company sends the same lawyer again. "What wild goose chase are you people on this time? Just because we collect your trash doesn't mean our people are felons."

157

During the questioning Trammel is composed although clearly angry under the surface. We admits he has guns and regularly goes to a shooting range. He denies that his guns match the shooter's. I try to catch him by asking how he knows that when he doesn't know what kind of gun fired the bullets found in the victims. He's not stupid because he replies, "It doesn't matter what type of gun fired the bullets. It wasn't one of my guns."

The questions go on for the next hour with no progress toward evidence of guilt. We ask Trammel if we can do a search of his apartment. He agrees. We call JAG to enlist someone to accompany us, but it's now after six o'clock and there is only a recording. So, in the company of this lawyer we drive to his place in Chula Vista about twenty minutes south. He lives in a plain apartment alone. There is no sign of a girlfriend or wife, but plenty of evidence that Trammel likes guns. He has magazines and photos and a framed copy of his membership in the National Rifle Association. There are also many photographs of kids' football and basketball teams with him in the picture. A framed thank you from the Chula Vista Boys Club hangs in his bedroom. Two hours of turning things over and we find nothing that links him directly to the shooting. Finally, his lawyer says, "Mr. Trammel has cooperated fully and this meeting is concluded. I'll take responsibility for Mr. Trammel if you release him to me. I'll drive him back to the company to get his car." Prince agrees and we leave. On the way back to the base I go over what we have beyond circumstantial evidence. The answer is not much. Still, we believe there is sufficient information to involve someone from JAG.

Late the next morning we are in Prince's office when a lieutenant from JAG arrives. His name is Lumpert. He introduces himself with, "Criminal law is my specialty. If this fellow is anywhere near the crime I'll find the evidence."

We explain to this modest fellow what has happened to date. He goes off, "Why didn't you involve me before you went to his apartment? You could have contaminated the scene."

I inform him that when we called JAG yesterday and no one answered. He claimed this is impossible because they are open 24-7 just for things like this. Prince jumped on him and told him to check for messages because we left one when no one answered. Seeing that he lost this round Lumpert shifted quickly to the main topic. We went through everything from the minute we met Trammell at the truck until his lawyer insisted the meeting was over. After repeated probes Lumpert finally accepts reluctantly that all we have is a thin circumstantial case. Nevertheless, he thinks we should arrest and prosecute. We contact Trammell's lawyer and ask for him and Trammel to come back for a conference. We strongly believe that we have found the shooter, but our case is very weak.

When they arrive we go right to the point, describing all the circumstantial evidence and asking Trammel how the shootings could have happened in his opinion. Despite his lawyer's objections he describes the hypothetical example. "It's a relatively easy thing to do for a person who knows how to handle guns. It's probably a case of someone on the base being the shooter. Here's the best way to do it. It's just like being a sharpshooter in war. Pick a time and a place and wait for a victim to appear. Have a stable firing platform."

I interject, "Like a tripod?"

He pauses. "A tripod could be used. So could any other stable base. If you're shooting a long distance stability is obviously critical. You also have to have a plan and a reason. You can't just go around firing like a madman. After that it's only a matter of waiting in a place where you can't be seen,"

Again I ask, "Like a truck?"

"The problem with a truck is its vibrating. You'd have to shut off the motor before attempting a shot. Then, you have to restart it, which could attract attention. That's all there is to it. It's not something that a lot of people couldn't do, especially here where there are thousands of professionals who know how to handle a weapon."

"But how do you explain the gun powder residue in the truck and on the tripod?"

"I use the tripod sometimes at the shooting range. As for the truck, it's like I said, five people drive that truck. Also, maintenance personnel are in it for test drives and the residue could have landed there any day, anytime, anywhere."

"But you drove it the day of each shooting."

"That doesn't mean that the shot came from the truck on that day."

For the moment there is silence. Then his lawyer speaks up.

"Commander, this is getting redundant and tiring. I think we both realize that there is no way you could convict Mr. Trammel of shooting one, much less several, people. All you know is that he was on base on the days of the incidents, there is gunpowder residue in a truck that is driven by all the drivers at the company, and it could have happened at any time over the two months since these incidents occurred. And you have no weapon. It seems to me that you have three choices. One, you give up and leave it as an unsolved crime. Two, you continue your investigation of other suspects without bothering my client again. Or three, you offer some way to resolve this in a way that is satisfactory to Mr. Trammel."

Prince is not about to bullied, and he strikes back. "We could shadow Mr. Trammel and make his life miserable with further investigation. His attitude toward the Marine Corps is well known. Some people would even be sympathetic to his taking revenge and that would stigmatize him for life. We can talk to people in Chula Vista about his activity there, and you know how that raises suspicion even when someone is totally innocent. How do those choices strike you?"

"Yes, you could be total assholes, excuse me ma'am, harassing a Navy Cross hero and a respected and involved member of his community. But I don't think the Navy needs any more negative publicity, do you? Can you visualize people at the gate of the base with protest signs and press coverage? Come on. Be reasonable. Make us a proposal that we can consider?"

Prince, Lumpert, Jenny, and I have prepared for just this scenario and we're formulated a deal. I state that if Trammel admits to one charge of simple assault, we will recommend clemency, recognizing his prior service, probation in consideration of this wounds, community service, and psychiatric help. It would be up the judge to set the limits. At first he objects. "You don't have anything on me and now you want to mark me as a felon for the rest of my life."

I counter, "We've got a pretty strong circumstantial case. If we look hard enough and talk to enough people in town and at work we are bound to find someone who remembers something you said that will incriminate you. Besides, do you want to spend the next year with this hanging over your head and going to court? Isn't it better to take a small punishment for what you know you did? If we can link you to these shootings you'll go away for a long time."

Trammel caves and we have solved the case. By the time Jenny and I get back to the BOQ it's too late for dinner. We just grab a couple sandwiches from the 24 hour grill and then call it a day. I'm greatly relieved. I wasn't prepared for this job. Yet, through luck and help from Prince and Jenny we pull it off. As I think about it I realize how much I love the chase so to speak. It's very stimulating to dig into a complex situation, weave through distractions and false leads to get to the source of the problem. When I think about it, that is mostly what I've been doing in my career. The Vietnam raid and Barton's fraud were scary, but intriguing. I think I could be happy focusing my career on investigative work.

Jenny and I have made our report to McMurray and McKay and with that officially wrap up our duties. We clean out our office and decide to go to a farewell dinner, as we will be reassigned by ONI shortly. I tell Jenny, "I know a nice place in La Jolla right on the beach. In fact, at high tide the spray hits the windows."

I make a reservation for 1900. Prince arranges a car for us. Out of courtesy and gratitude we invite him to come along, but he says he wants to get back to his family, something we can appreciate.

Once we are at our table by the window I ask Jenny, "What would you like to do next? Would you like to go to NIS?"

"That would be good, but I think I'd prefer DIS. I'm a lawyer and that would be more interesting than working in JAG, I think. From what I can see DIS would be largely field investigative work, which I like a whole lot better than writing briefs."

"For what it's worth, I'll make a recommendation to that effect."

"Well, what about you?" Where do you expect they will send you?"

"My guess is back to WestPac, for what I don't know. But I'll get a short leave to go back to see my son before they ship my butt out again."

The dinner goes very well. It's two comrades who have just finished a tricky assignment and grown to like each other. Our conversation shifts to the future and our personal dreams and hopes. We're both lonely in only slightly different ways. It feels very good to talk with someone who seems to genuinely care with nothing in it for them. We linger over dessert and coffee followed by a glass of very expensive brandy. Then, we head back to base. At the BOQ we linger for a few minutes not wanting the evening to end.

Jenny suddenly gets very teary-eyed. "Michael, I'm so proud to have served with you and gotten to know you. I believe you are an extraordinary man. I hope your situation gets resolved soon and you regain the peace of mind that I think you've lost. I'll never forget our time together. Thank you so much for teaching me, respecting me, and caring for me." Then, she puts her hands on my chest, comes close, and kisses me. She looks deeply into my eyes, then turns and walks quickly away. A warm feeling pulses through my body. It's not sexual, but it is loving. It's the type of feeling I had when I first met Lynda.

* * *

Two days later my request for leave comes through and I catch a plane for San Jose. Ramon picks me up at SJC.

It's a rainy day. California is very predictable about its short rainy season. It typically lasts from about Thanksgiving to Easter.

Then, they don't see a drop until November or even December again. Nevertheless, once in a great while a surprise storm hits and drops an inch just to settle the dust. That's all this one is doing. The streets are wet but not enough to slow the drivers who speed along like nothing is happening. It'll take us about an hour to Monterey, providing there are not traffic problems.

I'm very anxious to get home. Of course I want to see Davey. Lynda had said that Davey was often sick and was afraid to bring him to D.C., and we both knew the San Diego assignment would be relatively short. So it's been almost a year since I've seen them. Davey is walking now and is very playful, they tell me. I missed those precious early months and vow that I will do everything I can to make up for it in the future. Even more so I want to see Lynda and see if we can repair our relationship. By now I've realized the toll that my absence has taken on our marriage, the loneliness she must have been feeling and the struggle to raise a baby without a husband there. Her letters have become increasingly distant, and in my long absence in D.C. and San Diego, we've lost the ground that I'd felt we gained on our date night before I left. Jenny's companionship and parting kiss drove home the loneliness that I've felt for the last few years. In those few months I felt more closeness with Jenny than I had in my entire marriage with Lynda. I desperately want to find out if I can find that closeness with my wife.

When Ramon turns into 17-Mile Drive the smell of wet eucalyptus trees is very strong. It brings back mixed memories. Soon we pass the turnout where I was attacked and I wish the perps, and especially Paul, lifelong diarrhea. In a few minutes we drive up the stone driveway to the Arbuckles' house.

I walk to the door a little nervous about my reception, but before I can open it, Betsy flings it open with a big smile. "Michael, I'm so happy to see you! You look wonderful. How are you? A little tired from the trip?" A second later Fred comes down the stairs and gives me a bear hug. When this big man hugs you, you know you've been hugged. "Welcome home, Michael. We've really missed you." Fred isn't playing golf today because of the rain, but I like to think he stayed home for me as well.

Fred says almost forlornly, "Mike, we truly don't know what to do with Lynda. It's like watching someone who is deathly ill and not being able to help."

"Yes, I feel the same way and I'm so far away that I am truly helpless."

"Lynda doesn't spend much time with Davey. She hardly sees him and refuses to nurse him. Carmen and Josefa take care of him. She doesn't seem to have an appetite and never leaves the house. We've engaged a psychiatrist, a woman, to come to the house and talk to Lynda. We figured she could better relate to whatever is bothering her. She's been talking with Lynda for over a month on a regular basis here and in her office. We have an appointment with the doctor late this afternoon to find out what she has learned. Her office is in Monterey. You'll probably want to take a shower and put on some fresh clothes."

"Lynda wrote that Davey wasn't too healthy and was constantly getting the sniffles. That is one of the reasons why she didn't want to move to D.C."

"No. He is doing well." Betsy says, "He's the sunshine in the house. He is such a sweet boy. Go ahead and see him. He's in his room with Carmen or Josefa. They never let him out of their sight."

I take the stairs two at a time to Davey's room on the second floor. I try to enter quietly but Josefa hears me coming and opens the door before I reach it. I give her a little hug and she puts her finger to her lips, "el niño está durmiendo"—the little boy's sleeping. I nod and tiptoe across the lush carpet to my son's crib. There he is, my beautiful boy. What a gorgeous child—blonde hair, blue eyes, rosy healthy skin, and smelling of baby powder. I am so blessed to see him and know he is my son. Now I feel even more guilty because I haven't been here to play with him or help him grow. I have to touch him, so I lightly brush his head and rub his back. He is so soft. It makes me tear up. I look up and see Josefa's eyes are wet also. Just about then Carmen comes quietly into the room and gives me a little hug. We all leave the room quietly so as not to awaken my beautiful son.

Once we're outside I suggest that the three of us go down to the kitchen and have a cup of coffee together. When we're settled over our cups I ask, "Carmen, please tell me everything about Davey."

She starts, "He's always been healthy. No esta un llorón --he's not a crybaby. He's very happy because everyone in the house pampers him. He doesn't ask about his mama because she doesn't spend as much time with him as Josefa and I do. Besides, he's too young to miss her. Because she's so withdrawn he doesn't know her as well as he knows us. We talk to him in English and Spanish, so he will be bilingual. He can already say several Spanish words. When he isn't sleeping he plays by himself with the toys in his room or with Josefa or me. We have a camera in his room and a sensor, so we can watch and hear him when he is alone."

Josefa breaks in, "He likes to play rollie ball. We sit on the floor facing each other and roll a plastic ball back and forth. He thinks it is so much fun that he laughs until he falls over. He likes to play hide and seek too. He's so happy when he finds one of us hiding behind his crib or in the closet. He started walking early. Now he can walk all over his room or anywhere we take him."

Carmen assures me that he only goes places with someone with him. "He's very quick and must be watched all the time when he's outside his room or he'll disappear and hide somewhere in this big house. Outside the house we take him out to the patio to ride his little scooter. Once in a while we take him to the stable. He loves to see the horses. Rubio – Blondie -- is not afraid of the horses. Es un pequeno caballero," she claims laughingly, and Josefa agrees that he is indeed a little cowboy. After a while Carmen says they have to start preparations for supper, so I give each of them a hug and go in search of Fred and Betsy.

They're in the den and ask me how Davey looks to me. "You mean Rubio?" I say laughing. "I'm very happy to see how good he looks. I never knew what to think from Lynda's letters, that is when she used to write. I can't thank you enough for the way you've cared for my son through all the problems. I better look in on Lynda now."

I walk tentatively into Lynda's room. Her parents had told me of her depression, and I could tell from her phone calls and letters that something was very wrong. She rarely talked about Davey and seemed extremely withdrawn. When I walk in her room, it's as bad as I was fearing. She's sitting staring out the window, still in her pajamas although it's afternoon. The room is a mess with clothes hanging out of drawers, Kleenex tissue on the floor and items all over the bathroom floor. I approach her slowly until I'm certain she knows I'm there. "Hi sweetheart, how are you? How is Davey?" She looks at me and starts crying. Soon she is sobbing and her body is trembling. I put my arms around her and she doesn't respond, just keeps sobbing. I take her over to the bed and make her lie down. I sit by her and hold her hand. "Is Davey alright?" She doesn't say anything, just lies there, and I don't know what to do next. After a few minutes, I leave her resting and go downstairs.

Fred and Betsy have made an appointment with Lynda's psychiatrist to talk with us alone. Ramon drives us to Monterey, where her office is in a modern medical building just off Munras Street. The reception area is painted in muted colors. Pictures on the walls are all of flowers. The carpet is even a soft brown. All together it is very restful. The receptionist shows us into the doctor's office who greets us graciously and beckons us to sit in comfortable chairs away from her desk. When we're settled and accept a glass of water she begins.

"Your daughter is very distraught, as you know. Actually, it did not take long to learn why. She is feeling extremely guilty for something that no one knows she did. You remember the day she discovered she was adopted, when she left the house and didn't come back until late the next morning? It turns out she went to Cannery Row and got involved with a group of young adults who were partying. One thing led to another and she got high and slept with one of the boys that night. That's why she didn't come home. Ever since, she's been torn apart with guilt—partly at her rage toward you, her parents, but even more for infidelity. She says she truly loves Michael and I believe her."

Fred and Lynda look stunned, and I'm speechless. But there's more to come. "The core of her problem is something beyond that, however. As a result of her liaison that night she found herself pregnant." Doctor Freiberg pauses for a moment as we all catch our breath. Fred and Betsy look at each other in amazement and disbelief. Doctor Freiberg continues: "She found out from a friend who had been in the same condition that there is a clinic in Salinas where she could have an abortion. Her friend took her, but after the abortion an infection set in. She has been having that secretly treated by her OB/GYN. Lynda gave me permission to speak with her physician who told me about the case. She told me that as a result Lynda can probably not have another child."

She lets this sink in. We are stunned. The doctor explains that the trauma and guilt have devolved into long-term depression. Suddenly we understand Lynda's condition.

The doctor goes on, "Lynda believes herself to be a terrible mother because of what she did. Of course, that episode doesn't make her a bad mother, but it adds to her general feeling of guilt. I believe she may be in danger of harming herself. I strongly suggest you put her in a place where they can keep her safe and help her deal with this huge burden that is growing just like an untended infection, which it really is. She needs daily intensive care at this point. If you agree, I know an excellent center in the hills above Palo Alto. It's called The Retreat and I would be glad to make arrangements."

There isn't a sound in the room except for Betsy softly crying. "Oh Fred, why didn't we tell her years ago. This never would have happened if we did." Fred has been staring at the floor with one hand on Betsy's arm. Finally, he says, "Is there anything you have left out? Is there more you haven't told us?"

"No, Mr. Arbuckle, you know the whole story."

I've been silent through the whole recitation. I don't know what to think or do. I never imagined she could go this far off track. She's very sensitive and I think somewhat frightened by the world, despite all the comforts and security she has in her home. My first reaction is to think of Davey. He is too young to understand or be hurt by this now. We'll see what to do for him after we get this problem fixed, if it is fixable. I suggest, "We need to go home and discuss this. Dr. Freiberg's recommendation is probably the best thing to do and do quickly, but we need to talk about all the ramifications of it." Fred and Betsy agree. We thank the doctor for finding the source of Lynda's problem, despite how painful it is to know.

It's early evening when we return to the Arbuckle house. When we come in Carmen is waiting and asks what we would like for dinner. She can see that we are in a state of shock so she suggests something comforting like her special enchiladas. We agree, retire to the library, and pour a round of drinks to numb some of the afternoon's sting. It is the first time I've ever seen Betsy accept a vodka martini. When Fred hands it to her she takes a good swallow, shudders, and relaxes. Fred is already working on his second. I join him.

No one talks for a few minutes, then Fred says to Betsy, "Are you alright, sweetheart?"

She nods but can't speak.

Then he turns to me, "Michael, I'm so sorry that we brought you in to this."

"Fred, Betsy, there is no reason to blame yourself for this or feel sorry for me. I knew that Lynda was a very sensitive girl, but I thought that we could work it out together. If anyone is at fault it's me. I truly love her, now more than ever. I should have insisted that she come east with me." When Carmen brings in some enchiladas, shredded chicken, sliced avocados, tomatoes, and sour cream, we stop and eat before facing up to the plans we know need to be made. Fred asks Carmen to sit down. He tells her the essential parts of the story. She says simply, "La Pobrecita" – Poor little girl.

In the morning when Lynda wakes up and comes downstairs, still in her pajamas, the four of us sit down at the kitchen table to talk. We tell Lynda about our visit with Dr. Freiberg and how worried we are for her. I tell her, "Sweetheart, I love you and I understand how you must feel. We don't blame you for anything that has happened. We just want you to get well."

Lynda just stares at the polished wooden floor for a long minute. No one speaks. Then, she looks up at us and bursts out in body-shaking sobs. I go to her to hold her. She is unresponsive. Finally, I take her up to her room and stay with her while Fred and Betsy arrange for Lynda to be admitted to The Retreat. When it's settled, they come to her room to tell her about the center. Lynda is almost catatonic. It is as though she can't see or hear us. A small nod is all we get.

The next morning, Fred, Lynda, and I drive to Palo Alto. On the way, I hold Lynda's hand and no one talks. At The Retreat her caretakers come out and help us bring Lynda inside. Lynda is still unresponsive. The head nurse says we should just leave Lynda with her rather than linger in awful silence. Dr. Levine, the chief of staff comes out to meet us and asks if we have any questions or can tell us anything about Lynda that Dr. Freiberg hasn't already disclosed. We've nothing to add. The ride back is silent.

Once home Fred offers and we all have a drink. I notice that Betsy, who seldom had anything stronger than white wine, is now into martinis with Fred. I can imagine them sitting in here nightly drinking and feeling deeply distressed. I'm struck by how different it is from when I first knew them. In just a couple of years the house that rang with laughter and joy and guests has become like an empty church following a funeral.

After dinner I excuse myself and go to my room for some much-needed rest. Once there I shower, change into pajamas, and lie down. I can hear the wind outside, and the bed is cool and lonely. My mind cycles between Hawaii, Monterey and Washington. I go over and over it wondering what I could have done or should have done to avoid this. In no time I'm crying, both for us and for Davey, this beautiful little boy who has been left without a mother or father for so much of his young life. I don't want to disturb the household or I would wail at the top of my lungs to release some of the pain I feel.

In the morning I get up, put on a bathrobe, and go to Davey's room. He is already up and playing with his little blocks and figures. I sit on the floor with him and we build a small rectangle with the blocks. He catches on quickly and laughs loudly when he sees he was successful. Next, we try a circle. That works too. I'm torn between the joy of being with him and the knowledge that soon I have to leave again. Shutting that out, we just play simple games and talk for an hour until Josefa comes in and says, "Esta tiempo para la banadera de Rubio." She picks him up and takes him for his bath.

I go downstairs to find Fred and Betsy to learn if they have anything planned. In turn, they ask me if there is anything I want to do besides be with Davey. I tell them no. I've just finished a couple of difficult assignments and don't mind the time to rest. They understand, but ask if they could invite some friends over for dinner tomorrow night. Of course I can't refuse. These people are so dear to me, and they need a distraction as much as I do. The people are Dr. and Mrs. Young, a retired couple who live farther down the Drive, and Admiral Klare and his wife, whose fantail I spilled my drink on. I'm worried about the admiral's reception of me, but they reassure me that he now understands Paul's part in the matter. "Besides," Fred says, "the admiral is aware of your exploits and wants to hear it from the horse's mouth."

The Youngs and the Klares arrive for drinks at seven p.m.. Carmen has made her special Mexican dishes, which is what the guests have requested. They have their fill of fancy cuisines and love the heartiness and flavors of Carmen's food. After dinner we return to the library for Mexican coffee and a few Mexican wedding cookies. Much of the conversation revolves around Davey and me, and the guests seem to be avoiding talk of Lynda. After about an hour the

Youngs excuse themselves saying they have an early morning trip to San Francisco.

After they leave Admiral Klare asks me about my kidnapping and Vietnam. In due course he says very directly to me, "Son, you are at a crucial point in your career; from here you either head for the top or slowly fade away. If you want to know the secret for the first choice, it's simply this: No matter who your report to or how you feel about the job, you have to go beyond just doing your duty. You must make your CO feel that you love working for him. Senior officers are egomaniacs. We have to be in order to compete for our star. When given an order, in addition to replying 'Yes, sir,' you have to convey the feeling that you are pleased to do it. The truly perceptive ones will know that you are bluffing, but that is okay because they need to feel that the men in their command actually like serving under them."

The conversation drifts away from me onto local political matters, but I continue to mull over what the admiral has said. I can see the wisdom in it, although it's not comfortable having to operate like that. I wonder if it is the same in the business world. In time, the Klares say goodnight, and Betsy goes to bed. Fred insists we have one more and pours us each a glass of port. We don't talk a lot, mostly just repeat what we've said earlier and enjoy the quiet companionship that we've always been able to share. Finally, we say good night, but not before I tell Fred how much I love him and Betsy and how comforting it is to know that Davey is in their care. We make our way up the stairs to our bedrooms and I lie in bed thinking about my talks with Fred, Dr. Freiberg, and Admiral Klare.

The next two weeks I spend every minute possible with Davey. We play a game where we sit on the floor facing each other. I have two small plastic balls. I palm one and hold my hands in front of him, letting him pick which hand. When I open both hands he giggles. We do it again and I switch hands. Again, he laughs. It's an exquisite sound, so pure, so uninhibited. Next, I palm both balls and when he picks one I open my hand and he is so excited. The day goes quickly

171

as we play and I read picture books with him when I get tired. Little ones have boundless energy, unlike adults.

One sunny afternoon Fred and I take Davey in the golf cart to the stables. He recognizes where we are going and jumps up and down. At the stables he points excitedly at the horses. "Caballos!, he yells. I guess Carmen and Josefa's Spanish tutoring has worked. We hold him up so that he can touch the horse. We feed the horse some apple but can't let Davey do it because he doesn't know how to hold the apple and we don't want him to lose a finger. I carry him on my shoulders as we make our way around the barn and into the exercise yard. He squeals with delight as the horses run and jump. After a half hour we go back to the house and Josefa gets him ready for his nap.

Fred and I go into the library for a little scotch on the rocks. He serves MacAllan's 21 Years Old. It is as sweet as kissing your grandmother. After a short silence I say to Fred, "I'm very unhappy about having to leave my son again so soon. It will be at least a year, maybe more, before I see him again. I'm being ordered to Hawaii and I suspect Japan. Now that I've had time with him I can't bear to think of not being with him. I'm beginning to wonder whether or not I should continue in the Navy."

Fred is a bit surprised but understands. "Yes, it is a big sacrifice. I can see how you feel and I feel for you. We love having Davey here. He is a bright spot in the lives of two old people. Of course, if your situation allows for it, you must take him with you. If you decide to leave the Navy I'm certain I can help guide you to some good positions. If you like, I would love to have you working at Watson Lines."

"Thanks, Fred. The problem is that I can't take him. I've no one to care for him and don't know where I'll be from day to day. Under the present circumstances he is best off with you. I can see how much everyone here loves and cares for him, so that is a comfort for me. It's just something I have to work out."

On Tuesday, I call Dr. Freiberg for an appointment to update me on Lynda. I know she's been checking with The Retreat on Lynda's state. The next afternoon I drive into Monterey to see her. After the usual pleasantries I ask, "What do you hear about Lynda? How's she doing?"

"Lynda is settled in and comfortable. Her anxiety seems to have lessened somewhat, they tell me. However, to be perfectly honest, this is going to be a very long journey and no one knows how, when or if she will come out of it. Tell me, how are you holding up?"

I repeat the conversation I had with Fred including my dilemma regarding my future in the Navy. We discuss that for a bit and in true psychiatrist style she asks how I would feel about leaving the Navy.

"I am torn about it. I truly like the service and I feel that I'm contributing to our nation. But I've a son who will grow up without seeing much of his father."

"There is no magic answer, Michael. You have to listen to your heart and hear what it tells you." I thank her for talking to me about this and drive back to the house.

When I get home, Fred wants to show Davey off at the Club, so we drive over and take Davey out on the putting green. He doesn't have the hand-eye coordination to swing a club yet. Still, he likes the feel of the putting green under his feet and would walk all over it if we let him. Davey gets a big kick out of sitting in a high chair in the nineteenth hole and sipping a drink while he takes in all the motion around him. He's such an easy child to be with.

My last week of leave flies by. I play with Davey every minute he is awake, full of joy at his presence but tormented by the knowledge that our time together is so short. If I decide to leave the Navy it will be after the upcoming assignment. On Friday I have to go. After a tearful goodbye with Fred and Betsy and a silent prayer for my wife, I'm on the plane to the Pacific.

10

DOUBLE DUTY

At the end of August 1971 I land in Honolulu. Hawaii's delicious plumeria-scented air brings back memories of the time with Lynda before I shipped out. The combination of brilliant sun, refreshing rain, and constant breeze are the hallmark of this paradise. They seduce one into wanting to just lie in a hammock and sip a mai tai. I don't go back to our house in Alewa Heights because I believe that I'll be deploying to WestPac soon.

I secure a room at the BOQ and report to the offices of CINCPACFLT in Honolulu. I'm assigned a temporary additional duty office. TAD means I won't be part of the staff at least for some time. Four days after I arrive I receive an order to meet the XO of the 7th Fleet, Admiral Braun, who is in Hawaii to conduct business with CINCPACFLT HQ. He starts out, "This is a joint services mission that you will lead. Although on the surface the mission looks much like an annual intel inspection, there is a much greater purpose. The end goal is to look for ways to improve joint intelligence operations."

After a short pause when he seems to be marshaling his thoughts, he says in a very serious tone, "The services have resisted joint operations since WWII when the Joint Chiefs began to take money from the departments. Budget is always the reason for resistance to change because it means that the services will have to give up funding and, more importantly, slots that will reduce the size of their command. The Army took a big cut when it lost the Army Air Corps to the creation of the Air Force in 1947. Surrendering to jointness always means a loss, even though everyone agrees that it might be a good idea. Congress doesn't allocate money for much that is outside of the direct focus of the mission. Remember, every change is judged by the amount of money gained and lost. It is always money and strength. Very basic, just like in business.

"We in the Navy have only ourselves to blame," the Admiral goes on. Officers sent to the Naval War College are penalized in the long run because the promotion and ship command boards feel the time can be better spent on the line. They are suspicious of officers who serve in joint slots. So we send over-the-hill or second-rate officers who often retire after the term. Thus, we totally waste the investment in those programs. Inside the Navy there has always been conflict between the deep draft sailor, the aviator, and the submariner. Adding jointness to the mix doesn't help. Intelligence has never been a hot path to promotion, even though the intelligence gathered during WWII was crucial to the battle of Midway and others. It made impressions on the historians, but not on the fleet or other services.

"Since WWII there have been numerous attempts at establishing joint intel commands, JICs. Somehow, every time the proposal rises to the Joint Chiefs it gets sent back. This mission is an attempt to change that by providing evidence, if it exists, that a joint focus will not only improve the quality of the intelligence but also not result in lost budget.

"You'll be receiving orders soon to report to Yokosuka to command a joint intel unit labeled JITPAC. This is a project supported by all the services in the Pacific theater. Your team will be staffed by officers from the Air Force, Army, Coast Guard, and Marines. The officers are Army Captain Park, a Korean American; Marine Corps Captain Busch, a Japanese American; Air Force Captain Philippe; and Coast Guard Lieutenant Grant. Of course, you represent the Navy. There will also be four chief warrant officers with a wealth of on-the-job technical experience in communications and intel, including cryptology.

"The mission is to inspect the intel operations throughout Korea, Japan, Taiwan, and the Philippines from three standpoints: equipment needs and utilization, operational efficiency, and quality of intelligence output. We're less interested in current levels of efficiency than in how things could be run better to generate intelligence jointly. Your unit is a prototype test as well as an inspection that hopefully will demonstrate the value of joint intel operations. It is the classic theory of 1 + 1 = 3.

"General Stone of the Air Force has generously assigned space for the initial organization of this team at Hickam. As soon as everyone can be assembled there will be a meeting of your team. The plan is that the team will be ready for its mission and on station in Japan before November. The Navy will provide a base for your team at the 7th Fleet at Yokosuka. Between now and the end of November you will organize the team, assign responsibilities, handle the logistics of moving your personnel and equipment, develop your plan, and generate your schedule.

"By now I think you must realize the importance of this assignment. You've been selected due to your previous experience in WestPac, your reorganization of NIS, your CIS training, and investigative work in San Diego.

"As soon as possible after your team is assembled you'll provide a basic description of the inspection schedule of your mission. This will be forwarded to all the intelligence functions in Korea, Japan, Taiwan, and the Philippines along with a directive signed by all the heads of Pacific operations ordering local units to cooperate to the fullest. Within the officer group you'll share the concept of joint intel command and the purpose of this mission. As you collectively feel out the warrant officers, you may choose to share the concept with them. It is up to you. Commander Still, I cannot emphasize too much how important this mission is to the structure of our nation's military services. If you can make the case for at least some level of joint intel operations it will provide the information we need to demonstrate it's economic as well as performance value. I will most likely see you again in Yokosuka."

On Monday I'm sitting in my new office at Hickam AFB roughing out a tentative schedule through the end of the year. I have briefing material on the team so I know by name and basic record who is on the team. There is a knock on the door and two officers walk in—one Air Force and one Army. The Air Force fellow is lean, about six feet tall with brown wavy hair. He speaks first.

"Commander Still, I'm Captain Augustin Philippe, United States Air Force."

I stand up and shake his hand, "Good thing you told me—I didn't recognize the uniform." We all laugh at my little joke. Then the second man speaks. He is Army, of Asian ancestry, probably Korean, about five eight at most. He says in a very matter-of-fact voice, "Commander, I'm Army Captain Hyun Ki Park. Most Westerners call me Ki, as in key," he says with a small smile.

I can see we're going to have a good time together. No stuffed shirts here. "Welcome, gentlemen. We're going to spend a lot of time together for many months, so I suggest we drop the formalities. Do either of you know where the Marine or Coast Guard members of this group are?" Both shake their heads. Just then, since the door is open, another man knocks on the door jamb and steps in.

"Commander, I'm Lieutenant Lawrence Grant, United States Coast Guard, reporting, sir."

"Welcome, Mr. Grant. I'm Mike Still, commander of this little team. I was just telling these gentlemen that since we are going to be living closely together for the foreseeable future we should drop the formalities. Do friends call you Lawrence or Larry or something else?"

"Larry, sir."

No sooner do we all sit down before there is another knock on the door jamb and I look up to see another officer. I motion him in, and standing at attention declares, "Captain Edwin Busch, United

States Marine Corps, reporting as ordered, sir." Busch is also of Asian ancestry, maybe a half inch shorter than Park and very muscular.

"Well, Mr. Busch, I was expecting a German; are you sure you're in the right place?"

He doesn't get the joke, "If you are Commander Still and this is the intel unit, I am, sir."

"Ed, it's just my little joke. Welcome aboard. Let's keep the formalities to a minimum. Introduce yourself to the rest of the team."

Once we resettle I suggest we get acquainted. "Mr. Phillipe, why don't you start and give us a familiar name we can use with you. Are you French?"

"Sir, I'm of French ancestry, Huguenot actually. Most people call me either Gus or Phil. I prefer Phil. I'm not sure why I'm here except that I speak Cantonese somewhat, I'm a pilot, and I have a background in intelligence with an emphasis on communications technology."

Park goes next. "I'm Ki Park. I was born to Korean parents living in the United States. I speak Korean fluently. My mother's family still lives in the north and my dad's in the south. That probably is a main reason for being assigned to the mission. My background is also in Army intel with experience in operations management."

Busch shifts in his chair and says, "Like Ki, I am born of Asian parents living in the United States. During the war my grandparents and parents were interned at Hart Mountain in Wyoming. I was born there. It is a bloody cold place in the winter. My name came after the death of my father at Hart Mountain and the subsequent remarriage of my mother. She had me take his name. It causes no end of confusion. My specialty is in coding and encryption. People call me Ed."

I ask, "Ed, do you have a Japanese name as well?"

"Yes, sir, it is Akio—the first-born son."

"Welcome, Akio. Very well. Our noncoms will be here later this week so we may as well start with planning and logistics. Did anyone receive a list of equipment that we will need to carry with us?"

Everyone shakes their head. Just like the military. "I've been assured by CINCPACFLT that whatever we need we will be given." At the end of the week I'm forwarded an initial requisition for our equipment. We go over the list and make a few changes. Then I transmit this to Yokosuka. Within a week I receive confirmation of receipt and assurance that all will be ready for us when we arrive. When the military gets going, it is an extremely effective organization. I assign Ki to be in charge of logistics.

The following Monday the warrant officers arrive together. One who seems to be informal leader speaks for the group. "Sir, I'm Chief Warrant Officer Seiichi Matsumoto, United States Army. Foreigners call me Sy. Sorry, we're a little late; problems getting orders processed and synched."

"I understand, Sy. Please give us a brief rundown on yourself."

"Very well, sir. I've been in the Army twenty-one years. Much of that time I've been working on logistics all over the Pacific. The last eight years I've been in Japan, most recently in supply corps in Yokosuka. I'm fluent in Japanese and pretty good in Chinese; my family lived on Formosa for many years. Whatever you need or want just let me know. I'll get it for you. No job too big or too small, sir.

"This young man is CWO Louis Tasca. He also has experience in logistics working largely with intelligence units. I can get a tank for you. Lou can get anything up to a destroyer, if you like. He's a specialist in communications technology, like our signal corps. Next is Chief Master Sergeant Harrison Carter. The Air Force doesn't like the CWO rank. His specialty is mechanics. He claims he can diagnose and fix any piece of equipment that the military owns even if he has never seen it before. He's a very handy man to have around in case your tank or destroyer breaks down. Last, but certainly not least, is Chol Lee, United States Marine Corps. We call him Chuck. This man is brilliant. I've come across him in Japan before. He's a signals intelligence/electronic warfare specialist. He's also got experience from VN in counterintelligence. Sir, I think together we can handle anything that comes up."

179

The next four weeks are spent laying out the itinerary. We discuss the roles each will play at each inspection point. Then I order these technical specialists to make a final review of the equipment list and make any changes they see fit. It'll be my job to obtain the changes from the people in Yokosuka. I emphasize that for all anyone knows this is just like an audit of equipment and operations, but with a focus on improving performance, not dinging someone for inefficiency. Once everything is ready we'll embark on a Navy transport plane to Yokosuka no later than 25 October prepared to launch the mission one week later.

We now we have a little less than a month before the team must leave. We organize as rapidly as possible and suggest that everyone make whatever personal arrangements are necessary since once we arrive in Yokosuka there won't be any time off for quite a while. I'll go out two weeks ahead of the team to make sure that all is ready for us and to receive a final briefing from Admiral Braun.

Before leaving for Yokosuka on the first of October I send a notice to each intelligence unit that we will visit outlining the inspection procedure and purpose. Again, I emphasize that this mission is to find better ways to gather and disseminate intelligence. I don't mention jointness directly. I'm certain that their commands have alerted them to our arrival, but I want them to become acquainted with my name. The notice lists the various activities we will be inspecting, such as administration/record keeping, operating procedures, periodic reports internal and external, intelligence gathering and processing equipment, general equipment utilization and maintenance, risk management plans, intelligence data records, any clandestine and counterintelligence operations, security, and budget data. This is their most definitive notice of the mission. Since it is an extraordinary joint inspection we cannot determine ahead of arrival precisely how long we will be on each site. I note that we will start in Korea no later than the first week in November. I tell them that if possible we will give them at least thirty days' notice before arriving, but they should begin to prepare for our arrival now. After Korea we should have a much better idea to timing to other sites. With that I leave for Yokosuka.

* * *

On my arrival at 7th Fleet headquarters I'm summoned to Admiral Braun's office. He says, "Commander, there has been a slight change of plans that should not affect your team's schedule very much. We've planned a very short but very important mission for a special ops team. Unfortunately, the team leader who spoke Chinese broke his leg last week and we need a new leader with Chinese language ability right now. That's you.

Naturally, I accept but ask why I was chosen. Braun tells me that it's because of my previous experience off Vietnam and my knowledge of Chinese. "Sir, that I understand, but I'm not qualified physically to serve with the people who train for this all the time." Braun says, rather pointedly, "Commander, I suggest you stop asking questions and report to Navy Special Operations Command immediately. They'll put you through a ten-day training session to get you in shape for this mission. Then you report back to me and be ready to go."

The commander of the special ops is not happy to see me. He believes that his men can carry out any mission that the Navy may have. I agree with him, but I have my orders for a physical training program. He understands and lays out a program aimed at getting me minimally prepared for the mission. The training is grueling. I'm certain they take out their frustration on me and my weakened knees. Nevertheless, in ten days I take my aching body back to HQ for my mission briefing.

Admiral Braun's deputy, Commander Porter Howell, tells me, "On Tuesday you'll fly to Naha, Okinawa. Your task is to board a Jones class destroyer escort DE 1037 where you'll meet your team, which is stationed in Naha. The ship will put out to sea for a designated station off Ningbo, China. It will appear to anyone on shore that this is just part of the Navy's patrol off the China coast. In order to maintain secrecy your team members will board separately in the middle of the night and in disguise as common seamen. Your equipment will have been boarded previously in mismarked crates. Once at sea at a designated point, under cover of night the ship will turn ninety degrees to port and steam directly to eight miles off Dawenchong. This is over the horizon and cannot be seen by anyone on shore. Obviously this is now within Chinese territory. This place is chosen because it is also in a radar shadow from the mainland. There are several mountainous islands in this area that make radar ineffective. The mission is for this small ops team to go ashore on the southeast corner of Dawenchong Island. There they'll rendezvous with an agent and be given a very important package to bring back. In return, you'll give this small packet to the agent. In addition, the agent has indicated he has very important, very recent information of the PLA's strategy. This needs to be conveyed in person since he doesn't have it on paper. That's why we need a Chinese speaker on the team. As soon as the agent has passed you the packet and relayed his oral information, the team will return to the ship and proceed at flank speed immediately back to Naha. There the package, you, and the team will be flown to Yokosuka. An armed escort will be waiting to accompany you to deliver the package and the briefing to the XO of the 7th Fleet." I'm thinking, this must be some package with all the secrecy and now an armed escort.

This is an extremely dangerous, highly sensitive special operation. The ship will drop my team in a power raft and then retrieve it once the mission has been carried out. My job is to make sure that the mission is carried out successfully. I'm glad for the physical training now because I have to participate directly on the pickup.

The raft has both gas and electric motors. The team will use the stronger gas motor until we're three miles from shore, then shift to the quieter electric motor. Should weather not permit a landing on Dawenchong Island, the captain is ordered to turn out to sea and wait until the next night. There is only a two-night window to meet the agent due to the extreme danger to the agent.

When I board the ship I meet Lt. Commander Madera, the ship's captain. He's obviously overqualified to command this vessel. He tells me that he knew something was unusual when he was transferred to 1037 and summoned to HQ for briefing regarding this voyage. As we go over the orders and the chart, he says he can calculate the current, wind, and tide to drop this ship on a dime exactly eight miles off the coast at 0200 two days from now.

Next, I meet the team. It is composed of four men, CWO Clemmons and three well-built and eager seamen named Slaughter, Walker, and Cohan. When we are two hours out from the drop point I make a last check with the team. Clemmons tells me, "Sir, we have a problem. Two of the men became deathly ill about two hours ago. The ship's medic was called and found they have temperatures over 102, continuous vomiting, nausea, diarrhea, and abdominal cramps. These are classic symptoms of food poisoning. One of the men brought some sushi on board and didn't keep it refrigerated."

I ask very pointedly, "Why, as the commanding officer of this critical mission, wasn't I advised when they experienced the first symptoms?"

Clemmons tells me, somewhat self-righteously, "Sir, we're not crybabies. We carry out our missions no matter what."

"They can't perform if their pants are full of shit and they're throwing up."

I have two choices. One is to scrub the mission. That is clearly untenable. The second is to go with a smaller team. I'm certainly not in as good a shape as the team members, but there is only this one choice. The good news is we don't plan on doing any swimming, even though we will have on life belts and thermal suits to ward off the cold. If everything goes right the mission should take about four hours, depending on sea conditions. The tides in this area are not strong. By launching at 0200 we will have the tide running with us on the escape.

The onshore agent has a group who will plant incendiaries on fishing boats in the harbor on the northwest coast to draw attention away from the landing point. When the team determines that it will be able to land at the designated point they will make contact with the agent who will in turn radio his group to detonate the explosives.

At H-hour we let the raft over the side and climb in—Clemmons, Walker, and me. We carry AK-47s for armament. There is a quarter moon providing just enough light to see what we're doing. We shove off and head toward Dawenchong. At approximately three miles off the coast I give the order quietly to Clemmons, "Switch to the electric motor." My knees are beginning to ache from the pounding the raft is taking. When we're one mile out, we send a weak radio signal toward the agent. He returns it promptly and we head in. Soon we see some light in the sky to the north from the fires his accomplices have set. When we hit the beach, two men come out of the shelter of the trees with a package in their hands. Clemmons and Walker position themselves to detect any undesirable movement. I double wrap the package in waterproof bags and give the small packet to the agent. I assume it's his payoff. I tell Clemmons and Walker to prepare to shove off as soon as the agent passes on the other intel about the PLA's strategy. The agent speaks clearly but hurriedly for about twenty seconds.

All of a sudden, Walker fires off several rounds into the trees. "I saw something move," he says. Now we have to get out fast. The agent and his accomplices take off immediately into the woods, cursing Walker as they run. Fortunately, there is no sign of life as we power out to sea using the electric motor. After three miles I order Clemmons, "Switch to the gas motor and head ninety degrees east at flank speed."

My knees are throbbing. The tide is still running out but a northwesterly wind is making the sea choppy. In about twenty minutes we spot the ship and signal it to turn toward us. Madera brings the ship up to us spot on and we clamber aboard. They have to pull me up as my legs are totally wasted. Once we're on deck he orders flank speed and we get out to sea before anyone on shore can possibly spot us. My knees are packed in ice to keep the swelling down.

The time is 0540 and dawn is just breaking in the east over the Pacific. We radio the code word to 7th Fleet HQ informing them the mission is successful and the merchandise is in hand. I put in writing what the agent told me, although it is very minimal information thanks to Walker. In one day we are in Naha with the prize. My legs are still aching and I have a noticeable limp. After thanking Madera, the team and I debark. Cohan and Slaughter are fully recovered, highly embarrassed and apologetic. We board a waiting plane and land in Japan before noon. The team returns to their command where I expect they will face disciplinary action for their lack of foresight in endangering the mission. The security escort picks me up and we head directly to the 7th Fleet HQ. On arrival I'm taken immediately to the executive officer. I debrief on the mission and hand over the package along with the limited intel that the agent gave me. The XO isn't too happy about missing something that was allegedly very important. Later I learn that the package contained highly confidential information on the buildup of the PLA, the People's Liberation Army. The short oral report mentioned that the PLA high command is turning attention to technological developments. What this means we don't know since the agent didn't have time to elaborate.

That business concluded I meet my intel team members who have arrived. We proceed with our planned mission. I report to Braun one last time. He asks if everything is on schedule and if there are any problems. Then he closes by saying, "Commander, I want to emphasize one more time how important this mission is and how secure the real purpose must remain. Commander Howell will be your main contact here. All arrangements have been made through his office. As you prepare for Korea he will provide transportation for your team. Good luck,"

A storm is coming in, making flying nearly impossible. For three days we're kept in Yokosuka by the storm off the Sea of Japan. Finally, our gear is loaded and on 4 November we take off for Seoul, Korea. From there we'll cover all the important bases that have intelligence operations. Korea is an important site. Here intel activity is at its highest level. The principle targets of interest are China and Russia, not North Korea. Air Force radar sites maintained by the Korean Air Force and Army monitor such sensitive missions as the U-2. They also monitor any unusually high amount of air or space activity.

Immediately on landing we head to Yongsan Garrison north of Seoul. This is the U.S.'s main Army base in Korea. It also supports the U.S. naval command with facilities. During the war it housed not only U.S. troops but soldiers from Thailand, Australia, and the Philippines. It is the site of the major intel ops in Korea. Yongsan also supports smaller local camps.

The reception is one that we know to expect: guarded. The first thing we do is meet with the senior staff and brief them on our purpose. My pitch is, "This is not a standard inspection. We are not here to critique or evaluate the effectiveness of your command. We assume operational excellence. Our job is to look, with you, for ways to fulfill your mission in the same or better processes without having to add or subtract staff."

This does not immediately change minds or manner. But as we show our true colors the staff comes to think and act differently. They ask for ideas, share their ideas and experiences. Gradually, by going through all aspects of the operation we build a sizeable list of possible improvements that might make joint intelligence more than a dream. Although the naval command is based at Yongsan Garrison, it runs its own intel operation. There the reception is more relaxed. It could be that through the walls from the Army side the Navy staff knew what was coming. Or the fact that a naval officer is heading the team makes it more palatable. All goes smoothly and in two weeks we move on.

The next stop is Osan Air Force Base about sixty kilometers south of Seoul. It's the more important of the two Air Force installations in Korea. Unlike many airbases on foreign soil Osan AFB was built by America in the early 1950s. Multiple bombing operations have been run from this base. Since it is close to North Korea, its positioning for intel operations is excellent. Although the number of personnel and equipment have been drawn down since the end of the Korean War, many of these operations are still important in maintaining a peaceful attitude in this part of Asia. Again we're met cordially but with some wariness. The CO, a decorated warrior, asks bluntly, "Commander, what do you think you can teach us about frontline intelligence activity?"

My reply is, "Sir, we're not here to tell. We're here to learn. We want to see how a well- run unit performs so that we can share it in our report. The goal is to collect the best examples from the region. From it we expect to find a more cost-effective field intel model."

This cools him off. We spend more than a week in Osan before moving to Kunsan AB for a short visit. By the time we finish there is not a Korean stone left unturned. We don't find any problems but do gather a wealth of ideas. How practical they are is a question for the high command. On 5 December we return to Yokosuka to debrief our operation among ourselves and pull together our individual perceptions. It is somewhat surprising that our team members share many of the same views about what they have seen.

When we've gathered our preliminary impressions, we move on to our next group of facilities, all in Japan. First is Fleet Activities Yokosuka, located on the southern end of Tokyo Bay in the immediate proximity of the Japanese capital. It is the most important military facility operated by the United States in Japan. It is very close to China and Russia. It's also the largest naval facility in the Pacific area.

The primary mission of Fleet Activities Yokosuka is to support all U.S. and allied units in the Pacific area. Our reception here is much better than in Korea, probably because Admiral Braun is supporting the mission. We find the staff is exceptionally sharp, as one would expect so close to the seat of power. They are full of ideas that could improve operations. To date, many of the ideas have to do with greater efficiency through scaling the operation. That is, through greater size they can find efficiencies, better intel speed to field, and overall higher effectiveness. This is not a great surprise. It's common sense that has been over ridden by interservice rivalry.

After we finish in Yokosuka we fly north to Misawa AB. Misawa is located on the far northern end of Honshu Island, about 425 miles from Tokyo. Prior to World War II, the base was used for the training sessions of those who attack Pearl Harbor. It is isolated and very cold from the freezing winds off Siberia. During the latter days of the war Misawa experienced almost total damage, with up to 90 percent of the base completely destroyed by U.S. bombardments.

The base has supported many flights during the Korean and Vietnam Wars. Its northern location makes it an excellent spot for secret surveillance missions in Russia and China. Maybe because it is so isolated the staff is happy to see friendly faces. We find the reception very cordial. The CO is a Japanese American Army major. He's very sharp.

"Welcome, Commander. We've been looking forward to your visit. We don't see many VIPs here. I guess we need to build a Marriott Hotel around our hot springs. We can provide plenty of Suntory scotch, though, to keep you warm."

Since Misawa has a major intel mission and operates on its own, away from HQ, there is great esprit de corp. Everyone feels like comrades. Our work there lasts nearly a month and we spend Christmas there. We're so far north that some of the staff produce a visit by Santa Claus to everyone's delight. I'm induced to give a short speech to mark the holiday.

"Christmas is more than a Christian holiday. It marks a time of year for many people of different faiths, cultures, and nationalities to share the joy of giving. Giving is a gift in itself. It reminds us of how much we love family and friends—well, some of them anyway." The group laughs heartedly. "It feels good to make someone else happy, doesn't it? Giving brings love and good will from the depths of our hearts. It makes us better people. Our group knew we would be here to share the holiday with you so we want to give you something. Through the acquisitive skills of our CWOs, we've managed to secure some special victuals that you might not get from the commissary in Zama. On New Year's Eve we're going to take over the kitchen, assuming the cooks don't mind a day off. We are going to cook for you and serve you. We'll even do the dishes. The menu will consist of fresh, handmade mac and cheese, homemade spaghetti with fresh beef and pork meatballs, pizza, apple pie, cherry pie, chocolate cake, and ice cream, plus wine from Napa Valley not ordinarily found in the commissary. This is our gift to you. Happy New Year and bon appetit."

The work at Misawa is very interesting. Their insights regarding western Russia and northern China are extremely useful. We gather a large amount of very rich and useful examples for improving remote intel services. When we finish here we fly to the other key airbase in Japan—Yokota AB, located just north of Tokyo. It is an important base but more for logistics than intelligence.

Our next stop is the Army base at Zama. Camp Zama is a huge facility, by far the largest U.S. base in Japan. Being the Army's HQ, Zama supports a large office building. It's two stories high, in the shape of an X. In front is a ceremonial entrance with two flag poles on a curved drive to a covered entrance. It sits on a ridge above a plain of rice paddies for as far as you can see. Zama is the head of a network of bases across southern Japan. We aren't there more than ten days when Sy Matsumoto comes to me and says, "There is something smelly here and it isn't the fish. Park and I agree that something big and bad is happening. We are going to ground on this, with your permission, sir. It may take a while to get the skunk out of the hole, if there is one, so please don't go any faster than is necessary to finish this site. We'll keep you informed, but at this point I recommend we keep this just between us. It wouldn't be helpful if all of a sudden we all start to act suspiciously."

I keep the rest of our team on their assigned tasks. Because Zama is so large and it supports other bases we don't have to work hard to keep busy. One night three weeks later Matsumoto and Park come in with grim smiles on their faces. "We got the bastards!" says Sy.

They go on to explain, "There is a large black market network operating out of Zama and into the surrounding bases. The way it is working is they chip away a small piece here and a small piece there so it isn't noticeable. For example, a shipping manifest shows 200 cartons of something. Only 198 show up with the explanation of breakage or pilferage on route. It's not uncommon and the shortfall is too small to make it worth the time and effort to go through the paperwork to report it. Shortages, breakage, and pilferages are a thousand drops of blood coming out of all the bases. We don't know the volume or how long it has been going on. We find no evidence that the Army supply troops are in on the deal. The losses take place during transport to or from a base. Make no mistake about it: this is a big deal. We've got the names and even pictures of the top guys. We even took them to dinner and drinks at a sushi bar to oil them up. They believe that we're interested in getting in on the take and cutting them into a network we're operating out of Yokota. Park doesn't talk much so they don't get his Korean accent. He tells them he is from Hokkaido and part of the aboriginal Ainu clan. They've never met an Ainu before so they didn't know what he should look or sound like."

"Great job! Congratulations. Are you at a point where I can bring in the MP commander and the local police?"

"Better wait on the police, sir. We're not certain that some of the local constabulary might be getting a piece of the action."

As we finish our work at Zama in the next couple weeks the bad guys are caught and are being held for trail. The word gets out and Park and Matsumoto are heroes. They are hounded for details that can't be divulged because of the upcoming trial.

Our last Japanese base is Kadena AFB on Okinawa. The island of Okinawa is 1,000 miles south of Tokyo. Kadena is the biggest

Air Force installation in the Pacific. It is a large and important base because of its location just few hundred miles off the east China coast. It is a major storage facility for munitions and is also an important intel center. From their proximity to China's central coast, recon and electronics surveillance operations are extremely valuable. We get nothing but cooperation there. They are happy to show what they can do and could do under better circumstances.

By the end of March we depart Okinawa for Taiwan, which houses the sub-unified command of the U.S. armed forces in the Pacific. It was originally formed as the Formosa Liaison Center after the first Straits crisis of September 1954. In November 1955, the FLC became the Taiwan Defense Command. The command reports directly to the CINCPAC. The command is composed of personnel from all branches of the U.S. armed forces and has its headquarters in Taipei. Taipei is the capital of Taiwan and is located on the north end of the island. This is the base that is the closest to mainland China, less than 200 miles away.

Given its proximity to China there is an intense intelligence function around Taipei. Our reception is guarded to say the least. The intel CO, a Chinese American army colonel named Wong, greets me with the admonition, "Commander, we have probably the best intel staff and function in the Pacific, if not the world. Over the past ten years there isn't anything that we have not considered, whether in the end we adopt or disregard it. This group knows its strategic importance and performs at the highest level 24/7/365. I doubt that you will find anything that is not superbly managed by me or my predecessors in this command. What do you think you can tell us about field intelligence operations?"

It's very clear that he's not happy to see us and does not intend to make this a cordial visit. By now I'm pretty tired of provincialism. "Sir, I assure you that this is not an inspection. Rather, it is a research project aimed at improving intelligence operations across the Pacific region. It has the full support of all service commands and the mandate for all to cooperate."

We are not here to disrupt your operation or usurp your power. However, we do intend to fulfill our mission and expect that your staff will cooperate."

He takes a step back and a deep breath. He's probably never had a junior officer talk to him this way. Still, he's smart enough to see that I hold all the cards. He reluctantly loosens up, but only slightly. "Commander, you will have our full cooperation, but operational effectiveness must not be hindered. That cannot be tolerated and a breach in intelligence cannot be allowed." It's his way of saying, Okay, you SOB, but don't get in our way.

This group is the least cooperative we've encountered. We have to pull teeth to elicit any substantial information. We're given the runaround. Our requests for meetings or information are delayed and must be repeated. When we ask to see how they operate we are given only summary views and nothing that a fresh intel grad wouldn't already know. What could have been a treasure trove turns out to be a frustrating and lengthy exercise. This place is a prime example of how intel should be a joint operation that fits into and supports the larger strategic picture. I'm only one step away from filing a complaint with Admiral Braun. But my job is to survey intel ops and, by god, that's what we are going to do no matter how difficult the Taipei commander makes it. My dilemma is how to describe their recalcitrance without creating another NIS-type incident. In the end, we'll probably just gather what we can and get on with the mission, but I would sincerely like to kick this colonel's ass clear back to D.C.

As we prepare to depart from Taipei after nearly two frustrating months I receive an unexpected courier envelope. It is not government business so I can only guess that it might be from Fred. I take it back to my room and open it with great trepidation. In it are two envelopes, one large and one small. The small one bears Fred's letterhead. I open it first. It reads:

Wilfred A. Arbuckle
Seventeen-Mile Drive
Carmel, California 93922

Dear Michael,

Betsy and I hope you are doing well and are keeping your health during your travels.

We have given a great deal of consideration to what I am about to propose. We hope you will agree with our conclusions.

Drs. Levine and Freiberg concur that Lynda's state is highly unlikely to change now or in the distant future. They will continue to work with her at The Retreat. But there is little hope. Eventually, we will find a permanent facility that is designed for cases such as hers. Clearly, this is a painful, heartbreaking decision, but the only practical one.

Therefore, since I have Lynda's power of attorney, we plan to file for dissolution of your marriage to Lynda. We know this is another awful decision for you. However, it is only reasonable that you be free to pursue the rest of your life without this hanging over you. Choosing not to do it will not in any way improve Lynda's situation.

Please read the papers in the other envelope. There are two copies of the Petition to Dissolve. Our attorney has provided counsel on how to do this as quickly and painlessly as possible. If you agree to our proposal please sign where indicated. A return, prepaid courier envelope from DHL is included. In due course you will receive the completed transaction.

We love you, Michael, and only wish that you had not been so afflicted by this. Of course we will continue happily to care for Davey until such time as you can take him. If you come through San Francisco on your travels, please stop to visit with us. We miss you very much. Davey is doing very well and needs to see his daddy too. Take care of yourself.

Affectionately,
Fred

I'm trembling as I reread this. What courage it must have taken for Fred and Betsy to recommend this. How I hurt for them. These two wonderful people have had nothing but grief since I came into their lives. Despite the fact that it makes no sense, I feel very guilty for everything that has happened. Divorcing Lynda while she is incapacitated feels like cowardice to me. On the other hand, given my constant movement and the very high probability that she will never recover, what can I realistically do for her? It's not an easy decision. In the end despite their offer I must take responsibility for this decision. After a couple days of rereading the letter, sleepless nights of running the pros and cons of the situation and putting off the inevitable, reluctantly I sign the documents. I include a personal note in the envelope.

Michael C. Still
Lieutenant Commander
United States Navy

Dear Fred and Betsy,

I am very moved by your decision. You are the two most courageous people I have ever known. My life has been greatly enhanced by knowing and loving you.

I am profoundly sorry that so much of our time together has been in such painful circumstances. There seems to be no reason to go against your wishes. The papers are signed as required.

At the end of this assignment I expect and hope to return to the States to a new duty station. I am most anxious to see Davey again. You can be absolutely certain that the next time I am in California of course I will stop to see you and Davey. We can discuss his future at that time.

With great love and admiration,
Michael

I leave the envelope with instructions to arrange a pickup by DHL as quickly as possible.

Now, we must continue our mission. Our last group of bases is in the Philippines. The Philippines provided the fourth largest force under the United Nations Command during the Korean War. During the Vietnam War, it supported civil and medical operations. The two principle U.S. bases are the Subic Bay Naval Base and Clark Air Force Base.

We begin our mission at Clark forty miles northwest of Manila. Clark AFB is a very large facility that covers over 200 square miles. The Bataan Death March came north from Corregidor in early 1942 and passed the gates of this base. The Philippines is a rugged landscape of rainforest and mountains. It's easy to see how difficult a forced march of eighty miles without food or water would have been a trail of agony and death. Now, Clark is the focal point of the combined Filipino and American forces. It is a backbone of logistical support for Vietnam.

We arrive at the beginning of the rainy season. The temperature is in the low ninety degrees and the rain turns everything into a steam bath. Still, the reception is cordial. Perhaps the word has filtered down from our other stops and people have finally accepted our mission for what it is. I'm asked to see the base commander, General Vernon. The intel commander takes me to him.

"Mr. Still, we're happy to have you here. Personally, I agree with your mission to improve intel across the region and among the services. Be assured that Colonel Evers here will provide all the cooperation you require." Clark is a major intel center with the latest equipment and excellent personnel. The senior staff and their personnel are cooperative and our three-week visit runs quickly and smoothly.

We go south from there to Subic Bay, which is west across the bay from Manila. Subic is a major ship-repair, supply, and rest and recreation facility. The Naval Supply Depot here handles the largest volume of fuel oil of any naval facility in the world. The naval base is the largest overseas military installation of the U.S. armed forces after Clark. This is a significant intel center. On the surface it seems a prime candidate for synergetic operations. Surprisingly, despite General Vernon's statement, we note a competitive edge that probably impedes the flow of information between the two facilities. It could be that he's just playing the game of support. When questioned in private a number of officers agree with that assessment. In retrospect, the info that we obtained at Clark is not all that enlightening. After Taipei we were so relieved to be treated well that we might have relaxed a little. I think we've been taken for a ride.

* * *

After six weeks in the Philippines, we fly back to Yokosuka to organize our data and prepare our report. In the end we believe we have a solid case for a joint intelligence system. We have recommendations as to how this can be accomplished through economies of scale. In the end no command should have to lose positions or operating budgets. As the commanding officer of this little group, I'm responsible for the final report. Everyone has given me their input and we've discussed the findings in depth. Now I put it all together and turn it over to Admiral Braun. I don't know if we can claim any credit for this, but a year later after thirty years of discussion and frustration a joint intelligence system is launched in 1973.

Once the report is handed in, I plan to take a few days leave before I fly back to California. Before that happens, I receive an urgent summons to Porter Howell's office. Whatever craft of peace and happiness I'd built in my work is about to be capsized.

11

S.O.S

The late summer morning is crystal clear with a brilliant sun bouncing its light off the ocean. Living in Carmel is the next best thing to heaven, except for the taxes. Carmen comes into the breakfast patio where Fred is waiting for Betsy. She's is clearly upset. "Señor, el niño no está bien."

The trio start for Davey's room as Carmen describes Davey's symptoms: labored breathing, pale skin, dizziness. When they enter the room Josefa is at the crib side talking to Davey and trying to console him. Fred and Betsy ask simultaneously, When did this start?

Carmen says, "This morning when Josefa came in he was still asleep. She came back after getting his bath ready and he is trying to sit up and can't. He keeps falling to one side or the other. It's like he can't get his balance. He's almost three years old and has always had good balance."

The baby is clearly in distress. "Josefa, call an ambulance immediately," Fred orders. In ten minutes the security cruiser leads an ambulance into the driveway. Josefa lets the paramedics in and leads them quickly to Davey's room. The security men wait outside in case they might be needed. The paramedics quickly check vital signs and confirm that Davey is having trouble breathing and his heart beat is slow, labored, and irregular. They confirm he needs to go to the hospital immediately. Within twenty minutes Davey is in

ER at Community Hospital. Fred, Betsy, and Carmen follow quickly behind. When they arrive the admitting nurse says he is being seen already. She shows them to the waiting room just off the ER lobby.

In about thirty minutes a doctor comes out. "We're running tests on the baby's heart, lungs, and other vital organs. We should have a preliminary diagnosis within an hour." The three sit with hardly a word until Betsy asks Carmen, "How was Davey last night when you put him to bed?"

Carmen replies, "We were playing with him and he seemed to be tiring, so we got him ready for bed and watched him until he went to sleep like we always do, pobrecito." She starts to cry softly. "I'm so sorry. Lo siento tanto. He didn't look different other than seeming to be tired, cansado."

In less than an hour the doctor comes back. He reports, "We're going to transfer him to the pediatric ward. Both sides of his heart seem to be laboring. We've called Dr. Rashkin, the head of pediatrics, to come in right away. He should be here soon. I suggest you go to the café and have a cup of coffee. By the time you get back we should know a lot more."

"What's wrong, doctor?" Fred asks.

"At this point we don't know for certain. I don't want to upset you with only a partial diagnosis. One thing is clear, and that is his heart is laboring. It could just be an infection that can be treated with antibiotics, but at this stage we don't know and we don't want to take any chances."

No one wants to leave the waiting room until Fred says, "I think we should go for coffee and maybe something to eat, Betsy. We've not had any breakfast." Betsy nods and the three walk somberly toward the café. Within forty-five minutes they are back in the waiting room.

In about thirty minutes another doctor comes out, sits down in the group, and introduces himself. "I'm Doctor Rashkin. I've checked the baby thoroughly. We've run an electrocardiogram on this heart. There clearly is a problem in both the left and right ventricles. His blood pressure, both systolic and diastolic, are low and somewhat erratic. His heart is working very hard to move blood through. This might be a small, undetectable birth defect that is simply worsening as he grows. Now, they are conducting an ultrasound and an MRI. Then, we'll do a CAT scan to see if there was any damage to his brain from insufficient blood flow. I don't see any symptoms there, so it should come back negative. These are going to take a few hours. You can wait or go home and we will call you just as soon as we have a clear diagnosis. Do you have any questions?"

They were too stunned to ask. After a long pause, Fred responds, "Do you have any idea what might have happened so suddenly? Yesterday he was playing with Carmen without any apparent problems."

"It's hard to tell. Usually, the body is able to deal with some abnormality until it reaches a certain state. It's like walking along a cliff without a problem. Then there is a misstep and you fall off. In this case, preliminarily I caution, it may be a minor birth defect that just got worse until it is causing a partial failure of the heart. But we still don't know how severe it is. The moment that we are certain of the cause and treatment we will let you know."

"Doctor," Betsy asked, "How long might that be?"

"To be absolutely certain it could take most of the day. We've got a lot of tests to run and results to look at and correlate to know what the problem truly is. We want to be sure."

"Can we see him?"

"Yes, for a few minutes. He's sleepy but it might be a good thing for him to see familiar faces. I'll send the pediatric nurse to take you to him."

The nurse leads the way through the pediatric ward. Betsy looks in the doors to see children in several states of distress or recovery. She is an emotional and soft-hearted person and she is putting every ounce of her strength into dealing with these scenes. Carmen is close to her, holding her arm like the good friend she is. When they arrive at Davey's room Betsy can hardly hold back her tears. Davey is hooked up to a saline IV and has an oxygen mask over his nose and mouth. He appears to be asleep and his breathing is shallow. Betsy touches him and his eyes open. He sees her and Carmen and smiles faintly. He can't talk because of the mask. In a minute he goes back to sleep. The nurse comes back in and says, "After he has had a little more rest they will start the next battery of tests. He'll be very busy for the next few hours so I suggest you go home and rest the best you can. We will call you the moment that we have a clear and complete diagnosis." Carmen says tearfully, "I stay with Rubio."

Fred nods that is okay. He and Betsy know the close tie that she has with Davey. When they get home Josefa comes running to them, "Cómo está Rubio?" Fred tells her a short version of what has happened and she is about to burst into tears like everyone in the family.

Betsy asks Fred, "Should we contact Michael?"

"Not until we know more. It could be, hopefully will be, an easily fixable problem."

In mid-afternoon Doctor Rashkin calls and Fred puts the phone speaker on. "Mr. and Mrs. Arbuckle, it is clear that his heart is losing the ability to pump enough blood to the rest of the body. Although this is generally a long-term or chronic condition, it may have a sudden onset without any warning. What triggers the sudden change could be a number of things, but it often occurs after stress such as vigorous exercise or an infection. In his case I don't believe that is what happened. Whatever the cause, the tests indicate that the heart can't bear the strain anymore and is beginning to fail. What we have is failure on both sides of the heart. Systolic heart failure is when the heart is unable to pump blood out of the heart. Diastolic heart failure is when the heart muscles are stiff and do not fill up with blood easily. Over time the heart muscles can stiffen to the point where they can no longer fill with blood or expel sufficient amounts to keep the body healthy. As a result of a weakened heart, fluid can build up in the lungs, liver, and gastrointestinal tract; it's called congestive heart failure. Have you seen any fluid buildup or swelling in his hands or legs lately?"

Everyone looks at each other and shakes their head. "Heart failure may affect only one side of the heart. In this case it's apparent on both sides."

"What can we do, doctor?" Fred asks.

"Mr. Arbuckle, we need to operate as soon as possible to find and repair the abnormalities. If you agree I'll be the lead surgeon and Dr. Harmeet from Stanford will be in the process by video. He is a highly regarded cardio man who has years of experience with pediatric patients."

"By all means go ahead, doctor, quickly."

"We'll let him rest overnight and load him with antibiotics. The nurses will bathe him first thing in the morning, and then he'll be taken to the sterile pre-op at about 7:00 a.m. There his body will be bathed again in an antiseptic wash to ensure that nothing can get into the chest cavity. He'll have an oxygen mask to help him breathe. When he is fully prepped he'll be taken into the OR and we'll start the operation. In addition to myself and Dr. Harmeet looking in, there will be an anesthesiologist and pediatric and surgical nurses. All these people are very experienced. He'll be in good hands. The operation should start at 8:00 a.m. and take three to four hours."

"Thank you, doctor; we will be back in the morning."

Carmen says, "I stay with Rubio tonight."

The doctor says that's fine. "It'll be good for him to feel your presence. The room has a chair that turns into a bed, and the nurses will bring you blankets and pillows as well as something to eat."

Fred and Betsy drive home silently. They meet Josefa and bring her up to date. She says she'll prepare clean clothes that they can take to Carmen in the morning.

The night passes slowly and no one sleeps well. At 9:00 a.m. Fred and Betsy drive to the hospital. They have Carmen's clean clothes and toiletries in a small suitcase. Carmen is in the waiting room when they arrive. There is a coffee pot in the room along with the usual out-of-date magazines.

At 10:30 a nurse comes in and says Dr. Rashkin would like to see them. She takes them to a small room near the OR. As soon as they enter they know this is not going to be good news. It has only been two and a half hours since the operation was to start, and it was planned for three to four hours.

Dr. Rashkin motions them to sit down. "We encountered something unexpected. Just as we were about to start the operation David stopped breathing. Immediately, I applied CPR and the anesthesiologist increased the oxygen volume and pressure. When there was no response I injected adrenaline directly into the heart. Nothing happened. There was no time to lose so I opened his chest as quickly and safely as I could. I felt his heart. It was still. I started massaging it to force blood through it. He wasn't responding. I noticed that his heart in my hand was very thick and inflexible for such a young child. On closer examination we saw it was larger than normal. The muscle around the heart was quite thick and felt like heavy leather. Next, I opened his heart and saw that the septum, which is the wall separating the two ventricles, was almost rigid. The heart operates through a series of valves, like little gates. To function effectively these valves must be flexible to open and close at the right time, be synchronized. For some reason this boy's heart has gradually grown thicker and stiffer over time. The pressure was affecting the valves so they couldn't work correctly. I checked these and found some degree of shredding. Basically, they are wearing out from the stress. It must have been a slow process since his last physical did not show any abnormalities. This can happen, just like a stroke or heart attack. One day you are fine, the next day you aren't."

After taking a breath the doctor continued, "I kept massaging his heart and I asked Dr. Harmeet if he had a solution. He says he's never seen such rigidity in a young heart. It's called hypertrophic cardiomyopathy. This can occur in athletes, but I've never seen such a severe a case in a small child. We immediately checked the instruments for brain activity. I was concerned that with the heart stopping the brain was not getting any blood. It was confirmed: His brain had been over twenty minutes with little or no oxygenated blood. Nevertheless, I kept massaging the heart in the hope of restarting it. We gave the heart another shot of adrenalin. After thirty minutes with no response I knew for certain that his brain was severely damaged. The instruments showed no brain activity. I considered a heart transplant. But even if we can find one of a size he can handle, he will still have been without brain function. Basically, he'd be in a coma for the rest of his life."

Betsy and Carmen burst out sobbing. Fred drops his head into his hands and wraps his eyes in his handkerchief. The next message from the doctor is clear.

"Davey is gone. I'm so sorry. He's such a beautiful little boy. We did everything possible to save him, but his heart just failed. We'll keep him here until you can make arrangements."

Slowly, the trio walks out of the hospital to the car that Ramon has waiting. They drive home without a word. Finally, Fred says, "I have to call Michael in Japan."

Betsy asks, "What about Lynda?"

"I don't know. We probably should call Dr. Freiberg for her opinion."

"It is now about noon in California; that would make it about 4:00 a.m. tomorrow in Tokyo. I'll put in a call to the Naval Intelligence Center in Yokosuka when it is 8:00 a.m. there. They will be able to find him if I tell them it is an emergency."

At 4 p.m. Fred picks up the phone and calls the number in the Tokyo that Michael had given him. An operator answers and Fred asks for Commander Howell.

"This is Commander Howell. Is this Mr. Arbuckle?"

"Yes, it is, commander. How did you know me?"

"Sir, late in the war I enlisted in the Merchant Marines and sailed some of your routes. When the war ended I transferred to the Navy. I've long admired your steamship line and know that you headed it. I know Commander Still is related to you. What can I do for you?"

"Commander, we had a tragedy here. I need to talk to my son-in-law right away."

"You say a tragedy, sir. I don't mean to pry, but can you tell me more so I know how to handle this when I pass the call on to Commander Still?"

"Yes, his son died of heart failure this morning. He was in OR prepping for open heart surgery and his heart simply failed."

"Oh my god. Does Commander Still know that his son was in trouble?"

"No. It happened so suddenly we haven't had time to contact him until now."

"That is absolutely horrible. Will you want an emergency leave for him?"

"Yes, I'm sure he'll want that."

"Very well, sir; I'll find him and have him call you ASAP. Please accept my most heartfelt condolences."

Fred hangs up, trying very hard to maintain his composure. He goes into the library and pours himself a double shot of vodka. In two gulps he has it down and pours another. Then he settles down to wait for the dreaded call. Betsy, Carmen, and Josefa are in Davey's room, talking and consoling each other.

An hour later the phone rings and Fred grabs the receiver. The call is from a salesman offering who knows what because Fred slams the receiver down as soon as the pitch starts. Now he's breathing heavily and perspiring. He's very angry. He takes another sip and settles back in his chair again. In ten minutes the phone rings again. Fred hesitates and then answers it.

"Dad, its Michael. What's the matter? Commander Howell said it was important."

"Yes, son. It's important. There isn't any way to tell you this, Michael." He pauses, afraid to deliver this terrible blow. "Davey looked very tired yesterday morning when Josefa went to get him up. We called the EMTs immediately and they said he needed to go to the hospital because he was having trouble breathing. They took him into emergency right away, then into the pediatric ward for tests. To make a long story short, they had to operate and Davey died of heart failure in the OR this morning."

I scream into the phone. "What? No, no, how can this happen? He's a healthy little boy. How, why? It's not possible. My god, he's my baby, my son."

Fred waits for several seconds while I get myself under control. Then he goes through the whole story of the last two days from the time that Carmen called him in the breakfast patio to the last meeting with the doctor.

I'm out of control. I'm sobbing into the phone, murmuring, "No, no, no!" Finally, a minute later I calm down enough to discuss what to do next.

"Fred, have you told Lynda yet?" Fred says they haven't and believes that I'll want to do it personally. I agree.

"I've just finished my mission. I was going to take a couple days leave but I'm going to get out of here as quickly as possible. I'll send you info on my arrival time and airport, probably Oakland. Maybe Ramon can pick me up. Dad, I'll call you back tomorrow about an hour earlier."

Soon after, Fred and Betsy call Dr. Freiberg's private number. When she comes on the line and when she hears the news she's shocked as well. The doctor says she needs to talk to The Retreat to learn Lynda's state and how she might take the news.

I immediately put in my request for emergency leave. Then, I go back to my room and collapse onto my bed. I'm still in shock. I put a pillow over my face and scream, "No, no, no, no" into it over and over. I can't accept the loss of my son. It isn't right. Parents should go before their children. That is the natural order. There is something terribly wrong here. Did I dream this? At that moment the phone rings. It is Commander Howell. "Michael, how are you holding up? This is a horrible thing. Your request for emergency leave is granted and we will have a seat on a MATS flight for you this afternoon." In Monterey, Dr. Freiberg calls back within an hour. Fred and Betsy take the call together.

"How are you two doing? I'm very concerned about your mental health. You've had some heavy blows in the past year. Does Michael know yet? I've talked to the head psychiatrist at The Retreat. She says we should not keep it from Lynda until some future date. If she found out you didn't tell her when it happened, it would be a double blow. You should tell her within a couple of days at the most. Is Michael coming home immediately? If so you should wait and have him tell her." Fred thanks the doctor and hangs up. "Betsy, Michael should be home by tomorrow. I think he will want to talk to Lynda and break the news to her." Betsy agrees.

* * *

At 1800 I'm at the terminal at Yokosuka, not nearly as plush as a stateside commercial airport. I'm booked on a World Airways charter through MATS, the Military Air Transport System. I'm so upset that I can't sit still. I pace the terminal back and forth. There are other servicemen and their families waiting for the flight. When I see the little children laughing and playing my heart breaks again and I turn away and have to hold my breath so as not to cry. It's not fair to take a baby or even a child. They have a lifetime of joys and sorrows, triumph and failure to experience. This is a wound that will never heal.

Despite my pain as I pace the terminal, my eyes rest on a woman who is traveling with a baby and three youngsters all under ten. She is struggling to keep them entertained, so I go over to them and ask their names. They are Martha, Frank, and Billy. I ask them if they have a ball. When they say they have a tennis ball, I say, "Let's play circle ball. You toss it to me, I'll toss it to Martha, you bounce it to Frank and, Frank, you bounce it to Billy, Billy you toss it to me. The idea is to see if we can do it all the way around the circle without dropping the ball. Do you think we can?"

Of course, the kids all yell yes and start jumping up and down. Isn't it great how young children believe they can do anything and how eager they are to be challenged? If you walk into a kindergarten or primary grade class and ask if anyone can dance, all hands go up. They see no barriers. Unfortunately, life teaches us soon and often there seems to be nothing but barriers to overcome. My heart is pummeled by the contrast between the joy I feel in the presence of these children and the knowledge that I'll never experience such a moment with Davey again.

At boarding time there is an announcement, "Due to rough weather over the north Pacific there will be a short delay in departing." An hour later we're told it's time to board. I give the woman a hand with her baby and kid's luggage. By the time we finally get on the plane and take off I'm totally exhausted. I fall into a troubled sleep. Several hours into a very bumpy flight they serve what passes for dinner. I pass on it. I have no appetite. Finally, almost everyone falls asleep, even the small children. Sometime later the captain comes on the intercom and tells the passengers that there was a planned refueling stop in Anchorage, but there will be an unplanned stop in Cold Bay, Alaska, about 600 miles southwest of Anchorage. Cold Bay is at the beginning of the Aleutian Islands. It was established in World War II as a staging area for north Pacific flights. Despite its remoteness it is an active airport with a 10,000-foot runway.

The captain explains, "We saw an engine warning light from one of the starboard engines. The engine is still functioning with no signs to trouble, but to be safe we are diverting to Cold Bay. Customs and immigration officers are being flown to Cold Bay to process passengers so that you can go into the terminal until a replacement plane arrives." He closes with the news, "We should be landing in about three hours."

I calculate that it will take six hours or more to get a replacement plane here depending on where it comes from. By the time they transfer the baggage, reload the passengers, and refuel the plane we'll be lucky to get out of there before late afternoon. That means we won't get to California until after midnight if all goes well and it never does. When we get on the ground I'll check with the airline reps to see if they plan to call the emergency contact number of each passenger, explain the delay, and provide updated ETAs every couple of hours. I can't imagine that they won't but you can never be certain. God must really hate me by dealing this delay on top of Davey's death. If it's a test I think I'm clearly flunking.

In Alaska, it's cool to cold all the time. If you're in the Aleutian Islands it's cold to colder all the time. Cold Bay is mostly flat and enjoys the full effect of the arctic winds off the Bering Sea. There are only a couple hundred residents who mostly work at the airfield. When the passengers deplane, we'll face a temperature in the twenties with a strong wind that drops the wind chill factor into the low teens or worse.

Shortly before we land the chief purser comes on and says, "We can deplane and go into the terminal, but do not wander around. Remember this is our first landfall in the United States, so there will be customs and immigration agents to meet us and clear entry into the U.S. Once we arrive in Oakland, if you have been processed and have completed the customs card, you can go directly through to the public area of the terminal. Cold Bay is a busy transit point with full food services and rest areas." He apologizes for this inconvenience and reiterates that there is no danger. The pilot decided that in the interests of safety this was the best action to take. He goes on, "We've been told that the airline representatives will be calling your emergency contacts with the latest ETA. In addition, the arrival boards will be kept up to date."

I'm too tired to think about this anymore. "As you were, boy, better order a scotch and water and then relax."

I wake up to feel the plane decelerating and losing altitude. There is light on the horizon. I look at my watch and see it is a few minutes before noon local time. In the winter Alaska has only a couple hours of dim daylight at best. Looking out a window I see land in the distance. In a few minutes the plane makes a bumpy landing through a crosswind and then turns and taxis back to the terminal. The pilot comes on the intercom and welcomes us to the United States. He apologizes and assures us that the process is underway to get us to our destination as soon as possible.

The purser comes back on and reminds us that we have to stay in the terminal. Given the cold wind I doubt that will be a problem. He says the agents will arrive within the hour. In fact, they just learned that Cold Bay has one resident agent who will start processing as soon as we get settled in the terminal. There's no rush, he says, so we needn't form a long line. He closes by answering the question on everyone's mind: What about the replacement plane? He admits they don't have an ETA on that plane but have been told it's in the air and on the way from Seattle. I recheck my figures and estimate we should be out of here sometime in late afternoon, which is about dinner time in California. I look outside to see the weather; nothing special, just grey clouds and the normal wind.

When the door is opened, I grab Martha, Frank, and Billy and walk them head down into the wind toward the terminal. Once inside they catch their breath, jump up and down to get warm, and try to acclimate to this foreign place. Once again the resilience of children shines through!

When their mother, Carol, arrives behind us and unwraps the baby's face, I tell her I'll take the children on a walk around and find out what's happening as well as how prepared the station is to feed one hundred fifty travelers.

I find that already the kitchen is gearing up to feed the passengers and in general things look well organized. Undoubtedly, this is not the first flight that stopped here unexpectedly. It gives some comfort to know we're not on some isolated iceberg. The residents actually like to service the planes because they meet some new people and have something to do. I report back to Carol with the kids. When they have had enough running around I sit down next to her and ask her how she is holding up. Four kids under ten is a real load. She sighs and then starts crying.

"What's the matter? Did I say something inappropriate?"

"I'm sorry. I've just been under such a great strain the past couple of weeks. You see, my husband was killed in a plane crash in Korea last month. He was flying a little recon plane and a sudden gust of wind threw him into the side of a mountain. Now I have to get these babies home and find out how we're going to live."

"My god, that's terrible. You're actually doing a great job of holding them together." I decide not to add the burden of my loss to hers. There may be comfort in sharing problems, but I was raised to keep your troubles to yourself and work them out without saddling other people with them. It's very difficult not to share, but that's what I was taught. We talk for the next half hour as the kids play close by or doze off on the benches. Then there is an announcement. "The extra custom and immigration agents will be landing here within an hour. The replacement plane from Seattle should be here within three hours. As soon as the agents arrive we'll set them up in our customs area and you'll be able to start processing. We're sincerely sorry for this delay, but everything is moving along as rapidly as possible. In the meantime, the kitchen tells me they're ready to serve. Bon appetit."

After everyone has eaten, blankets and small pillows are distributed because the terminal is a bit chilly and we still have several hours to wait for the replacement plane. There are rooms for mothers to use to feed or change diapers. These people are truly ready for situations like ours. It's comforting to realize that some people really know and care about what they do. They even have a history and game room to entertain the children.

In time, everything winds down to waiting. When the kids come back we lay them down on the benches, cover them with a blanket, and let them go to sleep. This is just another adventure to them.

I offer to help Carol get the baby out of her seat and laid on the bench with a blanket wrapped around her. Carol says she is almost two and I start coughing to hide my emotion. I tell her I need to get a drink and leave. This is almost too much. How long will it be before I stop seeing Davey in other children?

By mid-afternoon we're told the replacement plane is in the landing pattern. Finally, the 707 lands and everyone gives out a big cheer. In an hour the plane is refueled, the baggage is loaded, and we prepare to embark. That's when the terminal staff come out to say what a pleasure it was to meet us. Some people take pictures with the staff. There are even a few tears on both sides. Then we are back out into the wind, onto the plane, and once again on our way after this ten-hour unplanned stopover.

The next six hours go slowly but uneventfully, thank god. About an hour out of Oakland across the bay from San Francisco, I get up and go forward to the purser's station. "Long night, isn't it?" The purser nods wearily. He's part of the replacement because the initial crew would have well exceeded their work day.

"We've a lady on board, a recent Air Force widow who is traveling with four children under ten, including a baby. She desperately deserves the best service you can provide. I'll help her off the plane and she'll need a wheelchair waiting on the ramp. She needs to be taken to a rest area. She is going on to Chicago as soon as you can book her a flight. Then she has another transfer, so she is going to be wiped out. She needs the best care we can give her."

He understands and assures me she'll be taken care of. These small opportunities to help Carol—and see others step up to help her—provide desperately needed moments of warmth in my battered heart.

We land in Oakland at about 0330. I help Carol and the kids deplane and place them in the hands of the airline service people. I give her a comforting hug and the kids as well. I've cleared customs and immigration in Cold Bay and show my documents to the few agents left on duty. When I get to baggage claim I go to a phone and dial Ramon's car phone. When he picks me up, I collapse in the back seat and fall asleep.

I wake up as we're entering the 17-Mile Drive Gate. In a minute we turn into the Arbuckle driveway. It is 0530 and still dark. I go up the steps into the great house. There's no one up so I tiptoe up the stairs to my room. A quick shower and I'm in bed and asleep. I don't even take time to rethink the unplanned two-day adventure.

At 9 a.m. I wake up again because my circadian clock is still thinking I'm somewhere on the other side of the international dateline. I wash my face, brush my teeth, put on a robe, and go downstairs without stopping in Davey's room. I'm not ready for that. Everyone is in the breakfast patio. There are lots of hugs and kisses all around and some teary eyes of both relief and pain.

Soon our thoughts turn to the terrible practical matters we have to face. Where will we lay Davey to rest? Fred says, "I believe he should stay here close to all of us. He's never known the outside world and this is no time to introduce him to it. I suggest that somewhere on the grounds there must be a little natural alcove where we could have the gardeners prepare a niche and a small shrine for him. We should cremate his body and put the ashes in the niche." Betsy looks up at him teary-eyed and says, "Yes, that way whenever I want to visit him I can go there." Fred suggests that we go over the grounds together before I have to leave. We'll find a site and together lay out the memorial. The decision is made but the pain remains.

The second issue is telling Lynda. "That's my job. Has Dr. Freiberg or The Retreat recommended how best to do this?"

"Yes, she called The Retreat and they recommend she be told as soon as possible."

"Okay, I'll call them today and set up a time and place there to tell her." Within the hour I make the dreaded call. The staff has been expecting me and assures me she is strong enough. A private, sunny alcove will be set aside for us tomorrow morning. I need a day to get my sea legs under me. We agree that about 10:00 in the morning is best. She's usually calmest then. They'll just tell her that I have come home on leave and am coming to visit her. I hang up the phone, one step closer to completing the tasks that we all have to do right now. But each step is one more step toward finality, toward eternity. I hate each and every one.

I have almost twenty-four hours to prepare myself for telling Lynda. I go downstairs and tell Fred that I have to get out and walk around. Fred suggests we walk the grounds searching for a place for Davey. We take off slowly on this vile mission, looking for a place to bury my son. After wandering about the property for an hour or so we find a sunny spot without much wind. It is around the corner from where most of the family walks, so it's naturally private.

When I come back, I finally have the courage to go to his room. As I enter, the shades are half drawn and the room is in twilight—nothing like it was the last time I was here. Immediately, the smell of baby powder assails my nostrils and I can't hold back. Slowly, haltingly, I cross the room to his crib. Here I believe I can smell him. When I look at the bed I know I can see him with his gleeful smile and chubby body dancing up and down. I rest my head on the rail and start to cry softly. In time, I look around the room, staring vacantly, seeing nothing. This is, but cannot be, true.

I go to my room, which also seems gloomy. Lying on the bed I let my mind wander. I slide over the events of the last three years: meeting Lynda, the assault at the beach, the adventure in WestPac, the kidnapping and lengthy rehabilitation, NIS and Captain Barton, visiting Davey here and then being gone again. I'm worn out with crying and soon drift off to sleep again. In late afternoon I wake up, splash some water on my face, and go back down stairs. I see Carmen out of the corner of my eye and walk slowly toward her. Her eyes are full of pain. Davey was like her own son. I give her a long, soft, rocking hug and then retreat to the library.

I turn on the television to have something to engage my mind, however faintly. In an hour or so Fred and Betsy come into the room looking like two old people who have been beaten down, which they are. I rise and give Betsy a long hug. Fred and I hug and pat each other on the back. Then, we all sit down. Fred suggests a drink and we agree.

"Betsy, did you see the place Fred and I chose?" She nods slightly and murmurs almost incoherently that it's a good spot. We sit in the late afternoon shadows without saying a word. Finally, I tell them that I have an appointment to see Lynda at 10:00 next morning. This too passes with almost no response. Then Betsy asks quietly what am I going to say to Lynda—how I'll get into the topic and tell her what happened. I have to admit that I don't know. I've run a number of scenarios through my head and each one breaks down at the moment of truth. I'm thinking that I cannot plan this verbatim. The exact words will depend on what is happening with Lynda when we meet. Will she be positive, negative, alert, or unresponsive? Soon the three of us go to a very quiet dinner and then return to our respective bedrooms. We are together in pain but alone too, stunned into silence.

Morning comes early because of the task ahead. I dress slowly, have a cup of coffee, some toast, scan the paper absentmindedly, and pick up the car Fred told me to take. Very slowly I drive up route 101 toward Palo Alto. In San Jose I turn west onto Route 280, I pass scenic views of the Santa Cruz Mountains to the west and, at a few points, San Francisco Bay to the east. Through much of this segment, the freeway is actually running just inside the eastern rim of the rift valley of the famous San Andreas Fault. As I approach Palo Alto I take Sand Hill Road west into the foothills of the Santa Cruz Mountains. Soon I've gained the seclusion of the valley and find The Retreat. It is not yet 10:00 so I turn into a corner of the parking lot and shut off the motor. Once again I go through possible scenarios. Before long I take a deep breath, get out of the car and head toward the most difficult, sensitive, challenging task of my life.

The chief of staff, Dr. Levine, tells me that Lynda seems quiet and somewhat serene today. She ushers me to a leafy, sunny niche in the south side of the garden. The only sounds are the slight rustling of the trees and occasional bird song. Dr. Levine assures me no one will come by to disturb us. She'll have an attendant waiting on the patio if I need assistance. I'm as nervous as can be while I wait. In a few minutes she appears with Lynda on her arm. She has already told her I am here so she won't be startled.

I stand up and slowly put my arms out to her. She comes to me and once in my arms seems to slowly relax. We don't say anything as the doctor leaves. Then, we pull back a few inches and look into each other's eyes. A small breeze rustles the trees and the shadows of the leaves fall over our eyes. She is shivering. "How are you, sweetheart? Are you cold? Here, put on my jacket. I've missed you."

She just looks at me, a little quizzically I'm thinking, but says nothing. I take her hand and lead her to the padded bench and we sit. I continue to talk softly, asking her how the staff has been treating her, if she feels better now than when she came here. One question after another I lay in front of her with little or no response. It is almost as if she can't hear me or isn't listening. I know she can hear me because nearby a squirrel chatters and runs across the leafy path and she turns her head to look at it. Frankly, I don't know where to go next.

I start, "Sweetheart, I wasn't scheduled for a leave, but three days ago Dad called me and told me that Davey was quite ill." As soon as I said Davey's name she seems to wake up.

"Davey?" she asked.

"Yes. As soon as I talked to your dad I got emergency leave and started for home. I went right to the hospital and found the head of pediatrics, Dr. Rashkin. He told me that Davey had a major heart problem, which had apparently worsened rather quickly. After diagnosis, they took him immediately into OR and performed open heart surgery. But . . ." Here I falter. Holding her hand tightly and after taking a deep breath, I say, "But he didn't make it. He's with the angels now."

Lynda looks at me with the first signs of comprehension. She looks for a long moment, then drops her eyes and stares at our hands together. I hold her and wait. She looks up again: "Davey's gone? He's dead?" Her eyes are beginning to tear. "Is that what you are telling me?"

"Yes sweetheart, I'm afraid so."

The look in her eyes is awful. She begins sobbing and starts repeating "I've been such a bad mother, such a bad mother, such a bad mother." I reach out and hold her. "Sweetheart, it has nothing to do with that. He just had a bad heart defect and it couldn't function anymore." We sit like that for quite a while, Lynda murmuring her mantra of regret and me holding her, feeling helpless. I hear the chief of staff tiptoeing toward us to check. We've been there for the better part of an hour. She peeks discreetly around the corner and I motion her to come over. I say almost in a whisper, "I don't know what to do."

She replies just as quietly, "I'll take her. Stay here."

Lynda doesn't look back as the doctor walks her gently back toward her room. In a few minutes, while I break into a massive sweat and then simultaneously shiver, she returns and we sit down. But I'm so nervous I get back up and pace around in front of her while she talks.

"Commander Still, Lynda is showing signs of what are called dissociative disorders. These types of disorder may emerge with overwhelming stress, as the result of traumatic events, accidents, or disasters that may be experienced or witnessed by the individual. Her brother's attempts to hurt you, learning that she is adopted, and your injuries here and in Hong Kong are examples of events that can lead to one or another form of severe depression. Now the loss of her son may be a final blow. Such a patient may suffer from an abysmally low and hopeless outlook on life. Lynda is clearly suffering from depression, but she may be on the path to a dissociative disorder as well. This is nothing that anyone can be blamed for, with the possible exception of her brother's crime. I'll talk to Doctor Freiberg and ask her to help you to tell the Arbuckles."

The next few days are a struggle as everyone at the house tries to deal with this seemingly final phase of a terrible story. I feel like I've fallen into my own personal San Andreas Fault.

12

CALM SEA

I t is a blustery September 1972 morning in Yokosuka. The sun is bright but the wind demands a jacket for comfort. Now that the joint intelligence report is finished, I'm expecting to be reassigned. Knowing I'll be moving on soon, I decide to take some time to see the real Yokosuka. I'm strolling one of the many narrow lanes found in Japanese cities. They're barely wide enough for a small delivery truck yet there you can find a wide variety of businesses. The shops carry everything from plumbing supplies to groceries, clothing, electronics, cosmetics, jewelry, and furnishings, plus bars and restaurants. You name it, it's there

The cloth signs in front of the shops are fluttering. Since I can't read the characters I just admire the bright colors. On one of the less busy lanes I see an old man in a paint-spattered gray smock sitting in the sun, smoking a cigarette. He smiles and gives a little bow, so I try my very limited Japanese on him,

"Konichi wa, Ikaga desu ka." [Good day, how are you?]

"Genki desu. Anata wa." [I'm fine, healthy. And you?]

Having run through 90 percent of my vocabulary I spread my hands and point to the sky with a happy look.

"Yes, it is a beautiful day," he says. The old gentleman speaks English!

Somewhat chagrined and not knowing where to go next, I ask him what is his business. He tells me it is art. When I ask how it's

217

going, he says business is okay but not great. Then he asks if I am in the military, since I am in mufti.

"Yes, sir. I'm a naval officer."

His smile brightens. "I was a sailor for a short time at the end of the war. You see I was born in 1900, so at the beginning I was too old. But by 1944 so many of our young men had been killed or captured that I was drafted into the navy. I was running a piano store in Formosa, so I had no military skills. They made me a cook at the navy base until the war ended. After the war Formosa became Taiwan and Chiang Kai-shek's followers came from the mainland and took it over. I moved here where I had family. Do you have family, a wife or children?"

"I did but my wife is quite ill and my son died recently."

"Please forgive me. I did not mean to bring you grief. Do you have pictures of them that I might see?"

"Just my son," I reply as I reach for my wallet.

He squints at the picture of this beautiful baby boy who's looking at the camera as though he wants to crawl out of the picture and onto your lap. You can see the pure joy of a small child. "Most beautiful. You must love him very much."

"Yes, I do, and I miss him terribly."

"Please come into my small shop. I have something to show you."

It's a tattoo shop, but all along the walls are dozens of paintings and drawings. "Did you make these?" When he nods I ask how he learned to draw so well. He said art has been his love since he was a child. Tattooing was a way to use his love and talent to make a living after the war.

I say, "You're very talented, sir."

He thanks me with a slight bow and asks if he can do a line drawing from the photo. I hesitate for only a moment, but realize he will not harm the photo, so I give permission. He is such a beautiful old man that I cannot deny him. Again he thanks me and pulls a piece of beautiful rice paper from a stack. With a tiny brush and a smooth, flowing motion he works slowly and meticulously. In about ten minutes he sits back, reviews his work, makes one small final stroke, and hands it to me.

It is exquisite. He totally captures Davey's joyous spirit. He asks, "Have I made a mistake?" because my eyes are tearing.

"No, sir. It's perfect."

"This is yours, sir, no charge. It is my great pleasure to capture the spirit of your beautiful son."

We sit and look closely at the rhythmic beauty of the lines for a minute. I grasp his drawing hand and hold it. He smiles shyly, but with appreciation.

"Would you like it as a tattoo? It will bring you constant joy wherever the Navy takes you."

"It is a nice idea, but the Navy doesn't like its officers to be tattooed."

"I am suggesting a small image, perhaps on your hip where no one can see it. Your son must be with you always. I know the pain of separation."

His sensibility and logic is impeccable, and I agree to it. He closes his shop door. We go into the back where I see he has a small studio. I choose my right hip for the image. The task takes about half an hour. It is a simple line drawing with no coloration to distract the eye. He says, "The Japanese have a saying that color is for children and idiots." He gives me a mirror. He found Davey's spirit again. The likeness is perfect and there is something special about it being on skin rather than paper.

He does not ask to be paid but I give him fifty dollars. The official exchange rate is 308 yen to the dollar in 1971, but on the underground market it is whatever you can get for it. Whatever the rate, I can never pay him enough for what he has given me.

When we finish he asks, "May I have the pleasure of you having tea with me?" I have no plans and am finding comfort in his gentle company, so I agree. As we sit in his small shop waiting for the water to boil I ask him if he lost anyone in his family to the war. He pauses and then, looking down at his wrinkled old hands, he says so quietly that I can barely hear him, "My son."

219

Now I apologize for rekindling his grief. He tells me not to worry, then goes on to say that his son died in battle at Guadalcanal. "They never found and returned his body. Each day my wife cries because she cannot close the book on his life."

I am so sorry for this poor man who lost a son and also a wife to the war.

He continues, "War is the most stupid act of humanity. It inflicts too much sorrow on too many people. It causes too much needless loss and it seldom solves a long-term problem. To understand war we need in think in terms of a century or more. What have the European wars taught the Europeans or the Asian wars the Asians? Is it just greed, or is man at heart a warrior?"

"Perhaps you're right. We never seem to learn from the last war before we start another one."

"Curiously, as a concept, war is pure."

"What do you mean? How can something as devastating to so many people be pure?"

"I only said, as a concept, it is pure. I mean that it is unequivocal. In a war there is a winner and a loser. The winner becomes the master and the loser becomes the slave or servant. The important lesson is how the master treats the servant. If he is vengeful, vindictive, cruel, or otherwise thoughtless, the servant will continue to hate the master. He will spend his time continually looking for ways to secretly harm the master. If, on the other hand, the master is thoughtful and caring, the servant will begin to see the master not as a conqueror but perhaps even as a partner in the rehabilitation of his country. General MacArthur understood this. At the end of the war, against the advice of some in power in America, he chose not to take vengeance on the emperor, because he understood, as they did not, how central the emperor is to the Japanese culture and identity. The people notice this because we are afraid that he would imprison or even execute the emperor. Can you imagine how the Japanese people would have responded to that? Another guerilla war would still be going on twenty-five years later. There would be no peace for either side today or maybe for generations. Take this idea to America. If America lost a war and the conqueror burned the While House as the British did in in 1812, knocked down the Washington Monument, and then destroyed the Lincoln Memorial, how would the American people respond?"

"You're very wise, sir." I couldn't say more as I tried to absorb this lesson.

He said, "No, I am not wise; I simply watch what is truly happening beyond the local, obvious scene. Reading the paper each day can be an opiate. It can dull your senses with mundane, pointless stories while missing the larger context of the time."

"Isn't that wisdom?"

He smiles and takes another sip of tea. I look at my watch and see that it's 5:00. "Will you do me the honor of having dinner with me," I ask?

"It would be a great privilege but I must get home to my wife who is so lonely by herself."

I take his hand in both my hands to let him know my regard for him.

He says, "Don't forget about washing the tattoo. Don't rub it for two weeks so the ink will set and won't smear."

I thank him and walk onto the lane. Now, it's getting cool and the wind is coming up. I walk rapidly up the lane with its fluttering pennants to the main street and hail a taxi to take me back to the base. I sit back and relax for the first time since Davey's death. He has given me a bit of comfort in the storm that has engulfed my life.

13

SAFE HARBOR

Ten days later I receive orders to depart Yokosuka for New York City and the United Nations. I'm to be part of the US delegation to the UN I have no idea why the Navy is sending me there, but it's a great place to serve. True to my promise to Fred and Betsy, I stop in Carmel to visit with them before reporting to the head of the delegation.

Fred sends Ramon to pick me up at the San Francisco airport and we take the familiar route to Monterey, which has grown so dear to me over the years. My arrival is greeted with big smiles and many hugs and kisses from everyone in the household. It's wonderful to see these beautiful people again. But underneath the congeniality there is a core of great pain. Fred and Betsy have endured three years of unending, compounding sorrow. It's amazing that they're surviving it and maintaining their health and good humor.

After bringing them up to date on my adventures we talk about their future plans. Betsy says that the life has gone out of things in Monterey for them. She no longer enjoys walking Carmel's Ocean Avenue through the familiar shops. The large house no longer rings with guests, parties or the laughter of a little boy.

Fred claims that he is getting too old to play golf competitively and, frankly, his heart isn't in it. He notes that the winters in Monterey can be "too damned wet", overcast, and cold. Every time they drive up to the big house they feel sad. So they have decided to sell the Monterey house and move back to their home in Sea Cliff. They have many long-term friends and former business associates still living there. If Fred wants to he can play golf at the Olympic Club out on Skyline Boulevard, where he has been a long-time member. San Francisco is a lively and beautiful place. Fred and Betsy have friends to dine with, to party with and generally revivify their lives. It is a splendid idea. There are too many bad memories in Monterey. It's been especially painful for them to go by Davey's room every day. They're going to take down Davey's shrine and find him a special place at Sea Cliff. Carmen and Josepha have always wanted to live in the city, and there is plenty of room for them at the Sea Cliff house. Ramon plans to live in the Mission District with relatives. I can tell that they are gaining energy from this move. The pain is still there, under the surface, but they seem to have made a turn away from the decline that had been aging them years every few months, it seemed.

Over the next couple weeks the house comes alive a bit. There are small dinners with friends such as the Klares and Youngs. It's very good to see Fred and Betsy smiling like old times.

All is going well until I get a call from Mom. In the years since I left home to go to UCLA I never really went back. Nothing much changed. Mom was as acerbic as ever and Dad just seemed to drop out. She tells me, "Dad is going into the hospital for another stomach operation. It shouldn't be anything special. You know he has a history of ulcers. Apparently, he's bleeding again and the doctor said he has to go in and repair the leak. He talks like a plumber. Anyway, your last letter said you were going to New York. If it's not too much of an inconvenience for you, it would be nice if you could stop on the way and see him. He really misses you." This is only a minor change of plans. I have time to spend a couple days in Nowhere with Dad.

The night before I leave, Fred and Betsy ask me to join them in the library. This room holds so many memories, both good and bad. I presume they want to have a farewell drink. Fred pours three glasses of a fine port. Then he starts by saying, "Michael, we have

223

enjoyed so much your company. You're truly an extraordinary young man. You're like a son to us. We love you very much. You deserve better than what you received here." I assure them that I've always made my own decisions and that I'm able to handle whatever destiny has in store for me.

"We know, Michael. However, there is one final financial matter to resolve. In the state of California marriages and divorces are driven by community property laws, as you probably know. In this case Lynda has no property except her share in the Hawaii house and the automobiles. Beyond that we just pay her bills. In her state, unless she recovers we will simply leave a trust to pay for her care. So Betsy and I have decided that we should, and did, file a quit claim in Lynda's behalf. This means the Honolulu house is now yours along with the two cars, if they are still around. In addition, we want you to have this check as a small symbol of our love and appreciation for you."

He hands me an envelope with a copy of the quit claim and the deed to the house along with copies of the pink slips for the cars. In addition, there is a cashier's check made out to me. It is for $500,000. I'm dumbfounded. "Fred, Betsy, this is ridiculous. I certainly appreciate your generosity, but this is absurd. You don't owe me anything. I should be paying you for all the goodness you've shown me. I can't accept this check."

"Well Michael, you have no choice. We want you to have it, period. It's not a hardship for us. In fact we've talked about doubling it. If you don't think it is your fair share we will be more than happy to do that."

I'm stunned. There is nothing I can say to that except to get up and give each of them a long, warm hug and tell them how much I love them. They are like a father and mother to me.

That night I lie awake for a couple hours recalling everything the Arbuckles have done for me and now this. It's overwhelming. My heart is so full I can't help lying there in the darkness and weeping softly. The sounds of the ocean, the wind rustling the trees, an occasional night bird calling all come together in a beautiful dream.

Early the next morning it's time to go. With many hugs and promises to visit whenever I'm in the city, Ramon takes me to the airport to catch a plane to Chicago. Vaya con dios amigo.

* * *

I land in Chicago in early afternoon rent a car and drive through the familiar cornfields to Nowhere. When I arrive I stop at the house before going to the hospital. Mom seems to have aged beyond her years. She asks how long I can stay. I tell her, "I've got a couple days before I have to report in New York."

"Well, it's good that you can spare us that." Good old Mom. Never misses an opportunity to share some good will.

When I get to the hospital I find Dad in a reasonably good mood. He says, "The plumber went in and fixed the leak, I hope. I'm very tired of dealing with this problem. So, how have you been, son?"

"I'm doing well, Dad. I'm excited about going to New York and working in the UN. I don't really know what I'm supposed to do there, but being part of that organization has got to be interesting to say the least. How are you, Dad?"

"My health isn't so bad, although the doc has cut my liquor down to one drink a day. I'm losing weight, which probably isn't a problem, but look at my arm. I haven't had an arm as thin as this since I was a freshman in high school."

"That's not a problem. When you get out of here and back on your feet you can get some dumbbells and build it back up."

"I guess so, but right now I've got a pain in my bicep and shoulder. It's getting worse, not better."

"Should I call a nurse to give you a shot?"

"I hate to be a cry baby, but it's really starting to hurt."

I hurry out into the corridor and down to the nurses' station. For a minute there is no one there, then one comes out of a room and back to the station. She asks rather wearily, "Is there something I can do for you?"

"Yes, my dad is in considerable pain and he says it is getting worse."

"Well, he shouldn't be suffering. The operation went very well. I'll take a look."

We walk back into Dad's room and he appears to be asleep. She tries to rouse him to check the pain level but he doesn't respond. After slapping him in the face and yelling "Albert" at him she brushes past me and calls out "Code Blue." Suddenly, two nurses and an intern appear with some machine and jam into Dad's room. They motion me to get out. In less than fifteen minutes of commotion in the room suddenly all goes quiet. The intern comes out with Dad's nurse and says, "I'm very sorry. Your Dad is gone. It looks like a blood clot broke off from the incision and got to his heart. That's why he was feeling increasing pain in his arm and shoulder. The clot was causing pressure. We couldn't give him a blood thinner because his incision would have starting leaking again. I'm very sorry."

Just then Mom arrives and asks, "What's all the commotion?"

I say, "Mom, let's go down to the waiting room and let these people do their job."

When we get there she sits down and the intern and surgeon come in. The surgeon tells her what happened. He repeats what the intern had already told me. Strangely, Mom doesn't say anything. She pulls out a handkerchief from her bag and wipes her eyes. We get up and go home. It's happened so fast we haven't had time to grasp it. Her husband and my dad is dead.

Mom wants to move quickly with the service, so I have the funeral home pick up Dad's body and prepare it for viewing. Mom makes a couple calls to old friends and the word quickly gets around town. The next morning she and I go to the funeral home and into Dad's room. He's lying in an open casket. I stand beside her for several minutes. There isn't a sound. Finally, she says, "What a fool I've been all these years. He's all I really wanted. I had two beautiful boys and a faithful husband and I acted like a witch." With that she finally breaks down and starts sobbing in my arms. This is as close to her as I've been since I was a small child.

The next two days before I leave for New York, Mom is a different person. For the first time in my memory she isn't caustic. Her sharpness is gone. Instead of sad and angry, she's sad and calm, sorrowful. I feel the same grief that she does, not just for the loss of Dad, but for the years wasted on anger and meanness.

Two days later at the end of September 1972 I leave for New York. I'm welcomed by the ambassador and staff and given a very nice office overlooking the East River. Within a few days I feel like an old hand here. A week later I get a letter from Mom. I'm more than a bit apprehensive as I open it. The letter starts out, "Michael, I'm sorry that I was so mean to you, Bob, and Dad all those years. I was just so angry that I never had a chance to make something more than a housewife out of myself. I took it out on you and you had nothing to do with it. I'm truly sorry and I promise you'll see a new Mom. I want you and Bob to know how much I love you. You take care of yourself. You boys are all I have left." After all these years, it is a beautiful thing to read, and it takes some of the sting out of our family's loss.

* * *

I'm very impressed with the site of the United Nation's Headquarters set along the East River of New York City. It gives me warm feelings of stateliness to walk through the UN building's several large meeting rooms and halls. Often there are meetings in session. I sit in the visitor's gallery and watch the deliberations. My favorite room is the General Assembly Hall. I stand at the back of the great hall marveling at the structure as well as the historic events that have taken place there. This citadel to peace seats 2,000 people in six sections each with more than a dozen rows all angled toward the speaker's platform. Behind the speaker is a golden shaft nearly twenty feet wide at the bottom and tapered as it rises to the ceiling. It's the background for the UN logo. The wooden acoustical shafts on the side walls angle up and inward from the floor past the translator's windows to the ceiling. The entire focus is on the speaker's stand. It's truly a most powerful room. The general assembly is not meeting today, so there's almost perfect silence broken only by murmurs from two men down in front working on some audio mechanism.

Suddenly I hear a voice. "Commander Still?" I'm startled because I'm lost in my thoughts and the atmosphere of this great room. Then it comes again: "Commander?" When I turn around I'm shocked, stunned. I can't believe what I see just ten feet from me.

"You're looking fit, Commander."

I can't speak. It is as if some mythic person is saying my name.

"What's the matter, Michael? Cat got your tongue?"

I'm stuck. Finally, I take a few steps toward her until we stand three feet apart. I'm afraid to go any closer for fear this apparition will disappear. "Grace, what are you doing here?"

"I work here. I heard your promotion to commander came through this morning and I wanted to be the one to tell you."

"What . . . what do you do here?"

"I'm a member of the United States delegation. I work on special projects related to Asia Pacific and I'm a backup translator."

"How long have you been here?"

"A little over a year. I saw that you were coming in a staff bulletin. I would have come to see you earlier but I was on a mission for the past month. I've been hoping to see you again."

"I don't know what to say. I thought I'd never see you again."

"If you're unhappy to see me, I'll leave you alone."

"My God, no! It's just a shock for you to appear out of nowhere after all these years. I read about your husband, and when I was last in Hawaii I tried to find you. I'm such a fool. I even drove by your old house like a high school kid. I saw that someone else had moved in. I asked about you but they didn't have any information. Finally, I went to the Chinese Cultural Center. I remember you said you worked there part-time. It had been a few years since you were there and all they could tell me was that you had moved to New York. What happened?"

"When Jerry went down I had a lot of time to think about the rest of my life. By '68 both my mom and dad were gone. I decided to change my name back to my maiden name, mostly out of respect for my parents, who never liked Jerry. When I was about to marry him my dad took me aside and said, 'That boy is self-centered, manipulative and insensitive . . . just like Chang.' He said, 'You can always come home. If he hurts you in any way I have friends who'll turn him into shark bait. He'll never be heard from again.'

"After a lot of soul searching I realized that the thing I know most about and truly enjoy studying is the political economics of Asia Pacific. So I went back to school at UH-Manoa and got a PhD in China Studies. Somehow it closes the loop for me."

"But how did you get here?"

"While I was at the Community Center in Hawaii I shepherded a group from the UN that held a meeting in Honolulu. The deputy for Asia Pacific suggested that I come to New York and talk to them about joining the staff. I had no reason to stay in Hawaii by myself. So I did as he suggested and they hired me." She smiled. "Any more questions?"

"I don't know what to say."

"I can see that. It's been a long time from Celia's party to now, almost ten years, right? I think about our conversation all the time and wish we had had more time together. But I was married and you left. Celia told me later that you really enjoyed meeting me and that still makes me feel good. Later, I heard about your wife and child and thought my presence would not be appropriate."

"I shipped out a week after we met. I didn't call you to say goodbye because, as you say, you were married and we had only a couple of hours together. I didn't know if you felt any connection."

"Men are so obtuse. If you couldn't tell that I truly liked you, you weren't paying attention."

I drop my folder, step up to her, and take her hands. It is just like ten years ago, but now things are different. We look at each other for what seems like eternity but is probably only five seconds. Then

I pull her into my arms so brutally that I knock the wind out of her. I relax a little. She leans back and takes a couple breaths. Then, says coyly, "Does this mean you still like me?"

"I've had a shrine in my heart for you since the night we met."

She slides her arms around my neck and gives me the softest, sweetest, most overwhelming kiss anyone has ever had. With her cheek next to mine she answers my unspoken question. "Yes."

I still can't speak. She says it again: "Yes."

We hold each other tightly and weep quietly.

* * *

This is the beginning of a new life. Suddenly, the pain of the past is no longer dragging me down. I can never forget, but I can learn to live with it.

ABOUT THE AUTHOR

Doctor Jac has worked in forty-six countries, is the author of a dozen books, and is a columnist for a business journal. In Rough Waters, he turns to his experiences growing up and serving in the navy as an intelligence officer to tell the story of a man's life, both personal and professional.

Made in the USA
Middletown, DE
13 January 2020

83141114R00144